GHOST KING

'I am not cut out to be a warrior', said Thuro.

'You are my grandson and the son of Aurelius and Alaida,' replied Culain. 'I think you will find that blood runs true. We already know you can swing an axe. What other surprises do you hold in store?'

Thuro shrugged. 'I do not want to disappoint you, as I disappointed my father.'

'Lesson one, Thuro: from now on you have no one to disappoint but yourself. But first you must agree to abide by what I say and obey every word I utter. Will you do this?'

'I will'.

'Then prepare to die,' said Culain. And there was no humour in his eyes.

Also in Legend by David Gemmell

LEGEND
THE KING BEYOND THE GATE
WAYLANDER
QUEST FOR LOST HEROES
WOLF IN SHADOW
LAST SWORD OF POWER
THE LAST GUARDIAN
KNIGHTS OF DARK RENOWN
THE LION OF MACEDON

GHOST KING

David A. Gemmell

LEGEND

First published in Legend 1988

9 10 8

First published in Great Britain in 1988 by Century Hutchinson Ltd

New Legend edition 1989
Random House UK Ltd, 20 Vauxhall Bridge Road, London SW1V 2SA

Random House Australia (Pty) Limited
20 Alfred Street, Milsons Point, Sydney,
New South Wales 2061, Australia

Random House New Zealand Limited
18 Poland Road, Glenfield
Auckland 10, New Zealand

Random House South Africa (Pty) Limited
PO Box 337, Bergvlei, South Africa

Random House UK Limited Reg. No. 954009

A CIP catalogue record for this book
is available from the British Library

ISBN 0 09 956550 1

Typeset by Input Typesetting Ltd, London
Printed and bound in Great Britain by
Cox & Wyman Ltd, Reading, Berkshire

Dedication

This book is dedicated with love to Stella Graham, to Tom Taylor and to Jeremy Wells for the gift of friendship.

Also to the ladies of the Folkestone Herald – *Sharon, Madders, Susie and Carol – for Rocky. And to Pip Clarkson who cast the pearls anyway.*

Acknowledgements

So much in the literary world depends on the skill of those who take the manuscript and edit it for publication. A writer can all too easily take the wrong direction, or lose the thread of the drama. A good editor will re-direct skilfully and enhance greatly the work that will then accrue credit to the author. Similarly a good copy editor can, with an inserted word, or a clever deletion, polish a dull sentence to diamond brightness.

My thanks to my editor Liza Reeves for making it all seem so easy, to copy editor Jean Maund for the fine tuning and the elegant polishing, and to my agent, Pamela Buckmaster, for bringing us together.

Foreword

Ghost King is a fantasy novel and not intended as historically accurate. However the cities of Roman Britain, as named, did exist in the areas suggested, as did certain of the characters who appear in these pages.

Cunobelin was certainly a powerful warrior king, who earned the title Brittanorum Rex from the Roman writer Seutonius. Cunobelin reigned for forty years from his base at Camulodunum, possibly giving rise to the Arthurian legends.

Paullinus was also a true man of history, and did defeat the Iceni of Boudicca during the ill-fated uprising. During the same period the Ninth Legion did indeed disappear. Some historians claim they were ambushed and destroyed, others suggest a mutiny that the Romans covered up.

The manoeuvres of Roman military units are detailed as accurately as research and the needs of drama allow.

The language used is relatively modern, and undoubtedly there will be some students who find it jarring to read of arrows being 'fired', when of course the expression evolved only after the introduction of matchlock muskets.

Similarly 'minutes' and 'seconds' appear ahead of their time.

Such arguments as may be offered can be overcome by pointing out that since the language being spoken is not English, but a bastardized form of Latin-Celtic, some licence in translation should be allowed.

Of the life of Uther Pendragon, little is known. This is not a history of the man, but a fantasy.

In other words it is not the story as it was – but as it *ought* to have been.

David A. Gemmell
Hastings, 1988

Principal Characters

(in alphabetical order)

ALHYFFA Daughter of Hengist, wife of Moret

BALDRIC Warrior of the Pinrae

CAEL Son of Eldared, King of the Brigante

CULAIN LACH FERAGH Warrior of the Mist, also known as the Lord of the Lance. Master of weaponry.

ELDARED Brigante King and Lord of Deicester Castle. Betrayed his brother Cascioc twenty years before to help Aurelius gain the throne.

GWALCHMAI King's retainer. Cantii tribesman

GOROIEN The Witch Queen, immortal and ruthless

HENGIST Saxon king, father to Horsa, the warlord

KORRIN ROGEUR Woodsman of Pinrae. Brother to Pallin

LAITHA Ward of Culain

LUCIUS AQUILA General of the Romano-British forces

MAEDHLYN Lord Enchanter to Aurelius

MORET Son of Eldared

PALLIN Half-man, half-bear, tortured by the Witch Queen

PRASAMACCUS Brigante tribesman

SEVERINUS ALBINUS Roman legate of the Ninth Legion

THURO Son of High King Aurelius Maximus and the MistMaiden, Alaida

VICTORINUS King's retainer and First Centurion

Roman Names of British Settlements

ANDERITA – Pevensey

CALCARIA – Tadcaster

LINDUM – Lincoln

LONDINIUM – London

CAMULODUNUM –
  Colchester
CATARACTONIUM –
  Catterick
DUBRIS – Dover
DUROBRIVAE – Rochester
EBORACUM – York
LAGENTIUM – Castleford
LONGOVICIUM – Lancaster
PINNATA CASTRA –
  Inchtuthill
SKITIS ISLAND – Isle of Skye
VENTA – Winchester
VINDOLANDA –
  Chesterholm
VINDOMARA – Ebchester

1

The boy stared idly at the cold grey walls and wondered if the castle dungeons could be any more inhospitable than this chill turret room, with its single window staring like an eye into the teeth of the north wind. True there was a fire glowing in the hearth, but it might as well have been one of Maedhlyn's illusions for all the warmth it supplied. The great grey slabs sucked the heat from the blaze, giving nothing in return save a ghostly reflection that mocked the flames.

Thuro sat on the bed and wrapped his father's white bearskin cloak about his own slender shoulders.

'What a foul place,' he said, closing his eyes and pushing the turret room from his mind. He thought of his father's villa in Eboracum, and of the horse meadows beyond the white walls where mighty Cephon wintered with his mares. But most of all he pictured his own room, cosy and snug away from the bitter winter winds and filled with the love of his young life: his books, his glorious books. His father had refused him permission to bring even one tome to this lonely castle, in case the other war leaders should catch the prince reading and know the king's dark secret. For while it might be well-known in Caerlyn Keep that the boy Thuro was weak in body and spirit, the king's retainers guarded the sad truth like a family shame.

Thuro shivered and left the bed to sit on the goatskin rug before the fire. He was as miserable now as he had ever been. Far below in the great hall of Deicester Castle his father was attempting to bond an alliance against the barbarians from across the sea, grim-eyed reavers who had even now established settlements in the far south from which to raid the richer northlands. The embassy to Deicester had been made despite Maedhlyn's warnings. Thuro had not wished to accompany his father either, but not for fear of dangers he could scarce comprehend. The prince disliked the cold, loathed long journeys on horseback and, more importantly, hated to be deprived of his books even for a day – let alone the two months set aside for the embassy.

The door opened and the prince glanced up to see the tall figure of Gwalchmai, his brawny arms bearing a heavy load of logs. He smiled at the lad and Thuro noted with shame that the retainer wore but a single woollen tunic against the biting cold.

'Do you never feel the chill, Gwalchmai?'

'I feel it,' he answered, kneeling to add wood to the blaze.

'Is my father still speaking?'

'No. When I passed by Eldared was on his feet.'

'You do not like Eldared?'

'You see too much, young Thuro; that is not what I said.'

But you did, thought Thuro. It was in your eyes and the slight inflection when you used his name. He stared into the retainer's dark eyes, but Gwalchmai turned away.

'Do you trust him?' asked the boy.

'Your father obviously trusts him, so who am I to offer opinions? You think the king would have come here with only twenty retainers if he feared treachery?'

'You answer my question with questions. Is that not evasive?'

Gwalchmai grinned. 'I must get back to my watch. But think on this, Thuro: it is not for the likes of me to criticise the great. I could lose the skin from my back – or worse, my life.'

'You think there is danger here?' persisted the prince.

'I like you, boy, though only Mithras knows why. You've a sharp mind; it is a pity you are weakly. But I'll answer your question after a fashion. For a king there is always danger; it is a riddle to me why a man wants such power. I've served your father for sixteen years and in that time he has survived four wars, eleven battles and five attempts on his life. He is a canny man. But I would be happier if the Lord Enchanter were here.'

'Maedhlyn does not trust Eldared; he told my father so.'

Gwalchmai pushed himself to his feet. 'You trust too easily, Thuro. You should not be shar-

13

ing this knowledge with me – or with any retainer.'

'But I can trust you, can I not?'

'How do you know that?' hissed Gwalchmai.

'I read it in your eyes,' said Thuro softly. Gwalchmai relaxed and a broad grin followed as he shook his head and tugged on his braided beard.

'You should get some rest. It's said there's to be a stag-hunt tomorrow.'

'I'll not be going,' said Thuro. 'I do not much like riding.'

'You baffle me, boy. Sometimes I see so much of your father in you that I want to cheer. And then . . . well, it does not matter. I will see you in the morning. Sleep well.'

'Thank you for the wood.'

'It is my duty to see you safe.' Gwalchmai left the room and Thuro rose and wandered to the window, moving aside the heavy velvet curtain and staring out over the winter land-scape: rolling hills covered in snow, skeletal trees black as charcoal. He shivered and wished for home.

He too would have been happier if Maedhlyn had journeyed with them, for he enjoyed the old man's company and the quickness of his mind – and the games and riddles the Enchanter set him. One had occupied his mind for almost a full day last summer, while his father had been in the south routing the Jutes. Thuro had been sitting with Maedhlyn in the terraced garden, in the shade cast by the statue of the great Julius.

14

'There was a prince,' said Maedhlyn, his green eyes sparkling, 'who was hated by his king but loved by the people. The king decided the prince must die, but fearing the wrath of the populace he devised an elaborate plan to end both the prince's popularity and his life. He accused him of treason and offered him Trial by Mithras. In this way the Roman god would judge the innocence or guilt of the accused.

'The prince was brought before the king and a large crowd was there to see the judgement. Before the prince stood a priest holding a closed leather pouch and within the pouch were two grapes. The law said that one grape should be white, the other black. If the accused drew a white grape, he was innocent. A black grape meant death. You follow this, Thuro?'

'It is simple so far, teacher.'

'Now the prince knew of the king's hatred and guessed, rightly, that there were two black grapes in the pouch. Answer me this, young quicksilver: How did the prince produce a white grape and prove his innocence?'

'It is not possible, save by magic.'

'There was no magic, only thought,' said Maedhlyn, tapping his white-haired temple for emphasis. 'Come to me tomorrow with the answer.'

Throughout the day Thuro had thought hard, but his mind was devoid of inspiration. He borrowed a pouch from Listra the cook, and two grapes, and sat in the garden staring at the items as if in themselves they harboured the

15

answer. As dusk painted the sky Trojan red, he gave up. Sitting alone in the gathering gloom he took one of the grapes and ate it. He reached for the other – and stopped.

The following morning he went to Maedhlyn's study. The old man greeted him sourly – having had a troubled night, he said, with dark dreams.

'I have answered your riddle, master,' the boy told him. At this the Enchanter's eyes came alive.

'So soon, young prince? It took the noble Alexander ten days, but then perhaps Aristotle was less gifted than myself as a tutor!' He chuckled. 'So tell me, Thuro, how did the prince prove his innocence?'

'He put his hand into the pouch and covered one grape. This he removed and ate swiftly. He then said to the priest, "I do not know what colour it was, but look at the one that is left." '

Maedhlyn clapped his hands and smiled. 'You please me greatly, Thuro. But tell me, how did you come upon the answer?'

'I ate the grape.'

'That is good. There is a lesson in that also. You broke the problem down and examined the component parts. Most men attempt to solve riddles by allowing their minds to leap like monkeys from branch to branch, without ever realising that it is the root that needs examining. Always remember that, young prince. The method works with men as well as it works with riddles.'

Now Thuro dragged his thoughts from the

golden days of summer back to the bleak winter night. He removed his leggings and slid under the blankets, turning on his side to watch the flickering flames in the hearth.

He thought of his father – tall and broad-shouldered with eyes of ice and fire, revered as a warrior leader and held in awe even by his enemies.

'I don't want to be a king,' whispered Thuro.

*

Gwalchmai watched as the nobles prepared for the hunt, his emotions mixed. He felt a fierce pride as he looked upon the powerful figure of his king, sitting atop a black stallion of seventeen hands. The beast was called Bloodfire and one look in its evil eyes would warn any horseman to beware. But the king was at ease, for the horse knew its master; they were as alike in temperament as brothers of the blood. But Gwalchmai's pride was mixed with the inevitable sadness of seeing prince Thuro beside his father. The boy sat miserably upon a gentle mare of fifteen hands, clutching his cloak to his chest, his white-blond hair billowing about his slender ascetic face. Too much of his mother in him, thought Gwalchmai, remembering his first sight of the Mist Maiden. It was almost sixteen years ago now, yet his mind's eye could picture the queen as if but an hour had passed. She rode a white pony and beside the warrior king she seemed as fragile and out of place as ice on a rose. Talk among the retainers was that their lord had gone for a walk with Maedhlyn into a mist-shrouded northern valley and vanished for eight days. When he returned his beard had grown a full six inches and beside him was this wondrous woman, with golden hair and eyes of swirling grey like mist on a northern lake.

At first many of the people of Caerlyn Keep had thought her a witch, for even here the tales were told of the Land of Mist, a place of eldritch magic. But as the months passed she charmed them all with her kindness and her gentle spirit. News of her pregnancy was greeted with great joy and instant celebration. Gwalchmai would never forget the raucous banquet at the Keep, nor the wild night of pleasure that followed it.

But eight months later Alaida, the Mist Maiden, was dead and her baby son hovering on the brink of death, refusing all milk. The Enchanter Maedhlyn had been summoned and he, with his magic, saved young Thuro. But the boy was never strong; where the retainers had hoped for a young man to mirror the king, they were left with a solemn child who abhorred all manly practices. Yet enough of his mother's gentleness remained to turn what would have been scorn into a friendly sadness. Thuro was well-liked, but men who saw him would shake their heads and think of what might have been.

All this was on Gwalchmai's mind as the hunting party set off, led by Lord Eldared and his two sons Cael and Moret.

The king had never recovered from the death of Alaida. He rarely laughed and only came alive when hunting either beasts or men. He had plenty of opportunity in those bloody days for the Saxons and Jutes were raiding in the south and the Norse sailed their Wolfships into the deep rivers of the East Country. Added to this there were raiders aplenty from the smaller clans and tribes who had never accepted the right of the Romano-British warlords to rule the ancient lands of the Belgae, the Iceni and the Cantii.

Gwalchmai could well understand this viewpoint, being pure-blood Cantii himself, born within a long stone's throw of the Ghost Cliffs.

Now he watched as the noblemen cantered towards the wooded hills, then returned to his quarters behind the long stables. His eyes scanned the Deicester men as they lounged by the alehouse and he began to grow uneasy. There was no love lost between the disparate groups assembled here, though the truce had been well-maintained – a broken nose here, a sprained wrist there, but mostly the retainers had kept to themselves. But today Gwalchmai sensed a tension in the air, a brightness in the eyes of the soldiers.

He wandered into the long room. Only two of the king's men were here, Victorinus and Caradoc. They were playing knuckle-bones and the Roman was losing, with good grace.

'Rescue me, Gwal,' said Victorinus. 'Save me from my stupidity.'

'There's not a man alive who could do that!' Gwalchmai moved to his cot and his wrapped blankets. He drew his gladius and scabbard from the roll and strapped the sword to his waist.

'Are you expecting trouble?' asked Caradoc, a tall rangy tribesman of Belgae stock.

'Where are the others?' he answered, avoiding the question.

'Most of them have gone to the village. There's a fair organised.'

'When was this announced?'

'This morning,' said Victorinus, entering the conversation. 'What has happened?'

'Nothing as yet,' said Gwalchmai, 'and I hope to Mithras nothing does. But the air smells wrong.'

'I can't smell anything wrong with it,' responded Victorinus.

'That's because you're a Roman,' put in Caradoc, moving to his own blanket roll and retrieving his sword.

'I'll not argue with a pair of superstitious tribesmen, but think on this: if we walk around armed to the teeth, we could incite trouble. We could be accused of breaking the spirit of the truce.'

Gwalchmai swore and sat down. 'You are right, my friend. What do you suggest?'

Victorinus, though younger than his companions, was well respected by the other men in the King's Guards. He was steady, courageous and a sound thinker. His solid Roman upbringing also proved a perfect counterpoint to the unruly, explosive temperaments of the Britons who served the king.

'I am not altogether sure, Gwal. Do not misunderstand me, for I do not treat your talents lightly. You have a nose for traps and an eye that reads men. If you say something is amiss, then I'll wager that it is. I think we should keep our swords hidden inside our tunics and wander around the Keep. It may bc no more than a lingering ill-feeling amongst the Deicester men for Caradoc here taking their money last night in the knife-throwing tourney.'

'I do not think so,' said Caradoc. 'In fact, I thought they took it too well. It puzzled me at the time, but it did not feel right. I even slept with one hand on my dagger.'

'Let us not fly too high, my friends,' said Victorinus. 'We will meet back here in an hour. If there is danger in the air, we should all get a sniff of it.'

'And what if we find something?' asked Caradoc.

'Do nothing. If you can, walk away from trouble. Swallow pride.'

'No man should be asked to do that,' protested the Belgae.

'That may be true, my volatile friend. But if there is to be trouble, then let the Deicester men start it. The king will be less than pleased if you break the truce; he'll flay the skin from your back.'

Gwalchmai moved to the window and pushed open the wooden shutters.

'I do not think we need to concern ourselves about hiding weapons,' he said softly. 'The Deicester men are all armed.'

Victorinus swept up his blanket roll. 'Gather your gear now and follow me. Swiftly.'

'There are about a dozen of them coming this

way with swords in their hands,' said Gwalch-mai, ducking down from the window. Gathering his belongings, he followed his two companions to the rough-carved wooden door leading to the stables. Drawing their swords they stepped through and pulled the door shut behind them. Swiftly they saddled three horses and rode out into the yard.

'There they are!' someone shouted and soldiers rushed out to block the riders. Victorinus kicked his mount into a gallop, crashing into the crowding warriors, who scattered and fell to the cobbles. Then the trio were thundering under the beamed gateway and out into the snow-swept hills.

They had not travelled more than a mile when they came upon the bodies of their comrades, lying in a hollow by a frozen stream. The retainers had been armed only with knives, but at least eleven of the seventeen had been killed by arrows. The rest had been hacked to death by swords or axes.

The three men sat their horses in silence. There was no point in dismounting. They gazed at the dead faces of those who had been their friends, or at the least their comrades in war. By a gnarled oak lay the body of Atticus, the rope-walker. Around him the snow was stained with blood, and it was obvious that he alone of all the retainers had managed to inflict wounds upon the attackers.

'At lea~~ three men,' said Caradoc, as if reading the thoughts of his companions. 'But then

Atticus was a tough whoreson. What do we do now, Victorinus?'

The young Roman stayed silent for a moment, scanning the horizon. 'The king,' he said softly.

'And the boy!' said Gwalchmai. 'Sweet Juno! We must find them – warn them.'

'They are dead,' said Victorinus, removing his bronze helm and staring at his own distorted reflection. 'That is why the retainers were lured away and murdered, and why the king was invited on the stag-hunt. It was a royal stag they hunted. We must get back to Caerlyn and warn Aquila.'

'No!' shouted Caradoc. 'This treachery cannot go unpunished.'

Victorinus saw the pain in the Belgae's eyes. 'And what will you do, Caradoc? Ride back to Deicester and scale the walls to find Eldared?'

'Why not?'

'Because it would be futile – you would die before getting within a yard of Eldared. Think ahead, man. Aquila does not expect the king back until spring and he will be unprepared. The first sight he will see coming from the north is the Deicester army and any allies Eldared has gained. They will seize Eboracum and the traitor will have won.'

'But we must find the king's body,' said Gwalchmai. 'We cannot leave it for the crows; it is not fitting.'

'And suppose he is not yet dead?' offered Caradoc. 'I would never forgive myself for leaving him.'

'I know what you are feeling, and I grieve also. But I beg you to put aside emotion and trust Roman logic. Yes, we could bury the king – but what of Eboracum? You think the king's shade would thank us for putting his body before the fate of his people?'

'And if he is not dead?' persisted Caradoc.

'You *know* that he is,' said Victorinus sadly.

2

Thuro was lost. It had happened soon after the riders left the castle, when the dogs had picked up a scent and raced into the dark wood with the hunters thundering after them. Having no intention of galloping into the trees in hot pursuit, he had reined in the mare and followed at a sedate canter, but somewhere along the trail he had taken a wrong turn and now he could no longer even hear the hounds. The wintry sun was high overhead and Thuro was cold through to his bones . . . and he was hungry. The trees were thinner here, the ground slowly rising. The wind had dropped and Thuro halted by a frozen stream. He dismounted and cracked the ice, dipping his head and sipping the cold fresh water. His father would be so angry with him – he would say nothing, but his eyes would show his displeasure and his face would turn away from the boy.

Thuro cleared the snow from a flat rock and sat down, considering all the options open to him. He could ride on blindly in the hope of stumbling upon the hunters, or he could follow his own tracks back to the castle. It was not hard to find the right course of action with options such as these. He mounted the mare and swung her back to the south.

A large stag stepped lightly on to the trail and stopped to watch the rider. Thuro reined in and leaned forward on the pommel of his saddle. 'Good morning, prince of the forest, are you also lost?' The stag turned contemptuously away and continued its leisurely pace across the trail and into the trees. 'You remind me of my father.' Thuro called after it.

'Do you often talk to animals?' Thuro turned in the saddle to see a young girl, dressed like a forester in green hooded woollen tunic, leather leggings and knee-high moccasins fringed with sheepskin. Her hair was short and a mixture of autumnal colours – light brown, with a hint of both gold and red. Her face was striking, without a hint of beauty and yet. . . .

Thuro bowed. 'Do you live near here?' he asked.

'Perhaps. But obviously you do not. How long have you been lost?'

'How do you know that I am lost?' he countered.

The girl stepped away from the tree beside the trail and Thuro saw that she was carrying a beautiful bow of dark horn. 'You may not be lost,' she said, smiling. 'It may be that you found your tracks so fascinating that you decided you just had to see them again.'

'I concede,' he told her. 'I am seeking Deicester Castle.'

'You have friends there?'

'My father is there. We are guests.'

'A fortune would not induce me to be a guest of that foul family,' she told him. 'Continue on this path until you come to a lightning-blasted oak, then bear right and follow the stream. It will save you time.'

'Thank you. What is your name?'

'Names are for friends, young lordling, not to be bandied about amongst strangers.'

'Strangers can become friends. In fact, all friends were at some time strangers.'

'All too true,' she admitted. 'But to speak more bluntly, I have no wish to strike up a friendship with a guest of Eldared's.'

'I am sorry that you feel this way. It seems a great shame that to sleep in a cold and draughty castle somehow stains the spirit of a man. For what it is worth, my name is Thuro.'

'You do speak prettily, Thuro,' she said, smiling, 'and you have a wonderful eye for horses. Come, join me for the midday meal.'

Thuro did not question her sudden change of heart but dismounted and led his horse away from the trail, following the girl into the trees and up a winding track to a shallow cave under a sandstone rock-face. Here a fire had burned low under a copper pot perched on two stones. Thuro tied the mare's reins to a nearby bush and moved to the fire where the girl joined him. She added oats to the boiling water, and a pinch of salt from a small pouch at her side. 'Gather some wood,' she told him, 'and earn your food.' He did as she bid, gathering thick branches from beside the track and carrying them back to the cave.

'Are you planning to light a beacon fire?' she asked when he returned.

'I do not understand,' he said.

'This is a cooking fire. It is intended to heat the oats and water, and to give us warmth for an hour or so. The wood you need should be dry and no thicker than a thumb-joint. Have you never set a cooking fire?'

'No, I regret that is a pleasure I have not yet encountered.'

'How old are you?'

'I shall be judged a man next autumn,' he said, somewhat stiffly. 'And you?'

'The same as you, Thuro. Fifteen.'

'I shall fetch some more suitable wood,' he said.

'Get yourself a platter at the same time.'

'A platter?'

'How else will you eat your oats?'

Thuro was angry as he left the cave – an emotion he rarely felt and with which he was exceedingly uncomfortable. As he had followed the forest girl he had become acutely aware of the rhythmic movement of her hips and the liquid grace of her walk. By contrast he had begun to feel he was incapable of putting one foot in front of the other without tripping himself. His feet felt twice their size. He longed to do something to impress her, and for the first time in his young life wished he were a shade more like his father. Pushing the thoughts from his mind he gathered wood for the fire, finding also a round flat stone to serve as a platter for his food.

'Are you hungry?' she asked.

'Not very.' Using a short stick, she expertly lifted the pot from the flames and stirred the thick milky contents. He passed her his rock and she giggled.

'Here,' she said, offering him her own wooden plate. 'Use this.'

'The rock will be fine.'

'I am sorry, Thuro; it is unfair of me to mock. It is not your fault you are a lordling; you should have brought your servant with you.'

'I am not a lordling, I am a prince: the son of Maximus the High King. And doubtless were you to be sitting in the hall of Caerlyn, you would feel equally ill at ease discussing the merits of Plutarch's *Life of Lycurgus*.'

Her eyes sparkled and Thuro realised they echoed the russet tones of her hair – light brown with flecks of gold.

'You are probably correct, Prince Thuro,' she said with a mock bow, 'for I was never at ease with Lycurgus and I agree with Plutarch in his comparison with Numa. How did he put it? "Virtue rendered the one so respectable as to deserve a throne, and the other so great as to be above it".'

Thuro returned the bow, but without mockery. 'Forgive my arrogance,' he told her. 'I am not used to feeling this foolish.'

'You are probably more at ease chasing stags and practising with sword and lance.'

'No, I am rather poor in those quarters also. I am the despair of my father. I had hoped to impress you with my knowledge, for there is little else I have to brag of.'

She looked away and poured the cooling oats to her platter, then passed the food to Thuro. 'My name is Laitha. Welcome to my hearth, Prince Thuro.' He searched her face for any hint of mockery, but there was none.

He accepted the food and ate in silence. Laitha put down the pot and leaned back against the cave wall, watching the young man. He was handsome in a gentle fashion and his eyes were grey as woodsmoke, softly sad and wondrous innocent. Yet for all the gentleness Laitha saw, she found no trace of weakness in his face. The eyes did not waver or turn aside, the mouth showed no hint of petulance. And his open admission of his own physical short-comings endeared him to the girl, who had seen enough of loud-mouthed braggarts vying to prove their strength and manhood.

'Why do you not excel?' she asked him. 'Is your sword-master a poor teacher?'

'I have no interest in sword-play. It tires me and then I fall ill.'

'In what way ill?'

He shrugged. 'I am told I almost died at birth, and since then my chest has been weak. I cannot exert myself without becoming dizzy - and then my head pounds and sometimes I lose my sight.'

'How does your father react to all this?'

'With great patience and great sadness – I fear I am not the son he would have preferred. But it does not matter. He is as strong as an ox and as fearless as a dragon. He will reign for decades yet – and perhaps he will marry again and sire a proper heir.'

'What happened to your mother?'

'She died two days after I was born. The birth was early by a month and Maedhlyn – our Enchanter – was absent on the king's business.'

'And your father never remarried? Strange for a king.'

'I have never spoken to him of it . . . but Maedhlyn says she was the still water in his soul and after she had gone there was only fire. There is a wall around Maximus and his grief. None may enter. He cannot look me in the face, for I am much like my mother. And in all the time I can remember he has never touched me – not an arm on the shoulder nor the ruffling of a single hair. Maedhlyn tells that when I was four I was struck down with a terrible fever and my spirit was lost within the darkness of the Void. He says my father came to me then and took me in his arms, and his spirit searched for mine across the darkness. He found me and brought me home. But I remember nothing of it and that saddens me. I would like to be able to recall that moment.'

'He must love you greatly,' she whispered.

'I do not know.' He looked up at her and smiled. 'Thank you for the oats. I must be going.'

'I will guide you to the ford above Deicester,' she said.

He did not argue and waited while she cleaned her pot, platter and spoon. She stowed them in a canvas pack which she slung to her shoulder and then, taking up her bow and quiver, she set out alongside him. The snow was falling thickly now and he was glad she was travelling with him. Without tracks to follow, he knew he would have been lost within minutes.

They had gone but a little way towards the trail when they hear the sound of horses riding at speed. In the first second that he heard the horsemen, Thuro was delighted – soon he would be back at the castle and warm again. But then he realised it would mean saying goodbye to Laitha and on an impulse he turned from the path, leading the mare deeper into the trees and behind a screen of bushes below the trail.

Laitha joined him, saying nothing. There were four men all armed with swords and lances. They drew up a little way ahead, and were joined by three riders coming from the opposite direction.

'Any sign?' The words drifted to Thuro like whispers on the wind and he felt ashamed to be hiding here. These men were out in the cold searching for him – it was unfair of him to put them to further trouble. He was just about to step into view when another man spoke.

'No, nothing. It's incredible. We kill the father in minutes, but the beardless boy causes more trouble.'

'You are talking nonsense, Calin. The father killed six men – and that was with an arrow deep in his lungs. The boy is costing only time.'

'Well, I intend to make him pay for wasting

my time. I'll have his eyes roasting on the point of my dagger.'

Thuro stood statue-still until long after the riders had moved on.

'I do not think you should go back to Deicester,' whispered Laitha, laying a gentle hand on his shoulder.

*

Thuro stood unmoving, staring at the empty trail, his thoughts whirling and diving from fear to regret, from panic to sorrow. His father had been murdered and Thuro's world would never be the same again. This morning he had been miserable and cold, seemingly alone within a cheerless castle. But now he knew he had not been alone, that the giant strength of Aurelius Maximus, the High King, had covered him like a mantle and the companionship of men like Gwalchmai and Victorinus had shielded him from grimmer realities. Laitha was right; he was a spoiled lordling who did not even know how to set a cooking fire. Now the world was once more in turmoil. Eldared, as Maedhlyn had feared, was a traitor and a regicide. The prince was now a hunted animal, with no chance of escaping his hunters. Of what use would be his learning now? Plutarch, Aristotle and Seutonius were no help to a weakly boy in a perilous wood.

'Thuro?'

He turned slowly and saw the concern in Laitha's eyes. 'I think you would be wise to leave me,' he said. 'My company will bring danger to you.'

'What will you do?'

He shrugged. 'I will find my father's body and bury it. Then, I suppose, I will try to make my way back to Caerlyn.'

'You are now the king, Thuro. What will you do when you get there?'

'I shall abdicate. I am not suited to govern others. My father's general, Lucius Aquila, is also his second cousin. He will rule wisely – if he survives.'

'Why should he not?'

'Eldared has the equivalent of five legions and four hundred horsemen. At Caerlyn there are only two legions; the rest of my father's army is made up of militia men who return to their homes in winter. The killing of my father will see the start of a war no one can afford. With the Saxons invading the south, Eldared's ambition is lunacy. But then the Brigantes have always hated the Romans, even before Hadrian built the wall to torment them.'

'I was taught that Hadrian built the wall because he feared them,' said Laitha.

'If that were true, there would have been few north-facing gates. The gates were sally points for raids deep into Brigante territory.' Thuro shivered and noticed that the snow was quickening beneath a thunder-dark sky. 'Where is the nearest village?' he asked.

'Apart from Deicester Town there is Daris, some eight miles to the south-east. But Eldared will have men there looking for you. Why not come to my home? You will be safe there.'

'I will be safe nowhere. And I do not wish to place you in peril, Laitha.'

'You do not understand. I live with my guardian and he will allow no one to harm you.'

Thuro smiled. 'I have just told you that Eldared has five Legions. He is also the man who murdered the High King. Your guardian cannot be as powerful as my enemies.'

'If we stand and debate, we will freeze to death. Now, let your horse go and follow me. Trust me, Thuro, for I am your only chance for life.'

'But why release my horse?'

'It cannot go where I will lead you. And, perhaps more importantly, your hunters are seeking a boy riding and will not search the paths we will walk. Now come on.'

Thuro looped the mare's reins over her head and draped them over the saddle pommel. Then he followed the lithe form of the forest girl ever deeper into the trees, emerging at last at the foot of a high hill in the shadow of the northern mountains. Thuro's feet were cold, his boots wet through. A little way up the rise he stopped – his face white, his breathing ragged as he sank to the snow. Laitha had walked on maybe twenty paces when she turned and saw him beside the trail. She ran lightly back to him and knelt. 'What is the matter?'

'I am sorry – I cannot go on. I must rest for a while.'

'Not here, Thuro, we are in the open. Come on, just a little more.' She helped him to his feet and he staggered on for perhaps ten paces.

Then his legs gave way beneath him. As Laitha bent to help him, she saw movement some two hundred paces back along the trail. Three riders emerged from the trees; saw the travellers and kicked their horses into a gallop.

'Your enemies are upon us, Thuro!' she shouted, dropping the pack from her shoulder and swiftly stringing her bow of horn. Thuro rolled to his knees and tried to stand, but his strength had fled. He watched as the riders drew their swords and saw the gleam of triumph in their eyes, heard the malice in their screams. His eyes flickered to Laitha, who was standing coolly with her bow stretched, the string nestling against her cheek. Time seemed to slow and Thuro viewed the scene with detached fascination as Laitha slowly released her breath and, in the moment between release and the need for more air, loosed the shaft. It took the lead rider between his collar-bones and punched him from the saddle.

But the remaining riders were too close to allow such perfect timing again and Laitha's next shaft was loosed too swiftly. It glanced from the second warrior's helm, snapping back his head; he almost lost his balance and his horse veered to the right, but the last man hurled himself from his saddle to crash into the forest girl as vainly she strove to draw another arrow from her quiver. Her hand flashed for the hunting-knife in her belt, but he hammered his fist into her jaw and she fell to the snow, stunned. The other horseman, having gained control of his mount, stepped from the saddle and approached Thuro with his sword extended.

'Well, little prince, I hope you enjoyed the hunt?'

Thuro said nothing, but he climbed slowly to his feet and met the assassin's eyes.

'Are you not going to beg for life? How disappointing! I thought at the least you would offer us a king's ransom.'

'I do not fear you,' said Thuro evenly. 'You are a man of little worth. Come then, child-killer, earn your salt!'

The man tensed and raised his sword, but then his eyes flickered to a point behind Thuro. 'Who are you?' he asked and Thuro turned his head. Behind him, seeming to appear from nowhere, was a man in a white bearskin cloak. His hair was black and silver shone at the temples; his face was square-cut and clean-shaven, his eyes grey. He was dressed in a dark leather tunic over green woollen leggings and he carried a silver staff with two ebony grips – one at the top, the second half-way down.

'I asked who you were,' repeated the assassin.

'I heard you,' answered the newcomer, his voice deep, and colder than the winds of winter.

'Then answer me.'

'I am Culain lach Feragh, and you have attacked my ward.'

The man glanced at the unconscious girl. 'She is only stunned – and she killed Pagis.'

'It was a fine effort and I will compliment her when she wakes. You, boy,' he said to Thuro softly, 'move behind me,' Thuro did as he was bid and Culain stepped forward.

'I do not like to kill,' he said, 'but unfortunately you and your companion cannot be allowed to leave here alive, so I am left with no choice. Come, defend yourselves.'

For a moment the two assassins simply stood staring at the man with the staff. Then the first of them ran forward, screaming a battle-cry.

Culain's hand dropped down the shaft to the central ebony grip and twisted. The staff parted and a silver blade appeared in his right hand. He parried the wild cut and reversed a slashing sweep to the assassin's throat. The blade sliced cleanly free and the man's head slowly toppled from his shoulders. For one terrible moment the body stood, then the right knee buckled and it fell to rest beside the grisly head. Thuro swallowed hard and tore his eyes from the corpse.

The second assassin ran for his horse and, dropping his sword, vaulted to the saddle as Culain stepped over the corpse and retrieved Laitha's bow. He selected an arrow, drew the string and loosed the shaft with such consummate skill and lack of speed that Thuro had no doubt as to the outcome even before the missile plunged into the rider's back. Culain dropped the bow and moved to Laitha, lifting her gently.

After a while her eyes opened.

'Will you never learn, Gian?' he whispered. 'Another doe for your collection?'

'He is the son of the king. Eldared seeks to kill him.' Culain turned and as his eyes fastened on the prince, Thuro saw something new in his gaze, some emotion that the boy could not place. But then a mask covered Culain's feelings.

'Welcome to my hearth,' he said simply.

3

Eldared, King of the Brigantes, Lord of the Northern Wall, sat silently listening to the reports of his huntsmen. His sons Cael and Moret sat beside him, aware that despite his apparent tranquillity their father's mood was darkening moment by moment.

Eldared was fifty-one years of age and a veteran of dark intrigue. Twenty years before he had switched sides to support the young Roman Aurelius Maximus in his bid for the throne, betraying his own brother Cascioc in the process. Since that time his power had grown and his support for Maximus had earned him great wealth, but his ambition was not content with ruling the highlands. During the last five years he had steadily increased his support amongst the warring tribes of the high country, and solidified his power base among the Britons of the south. All he needed for the throne to fall was the death of Aurelius and his weakling son. After that, a surprise raid on Eboracum would leave him in an unassailable position.

But now a plan of stunning simplicity had been reduced to ashes by simple human error. Three retainers had escaped and the boy, Thuro, was at large in the mountains. Eldared kept his face calm, his hooded eyes betraying no hint of his alarm. The boy was not a great problem in himself, for he was by all accounts spineless and weak. However, if he managed to get back to Caerlyn then Lucius Aquila, the canniest of generals, would use him as a puppet to rally support against Eldared. Added to this, if any of the survivors lived long enough to warn Aquila, then the raid on Eboracum would become doubly perilous.

Eldared dismissed his huntsmen and turned his gaze to his elder son Cael, a hawk-eyed warrior just past his twentieth birthday.

'Suggestions?' invited the king and Cael smiled.

'You do not need me to state the obvious, Father.'

'No. I need you to show me you *understand* the obvious.'

Cael bowed. 'At present the boy is of secondary importance. He is hidden somewhere deep in our lands and we can deal with him at leisure. First we must find the three who escaped, most especially the Roman Victorinus. He is a man Aurelius had chosen for future command and I believe it was he who stopped the others from returning to seek the king.'

'Well and good, boy. But what do you suggest we *do*?'

'Concentrate our efforts in the south-west. Victorinus will cross the Wall at Norcester, and then cut east and south to Eboracum.'

'Why would he take the long route?' asked Moret. 'It only increases his danger.'

41

Cael's eyes showed his contempt for the question, but his voice was neutral as he answered it. 'Victorinus is no fool, brother. He knows we will send men south-east and he gains time by such a manoeuvre. We need to use Goroien.'

Moret cleared his throat and shifted nervously in his seat. Eldared said nothing.

'What choice do we have, Father?' Cael continued.

'Choice?' snapped Moret. 'Another dead Brigante babe for that foul woman!'

'And how many dead Brigante men will fall before the walls of Eboracum if we do *not* use the Witch?' replied Cael. 'If I thought it would guarantee victory, I would let Goroien sacrifice a hundred babes.'

'Moret has a point,' said Eldared softly. 'In this deadly game I like to control events. This Mist Magic of hers can be a boon, but at what price? She plays her own game, I think.' He leaned back in his chair, resting his chin on his steepled fingers. 'We will give the huntsmen another two days to catch the retainers. If they fail, I will summon Goroien. As for the boy . . . I believe he could be dead somewhere in a snow-drift. But send Alantric into the high country.'

'He will not like that,' said Moret. 'The King's Champion sent out after a runaway boy?'

'His likes and dislikes are mine to command – as are yours,' said Eldared. 'There will be many opportunities in the spring for Alantric to show his skills with a blade.'

42

'And what of the Sword?' asked Moret.

Eldared's eyes flashed and his face darkened. 'Do not speak of it! *Ever!*'

*

Victorinus sat near the narrow window of the alehouse tavern staring out at the remains of the Antonine Wall, built far to the north of Hadrian's immense fortifications and stretching from coast to coast over forty miles. It was a turf wall on a stone foundation and, as he stared, the young Roman saw the ruins as a vivid physical reminder of the failing Roman Empire. Three hundred years ago three legions would have patrolled this area, with a fortress every Roman mile. Now it was windswept and mostly deserted, except in remote villages like Norcester, on the well-travelled trade roads. He sipped his ale and cast a covert glance across the room to where Gwalchmai and Caradoc were sitting together, just beyond the six Brigante tribesmen. The three had been journeying for nine days; they had managed to buy provisions and a change of clothing from a Greek merchant on the road south. Victorinus was now dressed in the garb of an Order Taker: a long woollen robe and a fur jerkin. Across his shoulders hung a leather satchel containing stylus parchment and a letter from Publius Aristarchos naming him as Varius Seneca, an Order Taker from Eboracum.

The innkeeper, an elderly Romano-British veteran, moved on to the bench seat alongside Victorinus.

'How soon can delivery be made if I order goods from you?' he asked.

'They will be here in the second week of spring,' answered Victorinus, acutely aware of the Brigantes who sat nearby. 'Depending of course on what you need,' he continued. 'It's been a bad year for wine in Gaul and supplies are not plentiful.'

'I need salt a deal more than I need Gallic wine,' said the man. 'The hunting is good in these hills, but without salt I can save little meat. So tell me, what does your merchant charge for salt?'

Victorinus drew in a deep breath; he was no quarter-master and had no knowledge of such dealings.

'What are you charged currently?' he asked.

'Six sesterces a pound. Five if I take the bulk shipment and then resell to the tribesmen.'

'The cost has risen,' said Victorinus, 'and I fear I cannot match that price.'

'So what can you offer?'

'Six and a half. But if you can secure orders from surrounding villages, I will authorise a payment in kind. One bag in ten sold will come to you free.'

'I do not know how you people have the nerve to sell at these prices. It is not as if we were at war. The trade routes are as safe now as they have ever been.'

'Your thinking is a little parochial, my friend. Most of the trade routes in Brigantes territory may be open, but there is a war in the south, and that has cut our profits.'

A tall Brigante warrior with a deep scar across his cheek rose from his table and approached Victorinus.

'I have not seen you before,' he said.

'Is there any reason why you should have done?' replied Victorinus. 'Do you travel much to Eboracum?'

'You look more like a soldier than an Order Taker.'

'I earn more salt this way, friend, with a great deal less danger.'

'Are you travelling alone?'

'Even as you see. But then I carry little money, and there are few who would attack an Order Taker. They would much rather wait until I have fulfilled my duties and then raid the wagons on their way back.'

The man nodded, but his keen blue eyes remained fixed on the young Roman. Finally he turned his back and rejoined his comrades. Victorinus returned to his conversation with the innkeeper, while keeping a wary eye on the Brigantes. The scarred tribesman looked across at Caradoc and Gwalchmai.

'Where are you from?' he asked.

'South,' said Caradoc.

'Belgae, are you?'

Caradoc nodded.

'I thought I could smell fish!' The other Brigantes chuckled and Caradoc coloured, but tore his eyes from the warrior. 'I had a Belgae woman once,' continued Scarface. 'She charged a copper penny. She looked like you; perhaps it was your mother.'

Gwalchmai reached across the table and gripped Caradoc's arm, just as the tribesman was reaching for his sword. 'It could well have been his mother,' put in Gwalchmai softly. 'As I recall, she had a fondness for animals.'

The Brigante rose from his bench. 'Not wise to be insulting so far from your homeland.'

'It's my upbringing,' said Gwalchmai, rising smoothly. 'I was taught always to silence a yapping dog.'

Iron blades slid sibilantly from their scabbards. Gwalchmai up-ended the table and leapt to the right, drawing his gladius. Caradoc moved left, his sword extended.

'Six against two,' said Gwalchmai, grinning. 'Typical of the Brigantes!'

'The object of battle is to win,' said Scarface, his eyes gleaming, his colour deepening. Caradoc's left hand dropped to his belt, coming up with a heavy dagger. Just as the Brigantes tensed for the attack Caradoc's arm flashed forward and the dagger entered Scarface's throat below the chin strap of his bronze helm. With a gurgling cry he sank to the floor as Caradoc and Gwalchmai charged into the mass, hacking and cleaving.

Victorinus cursed, drew his gladius from within his robe and leapt to join them, plunging his blade deep into the back of a stocky warrior. The tavern was filled with the discordant sounds of battle – iron on iron, iron on flesh. Within seconds the fight was over. Victorinus despatched two of the men, as did Gwalchmai. Caradoc finished his own opponent and then sank to the floor. Victorinus knelt beside him, staring in anguish at the sword that jutted from the Belgae's belly.

'I think he's finished me,' said Caradoc, gritting his teeth against the pain.

'I am afraid that he has,' Victorinus agreed gently.

'You'd better leave me here. I have much to consider.'

Victorinus nodded. 'You were a fine companion,' he said.

'You too – for a Roman!'

Gwalchmai joined them. 'Is there anything I can do?'

'You could look after my woman, Gwal. She's pregnant again. You could . . .' His eyes lost their sparkle and breath rattled from his throat.

Gwalchmai swore. 'You think they guessed who we were?' he asked.

'Perhaps,' replied Victorinus, 'but it is more likely to have been the normal British penchant for tribal disharmony. Come, we had better be on our way.'

'How far is it to the Wall of Hadrian?'

'Too far – unless the Gods smile.'

*

Cael chuckled at his brother's discomfort as they walked across the cobbled courtyard to the carles' quarters. 'You should not have mentioned the Sword,' said the taller man.

'Go ahead – enjoy yourself, Cael. But I know what I saw. When he threw that blade out over the ice, a hand came up out of the water and drew it down.'

'Yes, brother. Was it a man's hand?'

'Your mockery does not upset me. Two other men saw the hand, even if you did not.'

'I was too busy putting the finishing blow to the Roman's neck,' snapped Cael.

'A blow, I notice, that came from behind. Even without his sword you did not have the courage to cut him from the front.'

'You speak of courage?' sneered Cael, pausing before the oak doors of the carles' quarters. 'Where were you? You did not land a blow.'

'I considered eighteen to one good enough odds even for you, Cael.'

'You miserable sheep! Bleat all you want. I did not hear your voice raised in argument when Father's plan was made known.'

'The deed was ignobly done. There is no credit in such a murder. And, by all the Gods beyond, he died well. Even you must admit that.'

'He had a choice then, you think? Even a cornered rat will fight for its life.'

Cael finished the conversation by turning away from his brother and pushing ahead into the dimly-lit quarters seeking Alantric. Moret turned back across the courtyard and returned to his apartments, where his young wife Alhyffa waited. She was dark-haired and sloe-eyed and Moret's passion for her grew daily. He had not wanted to wed the Saxon girl and had argued long into the night with his father. But in the end, as he had known he would, he gave in and the betrothal was secretly agreed. He had travelled by ship to meet his bride, all the way round the coast to the lands they were now calling the South Saxon.

Her father had met him in an inlet near Anderida forest and he had been taken to the Long Hall to see his bride. His heart had been heavy until the moment she entered the Hall . . . then it all but stopped. How could a barbarous animal like Hengist produce such an offspring? As she approached he bowed low, breaking all precedent. If she was surprised, she did not show it. He stopped her as she was about to kneel.

'You will never need to kneel before me,' he whispered.

And he had been true to his word – a fact that had surprised Alhyffa, especially after her father's disparaging comments concerning the treacherous family.

'Have no fear,' he had told her. 'Within a few seasons I shall be at Deicester Keep with an army and then we'll find a good husband for you.'

Yet now Alhyffa was not sure that she wanted her father riding north to take her back. Her husband was not a powerful man, nor yet a weak one, but he was gentle and loving and he aroused in her a feeling not unlike love. As he entered the room she watched his expression move from his perennial look of sadness to an almost juvenile joy. He swept her into his arms and swung her high into the air.

She draped her arms over his broad shoulders and kissed him lightly.

'I have missed you,' he said.

'You liar! You have not been gone an hour.'

'It's true, I swear it.'

'How went it with your father?'

He shrugged and released her, his face once more sad and wistful. 'I have no use for his lust for power. And my brother is as bad - if not worse. You know, Aurelius Maximus was not a bad High King.'

'My father spoke of him always with respect.'

'And yet your father connived in his murder?'

She pulled him to the window bench and sat beside him in the sunshine. 'The High King would have connived in the murder of Hengist, yet I do not doubt that he also respected my father. There has never been a king with clean hands, Moret. You are altogether too sensitive.' He grinned and looked so terribly young that she took his face in her hands and kissed his fair cheeks, running her fingers through his long blond hair. 'You have given me happiness. I pray to Odin that you receive a proper reward for it.'

'You are reward enough for any man.'

'You say that now, young prince, but what when my beauty fades?'

'Ask me that in twenty years. Or thirty. Or forty. Or a hundred!'

Her face became serious. 'Do not wish for the passing of time, Moret, my love. Who knows what the future holds for any of us?'

'Whisht! Do not look sad. The future is all gold, I promise you.'

Alhyffa pulled his head in to her breast and stroked his hair, while her sky-blue eyes stared out towards the south. She saw three horsemen riding and each was holding aloft a severed head. They came closer – riding across the sky towards the window where she sat – and the sky darkened, lightning flashing behind them. She could not see their faces, nor would she look at the heads they carried; she closed her mind's eye against them and heard the bitter laughter as they rode on: Odin's messengers, the Stormcrows, taunting her with premonitions of disaster.

She had never loved her father and thus never cared about his victories or his setbacks. But now she was torn. Moret's family was linked with Hengist and therefore she should wish him success. Yet once successful, her father would turn on Eldared and destroy him and all his get. Eldared with all his cunning could not fail to see this, therefore he must be planning the same tactic. And then what would be the future for Hengist's daughter?

'Do not think of tomorrow, Moret. Enjoy the Now, for it is all any of us ever have.'

4

Thuro awoke in a narrow room with log walls and a single window looking out over the mountains. The room was icy-cold and the young prince burrowed under the blankets, hugging them to his sleep-warm body. He could not remember coming to bed, only the seemingly endless journey to Culain's log cabin nestling in a wood of pine. At one point Thuro's legs had given way beneath him, and Culain had lifted him effortlessly and carried him like a babe across his chest. Thuro remembered being dumped in a wide leather chair as the warrior tindered a fire in the stone hearth, and he could recall staring into the growing flames. But somewhere about that time he must have passed out.

He looked out across the room and saw his clothes laid on a narrow chair. Glancing below the covers he saw that he was naked. He hoped fervently that Laitha had not been present when he was undressed.

The door opened and Culain entered. His long dark hair was tied at the nape of his neck, and he was wearing a high-necked shirt of thick wool and dark leather leggings over mountain boots of cured sheepskin.

'Time to be up, prince! And doing!'

He walked to the bed and dragged back the covers. 'Dress yourself and join me in the other room.'

'Good morning to you,' Thuro told his departing back, but Culain did not respond. The prince climbed from the bed and into his green woollen leggings and shirt of cream-coloured wool, edged with braid. Then he pulled on his boots and returned to sit on the bed. The events of the previous day washed over him like icy water. His father was dead, his own life in peril. He was hundreds of miles from friends and home, at the mercy of a grim-faced stranger he did not know. 'I could do with your help now, Maedhlyn,' he whispered.

Taking a deep breath and offering a prayer to the Earth Goddess, he joined Culain in the main room. The warrior was stacking logs in the hearth when he entered and did not look up.

'Outside you will find an axe and a hatchet. Chop twenty logs no bigger than you see here. Do it now, boy.'

'Why should I chop logs for you?' asked Thuro, disliking the man's tone.

'Because you slept in my bed and I don't doubt you'll want to eat my food. Or is payment above you, prince?'

'I will chop your logs and then I will leave you,' said Thuro. 'I like nothing about your manners.'

Culain laughed. 'You are welcome to leave, but I will be interested to know in which snow-drift you are planning to die. You are weaker than any boy I have ever known. I doubt you have the strength to walk down the mountain, and you certainly do not have the wit to know which direction to take.'

'Why should my fate concern you?'

'I'll answer that question when I'm ready,' said Culain, rising to his feet and moving to tower over the youngster. Thuro stood his ground and answered the firm gaze with uplifted chin, giving not an inch.

Culain smiled. 'Well, boy, you may have no strength in your arms but your spirit is not lacking, thank the Source. Now chop the logs and we'll discuss your departure over breakfast.'

Thuro felt he had won a small victory, but he was not sure what the prize might be or whether the win was worth a lick of salt. He left the cabin and located the wood-store some eighty feet away, near a stand of trees.

He found the axe embedded in a log and wrestled it clear. Then he lifted the log to stand upon a thick ring of pine and hefted the axe over his head. His first swing saw the axe-head miss the log, burying itself in the snow-covered ground. He wrenched it clear, steadied his feet and tried once more. This time the head glanced from the log, tearing the axe from Thuro's slender fingers; he retrieved it. On the third swing the axe hit into the log, stopping half-way through and trapping the head. After several minutes he worked it loose, then he stood and thought about the action necessary to complete the task. He planted his feet wider apart, with his right leg slightly ahead, swung the axe – and split the log. He continued work for some time, until his breathing became ragged, and his face was white with exhaustion. He counted the logs. Eleven . . . and Culain had asked for twenty! More slowly now, he continued the chore. His hands hurt him and he put down the axe to check the skin; four large blisters decorated his palm. He glanced towards the cabin but there was no sign of Culain. Once more he counted the logs: eighteen. He took the axe in his injured hand and set to work until twenty had been split, leaving forty solid chunks.

Returning to the cabin he found Culain sitting in the wide leather chair, his feet raised on a small table. The warrior looked up as he entered.

'I thought you'd fallen asleep out there, prince.'

'I did not fall asleep, and I dislike the tone in your voice when you use my title – you make it sound like a dog's name. My name is Thuro; if you are uncomfortable around royalty, you may use that.'

'May I indeed' What a singular honour! Where is the wood?'

'It is all chopped.'

'But it needs to be in here to be of any use, boy.'

Swallowing his anger, Thuro returned to the wood-store and hefted three chunks which he carried with ease back to the cabin, up the three steps and in to the hearth. He repeated this maneouvre eight times, before his arms burned like fire and his feet dragged in the snow. Culain merely sat, offering no assistance. Twice more Thuro stumbled back bearing wood, then he staggered and fell to the cabin floor. Culain leaned from his chair and tapped the boy on the back.

'Seven more chunks, I think, young Thuro?'

The prince rolled to his knees, anger giving him strength as he staggered out into the snow and this time hefted four pieces which he carried slowly back. His right hand was hot and sticky and as he dumped the wood in the hearth he noticed blood was leaking from the torn blisters. He returned to the wood-store and with a supreme effort carried the last of the chunks back to the cabin.

'Never leave an axe naked to the air,' said Culain. 'Always embed it in wood; it protects the edge.'

Thuro nodded, but lacked the strength for a retort. Once more in the open, he took the axe and plunged the head into a log.

'Anything else?' he called. 'Or is it part of the game that I return first?'

'Come and eat,' called Culain.

The two broke fast with cold meat and cheese, and Thuro wolfed his small portion swiftly. This was followed by a dark ale, so bitter that the prince choked. Culain said nothing, but Thuro finished the foul brew to pre-empt any sneer.

'How do you feel?' asked Culain.

'I am fine.'

'Would you like me to tend to your hand?'

Thuro was about to refuse when he saw that this was what the other man expected. He recalled the advice of Ptolemy, as reported by Plutarch: 'As long as you react, your enemy holds your destiny in the palm of his hand. When you force him to react, you hold his neck in yours.' Thuro smiled. 'That would be kind.'

Culain's eyebrows rose. 'Hold out your hand.' Thuro did so and the warrior tipped salt from the shaker directly on to the wound. It stung like needles of fire. 'That should suffice,' said Culain. 'Now I would like you to do me a service.'

'I owe you nothing. I have paid for my breakfast.'

'Indeed you have, but I would like you to carry a message to Laitha. I don't suppose you would want to leave without wishing her goodbye?'

'Very well. Where is she?'

'She and I built a cabin, higher in the peaks. She likes the solitude. Go to her and tell her I would appreciate her company this evening.'

'Is that all?'

'Yes.'

'Then I shall bid you farewell, Culain lach Feragh – whatever that title may mean – and thank you for your awesome hospitality.'

'I think you should delay your departure – at least until you know where to find Laitha.'

'Then be so kind as to tell me.'

Culain gave him simple directions and Thuro

left without another word. The morning was bright and chill without a trace of breeze, and he wandered through the bleak winter landscape for over an hour before coming to the path Culain had indicated, marked by a fallen tree. He turned to the right and continued the climb, stopping often to rest. It was almost dusk when the exhausted prince came to Laitha's small cabin. She helped him inside and he sat slumped before a log-fire for several minutes, gathering his breath.

'I thought I would die out there,' he said at last.

She sat beside him. 'Climb out of those wet clothes and get warm.'

'It is not fitting,' he replied, hoping she would offer an argument. She did not.

'I'll fetch you something to eat. Some bread and cheese, perhaps?'

'That would be wonderful. I haven't been this hungry since . . . I can't remember.'

'It's a long haul to my home. Why did you come?' She offered him some dark bread and a round of white cheese.

'Culain asked me to give you a message. He said he wanted your company this evening.'

'How strange.'

'The man is strange, and quite the most discourteous individual I have ever met.'

'Well, I think it best you gather your strength and feed a little warmth into your body before we head back.'

'I shall not be going back. I have said my farewells,' Thuro told her.

'You must go back. It is the only way off the mountain and it will be well after dark before we reach his cabin. You'll have to spend at least one more night there.'

'Can I not stay here? With you?'

'As you said, Prince Thuro, that would not be fitting.'

'He knew that,' said Thuro. 'He knew I would be trapped here. What evil game is he playing?'

'I think you presume too much,' she snapped. 'You are speaking of a friend of mine – the greatest friend anyone could ever have. Perhaps Culain does not like spoiled young princelings. But he saved your life, as he saved mine ten years ago – at no small risk to himself. Did he ask you for payment for that, Thuro?'

Instinctively he reached out and touched her hand. She withdrew it as if stung. 'I am sorry,' he said. 'I did not mean to offend you. North of the Wall, you are now the only friend I have. But even you said it was strange that he asked me to come here. Why was that?'

'It does not matter. We should be going.'

'But it *does* matter, Laitha. Let me hazard a guess. You were surprised because you were going to him anyway. Is that not true?'

'Perhaps. Or perhaps he forgot.'

'He does not strike me as a forgetful man. He knew I would be forced back to his cabin.'

'Ask him when you see him,' she countered, donning a heavy sheepskin jerkin and opening the door of the cabin. Outside, a heavy snowfall was in progress and the wind was picking up alarmingly. With a curse Thuro had last heard from a soldier, she slammed the door. 'We cannot leave now,' she said. 'You'll have to stay the night.' Thuro's mood brightened considerably.

Just then the door opened and Culain stepped inside, pausing to brush a dusting of snow from his shoulders.

'Not a good night for travelling, prince,' he said. 'Still, one or two chores in the morning and you'll soon pay for your keep.'

*

Victorinus and Gwalchmai had been riding for four days, and for the last two they had been without food. The Roman was more concerned about the state of their supplies than the possibility of capture, for the horses needed grain and without horses they had no chance of leaving the land of the Brigantes.

'What I would not give for a good bow,' said Gwalchmai, as they spotted several deer on the flanks of a low hill.

Victorinus did not respond. He was tired and the growth of beard on his square chin made him irritable. A man who liked to be clean, the smell of his own stale sweat also galled him as he scratched at his face, cursing the lack of a razor.

'You are beginning to look human,' said Gwalchmai. 'Another few months and I'll braid the beard for you – then you can walk in respectable company.'

Victorinus grinned and some of his ill-humour evaporated. 'We have no coin left,

Gwal, but somehow we must find food for the horses.'

'I suggest we aim for the high ground,' said Gwalchmai, 'and try to spot a village or settlement. We can trade some of Caradoc's gear; his sword should fetch a good price.' Victorinus nodded, but he did not like the idea. The saddest fact about the British tribes was that they were incapable of mixing together without bloodshed. The thought of Gwalchmai riding in to any Brigante or Trinovante settlement filled him with apprehension.

They camped that night in a glade nestling in the bowl of the hills and out of the wind. It snowed heavily, but the two men and their mounts were snug within the shelter of a heavily laden pine and the fire kept their blood from freezing.

The following morning they located a small settlement consisting of some twelve huts and rode warily in. Gwalchmai seemed unconcerned and Victorinus marvelled anew at the British optimism which pervaded the tribes. They had a total inability to learn from past mistakes, and greeted each new day as an opportunity to replay the errors of the past twenty-four hours.

'Try not to insult anyone,' urged Victorinus.

'Have no fear, Roman. Today is a good day.'

They were met by the village head man, an elderly warrior with braided white hair and a blue tattoo on his forehead in the shape of a spider's web.

'Greetings, Father,' said Gwalchmai, as a small crowd gathered behind the head man.

'I am no father to you, South Rat,' answered the man, grinning and showing only one tooth at the top of his jaw.

'Do not be too sure, Father. You look like a man who spread his seed wide as a youngster, and my mother was a woman who attracted such men.'

The crowd chuckled and the old man stepped forward, his blue eyes bright. 'Now you mention it, there is a certain family resemblance. I take it you've brought a gift for your old father?'

'Indeed I have,' said Gwalchmai, stepping down from the saddle and presenting the old man with Caradoc's best knife, an oval-bladed weapon with a hilt of carved bone.

'From across the Water,' said the old man, hefting the weapon. 'Good iron – and a fine edge.'

'It is pleasant to be home,' said Gwalchmai. 'Can we rest the night and feed our horses?'

'But of course, my son.' The old man called forward two youngsters and they led the horses back towards a paddock east of the settlement. 'Join me in my hut.'

The hut was sparsely furnished, but it was a welcome respite from the wind. There was a cot bed and several rugs, and an iron brazier was burning coal. An elderly woman bowed as they entered and fetched bowls of dark ale and some bread and cheese. The three men sat by the brazier and the ancient identified himself as

Golaric, once the champion of the old King Cascioc.

'A fine king – good with sword or lance. He was murdered by his brother and that cursed Roman, Aurelius.' Golaric's bright eyes switched to Victorinus. 'It is not often that an Order Taker bothers to visit my small village.'

'I am not an Order Taker,' owned Victorinus.

'I know that. My teeth may be gone, but my mind is unaffected. You are Victorinus, the Centurion. And you, my wayward son, are Gwalchmai the Cantii, the Hound of the King. Word travels with exceptional speed.'

'We are hunted men, Father,' said Gwalchmai.

'Indeed you are. Is it true that bastard Roman is dead?'

'Yes,' said Victorinus, 'and I'll not hear that term used of him - alive or dead.'

'Short-tempered, is he not?' asked Golaric, seeing Victorinus' hand straying towards his gladius.

'You know these Romans, Father. No control,' said Gwalchmai. 'Why are you so open with your knowledge?'

'It pleases me to be so.'

Gwalchmai smiled. 'I know something of Brigante history. Cascioc was Eldared's elder brother; he was slain in his bed. There was almost a civil war amongst the tribes of the old Caledonian Confederacy. What part did you play in that, Father?'

'As I said, I was the King's Champion. I had a good arm in those days and I should have gone to Eldared and cut his throat, but I did not. The deed was done and I was sworn on Blood Oath to defend the king with my life. But Eldared was now the king so I left his service. And now he offers good gold to kill the men who are a danger to him. I am not interested in his gold; I am interested only in his downfall.'

'I cannot promise that,' said Victorinus. 'All I can say is that he will succeed if we do not reach Eboracum. Eldared bragged of having around fifteen thousand men at his call. Lucius Aquila has only four thousand at Eboracum. Taken by surprise, he would be routed.'

'I do not care whether a Roman survives at Eboracum, but I understand the point you are making. Your horses will be fed and watered tonight, but tomorrow you will leave. I will give you food to carry – not much, for we are a poor village. But be warned, there are hunting parties south and east of you. You must move west and then south.

'We will be careful, Father,' said Gwalchmai.

'And you can stop calling me "Father". I never slept with a Cantii woman in my life – they were all bearded.'

Gwalchmai chuckled. 'He's right,' he told Victorinus. 'It's one reason I joined the king's army.'

'There's something else for you to think of,' said Golaric. 'The huntsmen seem unconcerned about your capture; they say that Mist Magic is being used to track you. If that is true, I pity you.'

The colour drained from Gwalchmai's face.

'What does he mean?' asked Victorinus.

'Death,' whispered Gwalchmai.

*

Throughout the long day the two men rode together and Victorinus grew steadily more uncomfortable with the silence. The land was open, the wind bitterly cold, but it was Gwalchmai's frightened eyes that dominated the Roman's thinking. He had known Gwalchmai for four years, since arriving at Camulodunum as a raw eighteen-year-old fresh from Rome. In that time he had come to hold the man in high regard for his eternal optimism and his reckless bravery, but now he rode like a man possessed – his eyes unseeing, his manner echoing his defeat. They camped in the lee of a rockface and Victorinus prepared a fire.

'What is wrong with you, man?' he asked, as Gwalchmai sat passively staring into the flames.

'It is well for you that you do not understand,' said Gwalchmai.

'I understand fear when I see it.'

'It is worse than fear; it is the foreknowledge of death. I must ready myself for the journey.'

At a loss for a response, Victorinus laughed in his face. 'Is this Gwalchmai I see before me? Is this the King's Hound? More like a rabbit in the torchlight, waiting for the arrow to strike. What is the matter with you, man?'

'You do not understand,' repeated Gwalchmai. 'It is in the bones of this land . . . in the Gods of Wood and Lake. This land was once the home of the Gods, and they still walk here

65

within the Mist. Do not mock me, Roman, for I know whereof I speak. I have seen scaled dragons in the air. I have seen the Atrol walk. I have heard the hissing of dead men's breath. There is no escaping it; if the old gods walk our trail, there is nowhere to hide.'

'You talk like an old woman. What I can see, I can cut. What I can cut, I can kill. There is no more to be said. Gods, indeed! Look around you. Where are the Atrols? Where are the dragons? Where are the dead that walk?'

'You will see, Victorinus. Before they take you, you will see.'

A cloud obscured the moon and an owl swooped over the camp-site. 'There is your dragon, Gwalchmai. Out hunting mice!'

'My father angered an Enchanter once,' said Gwalchmai softly, 'and he summoned a witch woman. They found my father on a hillside – or rather, they found the bottom half of him. The top had been ripped away and I saw the fang marks on his back.'

'Perhaps you are right,' offered Victorinus, 'and perhaps demons do walk. But if they do, a man must face them. Fear is the killer here, Gwal.' A distant wolf howled, the sound echoing eerily through the glade. Victorinus shivered and cursed inwardly. He wrapped his blanket round his shoulders and stoked up the fire, adding fresh branches to the blaze.

'I'll keep watch for a couple of hours,' he said. 'You get some sleep.'

Obediently Gwalchmai wrapped himself in his blankets and lay down by the fire while

Victorinus drew his gladius and sat with his back to a tree. The night wore on and the cold grew. The Roman added more fuel to the fire until the last broken branch was all but finished, then he pushed himself to his feet and stretched his back, moving off into the darkness to gather more dead wood. He put down his gladius and had stooped to lift a long windfall branch when a low, whispering sound alerted him. Still on edge following the conversation with Gwalchmai, he dropped the wood, swept up his sword and dived to the right. Something touched the skin of his back and he rolled, gladius sweeping up into the darkness that threatened to overwhelm him. The blade struck something solid and a bestial scream followed. Victorinus rolled once more as a dark shadow loomed over him, then with a battle-cry he leapt to meet his assailant. His sword plunged home, then a blow to the side of the head sent him hurtling back into the camp-site to skid across the glowing coals of the fire. The clouds parted, the moon shining her silver light upon the scene. Victorinus came to his feet – and froze . . . Before him was a creature some nine feet tall, covered in long brown hair. Its eyes were red, shining like fresh-spilled blood, and its fangs were the length of daggers and wickedly curved. The creature's arms were disproportionately long, hanging almost to the ground, and from the end of each of its four fingers grew gleaming serrated talons.

A grey mist swirled around Victorinus' legs, rising even as he noticed it. The creature advanced. The Roman swiftly wiped his sword hand free of sweat and gripped the leather hilt of his gladius. It was the wrong weapon for this beast; he needed a spear.

'Come forward and die!' he called. 'Have a taste of Roman iron!'

The creature stopped – and spoke. Victorinus was so surprised that he almost dropped his sword.

'You cannot fight destiny, Victorinus,' it said, its voice sibilant. 'This is the day of your passing. Cease your struggle. Rest and know peace. Rest and know joy. Rest . . .' The voice was hypnotic and as the beast advanced Victorinus blinked and tried to rouse himself from the lethargy it induced in him. The mist rose about his shoulders, billowing like wood-smoke.

'No!' he said, backing away.

Suddenly an unearthly scream pierced the silence. The mist parted and Victorinus saw Gwalchmai behind the beast, raising his bloody sword for a second strike. The Roman raced forward to plunge his blade into the hairy throat. The talons lashed at him, ripping the front of his robes and scoring the skin. Gwalchmai struck once more from behind and the creature fell. The mist thickened – then vanished.

The beast was gone.

Victorinus staggered back to the camp-site, gathering together the hot coals with his sword-blade and blowing flames to life. Gwalchmai joined him but they said nothing until the fire was once more lit.

'Forgive me,' said the Roman. 'I mocked in ignorance.'

'There is nothing to forgive. You were right – a man must fight for life, even when he believes all is lost. You taught me a lesson today, Roman. I will not forget it.'

'This is obviously a day for lessons. What was that thing?'

'An Atrol – and a small one. We were lucky, Victorinus. By now they will know they have failed and the next demon will not die as easily.'

'Maybe not – but it *will* die.'

Gwalchmai grinned and slapped him on the shoulder. 'I believe you.'

'One of us ought to,' said the Roman.

'I think we should leave this place,' offered Gwalchmai. 'Now they have the scent, they will be close behind us.'

As if to emphasise his words, a dreadful howling came from the north. It was answered from the east and west.

'Wolves?' asked Victorinus, dreading the answer.

'Atrols. Let us ride.'

5

Thuro stared at the unsmiling Culain and for the first time in his young life felt hatred swell inside him. His father was dead, his own life in ruins and now he was at the mercy of this strange mountain man. He stood up from the floor before the fire.

'I'll work for my keep tonight,' he said, 'despite your trickery. But then I leave.'

'I fear not, young prince,' said Culain, stripping off his leather jerkin and moving to stand before the fire. 'The lower valleys will be cut off by morning and the snow will be drifting over ten feet deep. I am afraid we are forced to endure your company for at least two months.'

'You are a liar!'

'Rarely is that true,' replied Culain softly, kneeling to extend his hands to the flames. 'And certainly not on this occasion. Still, look on the summer side, Thuro. You do not have to see much of me – a few simple chores and you can keep Laitha company. Added to this, you may not be able to leave but neither can your enemies come upon you. By spring you will be able to make the journey home a far less dangerous one. You may even learn something.'

'You have nothing to teach me. I need to acquire none of your ways.'

Culain shrugged. 'As you will. I am tired. I am not as young as once I was. May I rest my old bones upon your cot, Gian?'

'Of course,' said Laitha. Thuro saw the look in her eyes and wished he could inspire such a reaction. Her love for Culain was a radiant thing and Thuro was amazed that he had not realised it before. He felt like an interloper, an intruder, and his heart sank. Why should the forest girl not love this man of action – tall and oak-strong, mature and powerful? Thuro turned away from the love in her eyes and wandered to the far window. It was shut tight against the weather and he made a point of examining the wood, noting the neatness with which it fitted the frame. Not a breath of draught troubled him. When he turned back Culain had gone into the back room, Laitha with him. Thuro returned to the fire. He could hear them speaking in low tones, but could distinguish no words.

Laitha returned a few minutes later and lit two candles. 'He is sleeping,' she said.

'Forgive me, Laitha. I had not wished to intrude.'

Her large brown eyes focused on him, her look quizzical. 'In what way intrude?'

He swallowed hard, aware that he walked a dangerous path. 'On you and Culain. You seem happy together and probably did not need . . . more company. I will be gone as soon as I am able.'

She nodded. 'You were wrong, Thuro. There is much you can learn here – if you use your time well. Culain is a good man, the best I have known. There is no malice in him – whatever you may think. But there is always a reason for his actions that has little to do with selfishness.'

'I do not know him as well as you,' said Thuro in his best neutral tones.

'Indeed you do not. But you might, if only you would start thinking instead of reacting.'

'I do not understand your meaning. Thinking is perhaps the one strength I have. In all my life, my mind has never let me down as have my legs and lungs.'

She smiled and reached out to touch his shoulder and he felt an almost electric thrill in his blood. 'Then think, Thuro. Why is he here?'

'How can I answer that?'

'By examining the evidence before you and reaching a conclusion. Think on it as a riddle.'

Here was a situation in which Thuro felt comfortable. Even the word riddle made him feel more at home, remembering his evenings with Maedhlyn in the oak-panelled study. His mind switched effortlessly to a new path. Culain had asked him to visit Laitha, bringing a message, but then had come himself, thus negating the need for Thuro's journey. Why? He thought of the long arduous climb to this lonely cabin, and realised that the mountain man must have set out soon after he had. He looked up and found Laitha staring at him intently. He smiled, but her face remained fixed.

'Have you come upon the answer?' she asked.

'Perhaps. He was watching out for me – in case I collapsed in the snow.'

Now it was her turn to smile and he watched the tension flow from her shoulders. 'Do you still see him as an ogre?'

'The fact remains that there was no necessity for me to come here at all.'

'Think about that too,' she said, rising smoothly and moving to a long chest by the far wall. She removed two blankets and passed them to him. 'Sleep here before the fire. I will see you in the morning.'

'Where will you sleep?' he asked.

'Alongside Culain.'

'Oh. Yes, of course.'

'Yes, of course,' she repeated, the hint of fire in her eyes. He coloured deeply and looked away.

'I did not mean to offend. Truly.'

'Your words are not as offensive as the look in your eye.'

He nodded and spread his hands. 'I am jealous. Forgive me.'

'Why should I forgive you? What is your crime? You see and you do not see. You make judgements on the flimsiest evidence. Do not be misled, Thuro, as to your strengths. True, your body is not as strong as your mind. But what does that tell us? Your body is so weak that you have mistakenly inflated the true power of your intellect. Your mind is undisciplined and your arrogance unacceptable. Good night to you.'

He sat for a long time watching the fire burn, adding logs and thinking on what she had said. He should have known that Culain had followed him from the moment the tall warrior entered the cabin – just as he should have known why he had been told to come here. True, it was to trap him in the mountains for the remainder of the winter, but there was no gain in it for Culain; only for Thuro, safe now from his enemies. He lay on the floor with the blanket over his shoulders, feeling foolish and young and far out of his depth. Laitha first, and then Culain, had saved his life. He had repaid them with arrogance and lack of gratitude.

He awoke early, having slept dreamlessly. The fire was down to grey ash, with an occasional glowing ember. He carefully shifted the ash, allowing air to circulate, and added the last of the logs. Then he rose and left the cabin. Outside the snow had stopped and the air was fresh and bitterly cold. He located the woodstore and took up a long-handled axe. His first stroke sliced a thick log and he felt pride roar through him. He grinned and drew in a deep, searing breath. The blisters on his hand had dried, but the skin was still sore. He ignored the growing discomfort and continued to chop the wood until twenty logs had been rendered to forty-six chunks. Then he gathered them and sat down on the chopping ring, sweat dripping from his face. He no longer felt cold, he felt alive. His arms and shoulders burned with the raw physical effort, and he waited a little while until his breathing returned to normal. Then he took up three chunks and carried them back to the hearth. Just like the day before, he began to feel light-headed after several trips, so he slowed his action and rested often. In this way he completed his task without collapse, and felt a ridiculous sense of achievement when the hearth was full. He returned to the wood-store and hammered the axeblade into a log. His hand was bleeding again and he sat staring at the congealing blood, as proud of it as of a battle scar.

A brightly coloured bird fluttered down to sit on a branch above his head. Its breast was reddish brown, while its head was black, as if a little cap was perched there. On its back the feathers were grey, like a tiny cape, and the ends of its wings and tail were black with a white stripe – like the symbol of a Pilus Primus, a first centurion.

Thuro had seen birds like this before in Eboracum wood, but had never stopped to examine their beauty. It gave a soft, piping whistle and then vanished off into the woods.

'It was a Pyrrhula, a bullfinch,' said Culain and Thuro jumped. The man's approach had been as silent as the arrival of dawn. 'There are many beautiful birds in the high country. Look there!' Thuro followed his pointing finger and saw the most comical sight. It was a small orange bird with a white beard and black moustache, looking for all the world like a tiny sorcerer. 'That is a Panurus Biarmicus, a bearded tit,' said Culain. 'There are very few left now.'

'It looks like a friend of mine. I wish he could see it.'

'You speak of Maedhlyn – and he has already seen it.'

'You know Maedhlyn?'

'I have known Maedhlyn since the world was young. We grew up in the city of Balacris, before Atlantis sank. And you asked about my title – Culain lach Feragh: Culain the Immortal.' He smiled. 'But not any longer. Now I am Culain the man and the happier for it. I greet every new grey hair as a gift.'

'You are from the Land of Mist?'

'Maedhlyn and I, and several others, created the Land. It was not easy, and even now I am not sure it was worthwhile. What do you think?'

'How can I answer that? I have never been there. Is it wondrous?'

'Wondrous dull, boy! Can you imagine immortality? What is there that is new in the world to pique your interest? What ambitions can you foster that are not instantly achievable? What joy is there in an endless sequence of shifting seasons? Far better to be mortal and grow old with the world around you.'

'There is love, surely?' said Thuro.

'There is always love. But after a hundred years, or a thousand, the flames of passion are little more than a glow in the ash of a long-dead fire.'

'Is Laitha immortal?'

'No, she is not of the Mist. Are you taken

with her, Thuro? Or are you bored, stuck in these woods?'

'I am not bored. And yes, she is beautiful.'

'That is not what I asked.'

'Then I cannot answer. But I would not presume to approach your lady – even were she to receive me.'

Culain's grey eyes sparkled and a wide grin crossed his features. 'Well said! However, she is not my lady. She is my ward.'

'But she sleeps with you!'

'Sleeps, yes. Was life so sheltered for you in Eboracum? What can Maedhlyn have been thinking of?'

'And yet she loves you,' said Thuro. 'You cannot deny it.'

'I would hope that she does, for I have been a father to her – as best I could.'

For the first time in his short relationship with the Mist Warrior, Thuro felt strangely superior. For he knew that Laitha loved Culain as a man; he could see it in her eyes and the tilt of her head. Yet Culain could not see it; this made him truly mortal and Thuro warmed to him.

'How old are you?' he asked, switching the subject.

'The answer would dazzle you, and I shall not give it. But I will say that I have watched this island and its people for over seven hundred years. I was even the king once.'

'Of which tribe?'

'Of all the tribes. Have you not heard of Cunobelin?'

'The Trinovante king? Yes. That was you?'

'For over forty years I ruled. I was a legend, they tell me. I helped build Camulodunum. Seutonius wrote of me that I was the Brittanorum Rex – the king of all Britain – the greatest of the Belgic kings. Ah, but I had an ego in those days and I did like so to be flattered!'

'Some of the tribes believe that you will return when the land is threatened. It is taught around the camp-fires. I thought it a wonderful fable, but it could be true. You could come back; you could be king again.'

Culain saw the brightness of hope in the boy's eyes. 'I am not the king any longer, Thuro. And I have no wish to rule. But you can.'

Thuro shook his head. 'I am not like my father.'

'No, there is a great deal of your mother in you.'

'Did you know her?'

'Yes, I was there the day Maedhlyn brought your father home. Alaida gave up everything for him, including life. It is not a subject it pleases me to speak of, but you have a right. Alaida was my daughter, the only child I have fathered in my long life. She was nineteen when she left the Feragh, twenty when she died. Twenty! I could have killed Maedhlyn then. I nearly did. But he was so penitent I realised it was a greater punishment to leave him be.'

'Then you are my grandfather?' asked Thuro, savouring the feel of the word and seeing for the first time that Culain's eyes of wood-smoke grey were the image of his own.

'Yes,' said Culain.

'Why did you never come to see me? Did you hate me for killing my mother?'

'I think that I did, Thuro. Great age does not always ensure great wisdom – as Maedhlyn knows! I could have saved Alaida, but I refused to allow her to take a Stone from the Feragh.'

'Are the stones magical there?'

'Not all of them, but there is a special Stone we call the Sipstrassi, and it is the source of all magic. What a man can dream he can create. The most imaginative of men become Enhancers; they liven an otherwise tedious existence with their living dreams.'

'Maedhlyn is one of these,' said Thuro, 'I have seen him conjure winged horses no longer than my fingers, and whole armies to battle on my father's desk-top. He showed me Marathon and Thermopylae, Platea and Phillipi. I saw the great Julius fought to a standstill in Britain by Caswallon. I listened to Antony's funeral oration . . .'

'Yes, I too have seen these things,' said Culain, 'but I was speaking of Alaida.'

'I am sorry,' said Thuro, instantly contrite.

'Do not be. Boys and magic make for excitement. She had her own Stone but I would not allow her to take it from the Feragh. I thought, somehow, that when she needed me she would call. I knew I would hear her wherever I was. But she did not call. She chose to die. Such was her pride.'

'And you blame yourself for her death?'

'Who else would I blame? But that is in the

past and you are the present. What am I to do with you?'

'Help me get back to Eboracum?'

'Not as you are, Thuro. You are only half a man. We must make you strong; you will not survive a day as the weakling prince.'

'Will you use Stone magic to make me strong?'

'No. Earth magic,' said Culain. 'We will look inside you and see what we can find.'

'I am not cut out to be a warrior.'

'You are my grandson and the son of Aurelius and Alaida. I think you will find that blood runs true. We already know you can swing an axe. What other surprises do you hold in store?'

Thuro shrugged. 'I do not want to disappoint you, as I disappointed my father.'

'Lesson one, Thuro: from now on you have no one to disappoint but yourself. But you must agree to abide by what I say and obey every word I utter. Will you do this?'

'I will.'

'Then prepare to die,' said Culain. And there was no humour in his eyes.

Thuro stiffened as Culain stood and pulled a gladius from a sheath behind his belt. The blade was eighteen inches long and double edged, the hilt of leather. He reversed the weapon and handed it to Thuro. It felt blade-heavy and uncomfortable in his hand.

'Before I can teach you to live, you must learn to die – how it feels to be vanquished,' said Culain. 'Move on to open ground and wait.' Thuro did as he was bid and Culain produced a small golden stone from his pocket, closing his fist around it. The air thickened before Thuro, solidifying into a Roman warrior with bronze breastplate and leather helm. He seemed young, but his eyes were old. The warrior dropped into a fighting crouch with blade extended and Thuro backed away, uncertain.

The warrior advanced, locking Thuro's gaze. The blade lunged. Instinctively Thuro parried, but his opponent's gladius rolled over his own and plunged into the boy's chest. The pain was sickening and all strength fled from the prince. His knees buckled and he fell with a scream as the Roman dragged free his blade.

Moments later Thuro rose out of darkness to feel the snow on his face. He pushed himself to his knees and felt for the wound. There was none. Culain's strong hand pulled him to his feet and Thuro's head spun. Culain sat him on the chopping ring.

'The man you fought was a Roman legionary who served under Agricola. He was seventeen and went on to become a fine gladiator. You met him early in his career. Did you learn anything?'

'I learnt I am no swordsman,' admitted Thuro ruefully.

'I want you to use your brain and stop thinking with your feelings. You knew nothing of Plutarch before Maedhlyn taught you. There are no born swordsmen; it is an acquired skill, like any other. All it requires is good reflexes, allied to courage. You have both. Believe it!

Now follow me, there is something I want you to see.'

Thuro offered the gladius to Culain, who waved it away. 'Carry it with you always. Get used to the feel and the weight. Keep it sharp.'

The Mist Warrior walked out past the cabin and down the slope towards the valley below. Thuro followed, his belly aching for food. The return trip to Culain's cabin was made in less than an hour and the prince was frozen when they arrived. The cabin was cold and there was no wood in the hearth.

'I shall prepare breakfast,' said Culain. 'You . . .'

'I know. Chop some logs.'

Culain smiled and left the boy by the wood-store. Thuro took up the axe in his sore hands and began his work. He managed only six logs and carried the chunks into the hearth. Culain did not berate him and gave him a wooden bowl filled with hot oats, sweetened with honey. The meal was heavenly.

Culain cleared away the dishes and returned with a wide bowl brimming with clear water. He placed it before Thuro and waited for the ripples to settle.

'Look into the water, Thuro.' As the prince leaned forward, Culain lifted a golden stone over it and closed his eyes.

At first Thuro could see only his reflection and the wooden beams above his head. But then the water misted and he found himself staring down from a great height to the shores of a frozen lake. A group of riders was gathered there. The scene swelled, as if Thuro were swooping down towards them, and he recognised his father. A burning pain began in his chest, tightening his throat, and tears blurred his vision. He blinked them back. By the lake a man stepped from behind a rock, a long-bow bent. The arrow flashed into his father's back and his horse reared as his weight fell across its neck, but he held on. The other riders swarmed forward and the king drew his sword and cut the first man from the saddle. A second arrow took his horse in the throat and the beast fell. The king leapt clear and ran to the edge of the lake, turning with his back to the ice. The riders – seventeen of them - dismounted. Thuro saw Eldared at the rear with one of his sons. The group rushed forward and the king, blood staining his beard, stepped in to meet them with his double-handed sword hacking and cleaving. The killers fell back in dismay. Five were now down, two others retired from the fray with deep wounds to arm and shoulder. The king stumbled and bent double, blood frothing from his mouth. Thuro wanted to look away, but his eyes were locked to the scene. An assassin ran in to plunge a dagger to the king's side; the dying monarch's blade sliced up and over, all but beheading the man. Then the king turned and staggered on to the ice and, with the last of his strength, hurled the sword far out over the lake. The assassins swarmed around the fallen king and Thuro saw Cael deliver the death blow. And in that dreadful moment the prince watched as something akin to triumph flared in Aurelius' eyes. The sword hung in the air, hilt down, just above a spot at the centre of the lake where the ice had broken. A slender hand reached up from below the water and drew the sword down.

The scene fragmented and blurred and Thuro's own astonished face appeared on the surface of the water in the bowl. He leaned back and saw Culain watching him intently.

'What you saw was the death of a man,' said Culain softly, respectfully, as if conveying the greatest compliment. 'It was meet that you should see it.'

'I am glad that I did. Did you see his eyes at the end? Did I misread them, or was there joy there?'

'I wondered that, and only time will supply an answer. Did you see the sword?'

'Yes, what did it mean?'

'Simply that Eldared does not have it. And without it he cannot become High King. It is the Sword of Cunobelin. My sword!'

'Of course. My father took it from the stone at Camulodunum; he was the first to be able to draw it.'

Culain chuckled. 'There was little skill in that. Aurelius had Maedhlyn to guide him, and it was Maedhlyn who devised the Stone ploy in the first place. The reason no one could draw the sword was that it was always a heartbeat ahead in time. Draw it? No man could touch it. It was part of the legend of Cunobelin, a legend Maedhlyn and I established four hundred years ago.'

'For what reason?' asked Thuro.

'Vanity. In those days, as I have told you. I had a great ego. And it was fun, Thuro, to be a king. Maedhlyn helped me to age gracefully. I still had the strength of a twenty-five-year-old, within a body that looked wonderfully wrinkled. But then I grew bored and Maedhlyn staged my death – but not before I had dramatically planted my sword in the boulder and created the legend of my return. Who knew then, but that I might want to? Unfortunately events did not fare too well after my departure. A young man named Caractacus decided to anger the Romans and they took the island by force. By then I was elsewhere. Maedhlyn and I crossed the Mist to another age. He had fallen in love with the Greek culture and became a travelling philosopher. But he couldn't resist meddling and he trained a young boy and made him an emperor – conquered most of the world.'

'What did you do?'

'I came home and did what I could for the Britons. I felt somewhat responsible for their plight. But I did not take up arms until the death of Prasutagas. After he died, the Romans flogged his wife Boudicca and raped his daughters. I raised the Iceni under Boudicca's banner and we harried the invincible Roman army all the way to Londinium, which we burnt to the ground. But the tribes never learnt discipline and we were smashed at Atherstone by that wily fox Paullinus. I took Boudicca and her daughters back to the Feragh and they lived there in some contentment for many years.'

'And did you fight again?' asked Thuro.

'Another day, Thuro. How do you feel?'

'Weary.'

'Good.' Culain removed his own fur-lined jerkin and handed it to the boy. 'This should keep you warm. I want you to return to Laitha's cabin, restore yourself in her good grace and then return here.'

'Could I not rest for a while?'

'Go now,' said Culain. 'And if you can, when you come in sight of her cabin, run. I want some strength built into those spindly legs!'

6

Prasamaccus was proud of his reputation as the finest hunter of the Three Valleys. He had worked hard on his bowmanship, but knew that it was his patience that set him apart from the rest. No matter the weather, burning heat or searing cold, he could sit silently for hours waiting the right moment to let fly. No stringy meat for Prasamaccus, for his quarry dropped dead instantly, shot through the heart. No deer he killed had run for a mile with its lungs bubbling and its juices swelling the muscles to jaw-breaking toughness.

His bow was a gift from his clan leader Moret, son of Eldared. It was a Roman weapon of dark horn, and he treasured it. His arrows were straight as shafts of sunlight and he trimmed each goose-feather with careful cuts. In a tourney last Astarte Day, he had brought a gasp from the crowd when he sliced to the bull through the shaft of his last hit. It was a fluke and yet highlighted his awesome eye.

Now, as he sat hidden in the bushes of the hillside, he needed all his patience. The deer were slowly but steadily making their way towards him. He had been hidden here for two hours and his blood felt like ice even through the sheepskin cloak gathered about his slender frame. He was not a tall man, and his face was thin and angular, blue eyes set close together. His chin was pointed, emphasised by a straggly blond beard. Crouched as he now was, it was impossible to spot the deformity that set him apart from his fellows, which has deprived this finest of hunters from taking a bride.

The deer was almost within killing range and Prasamaccus chose a fat doe as his target. With infinite lack of speed he drew a long shaft from his doeskin quiver and notched it to the bowstring.

Just then the lead stag's head came up and the small herd scattered. Prasamaccus sighed and stood. He limped forward, his twisted leg causing him to hobble in a sadly comical manner. When he was a toddler he had fallen in the path of a galloping horse that smashed his left leg to shards. Now it was some eight inches shorter than the right, the foot mangled and pointing inward. He waited as the riders galloped towards him. There were two men and their horses were lathered; they ignored him and thundered past. As a hunter himself, he knew they were being pursued and glanced back along the trail. Three giant beasts were loping across the snow and Prasamaccus blinked. Bears? No bear could move that fast. His eyes widened. Lifting his hand to his mouth he let out a piercing whistle and a bay mare came galloping from the trees. He pulled himself into the saddle and slapped her rump. Unused to such treatment from a normally

gentle master, the mare broke into a run. Prasamaccus steered her after the riders, swiftly over-
taking their tired mounts.

'Veer left!' he shouted. 'There is a ring of
stones and a high hollow altar.'

Without checking to see if they followed him,
he urged the mare up the snow-covered hill and
over the crest, where black stones ringed the
crown of the hill like broken teeth. He clambered from the saddle and limped to the centre
where a huge altar stone was set atop a crumbling structure some eight feet high. Prasamaccus clawed his way to the top, swung his
quiver to the front and notched an arrow to his
bow.

The two riders, their mounts almost dead
from exhaustion, reached the circle scant
seconds before the beasts. Prasamaccus drew
back the bow-string and let fly. The shaft sped
to the first beast as it towered over a running
tribesman with a braided blond beard. The
arrow took the beast in its right eye and it fell
back with a piercing scream that was almost
human. The two men scrambled up alongside
Prasamaccus, drawing their swords.

A mist sprang up around the circle, swirling
between the stones and rising to stand like a
grey wall beyond the monoliths. The two
remaining Atrols faded back out of sight and
the three men were left at the centre in ghostly
silence.

'What are those creatures?' asked
Prasamaccus.

'Atrols,' answered Gwalchmai.

'I thought they must be, but I expected them to be bigger,' said the bowman. Victorinus smiled grimly. The mist around the stones was now impenetrable, but it had not pervaded the centre. Victorinus glanced up. There was no sky, only a thick grey cloud hovering at the height of the stones.

'Why are they not attacking?' asked the Roman. Gwalchmai shrugged. From beyond the stones came a sibilant, whispering voice.

'Come forth, Gwalchmai. Come forth! Your father is here.' A figure appeared at the edge of the mist, a bearded man with a blue tattoo on both cheeks. 'Come to me, my son!' Gwalchmai half-rose, but Victorinus grabbed his arm. Gwalchmai's eyes were glazed; Victorinus struck him savagely across the cheek, but the Briton did not react. Then the voice came again.

'Victorinus . . . your mother waits.' And a slender white-robed woman stood alongside the man.

An anguished groan broke from Victorinus' lips and he released his hold on Gwalchmai, who scrambled down the altar. Prasamaccus, understanding none of this, pushed himself to his feet and sent an arrow into the head of Gwalchmai's father. In an instant all was changed. The image of the man disappeared to be replaced by the monstrous figure of an Atrol, tearing at the shaft in its cheek. Gwalchmai stopped, the spell broken. The image of Victorinus' mother faded back into the mist.

'Well done, bowman!' said Victorinus. 'Get back here, Gwal!'

As the tribesman turned to obey the mist cleared, and there at the edge of the stones were a dozen huge wolves standing almost as tall as ponies.

'Mother of Mithras!' exclaimed Prasamaccus.

Gwalchmai sprinted for the stones as the wolves raced into the circle. He leapt, reaching for Victorinus' outstretched hand. The Roman grabbed him and hauled him up, just ahead of the lead wolf whose jaws snapped shut bare inches from Gwalchmai's trailing leg.

Prasamaccus shot the beast in the throat and it fell back. A second wolf leapt to the altar, scrabbling for purchase, but Victorinus kicked it savagely and it pitched to the ground. The wolves were all around them now, snarling and snapping. The three men backed to the centre of the altar. Prasamaccus sent two shafts into the milling beasts, but the rest ignored their wounded comrades. With only three shafts left, Prasamaccus refrained from loosing any more arrows.

'I don't like to sound pessimistic,' said Gwalchmai, 'but I'd appreciate any Roman suggestions at this point.'

A wolf jumped and cleared the rock screen around the men. Gwalchmai's sword rammed home alongside Prasamaccus' arrow.

Suddenly the ground below began to tremble and the stones shifted. Gwalchmai almost fell, but recovered his balance in time to see Victorinus slip from the shelter. The tribesman hurled himself across the altar, seizing the Roman's robe and dragging him to safety. The wolves also cowered back as the tremor continued. Lightning flashed within the circle and a huge wolf reared up, his flesh transparent, his awesome bone structure revealed. As the lightning passed the beast fell to earth and the stink of charred flesh filled the circle. Once more lightning seared into the wolves and three died. The rest fled beyond the stones into the relative sanctuary of the mist.

A man appeared from within a glow of golden light beside the altar. He was tall and portly, a long black moustache flowing on to a short-cropped white beard. He wore a simple robe of purple velvet.

'I would suggest you join me,' he said, 'for I fear I have almost used up my magic.'

Victorinus leapt from the altar, followed by Gwalchmai. 'Hurry now, the Gate is closing.' But Prasamaccus, with his ruined leg, could not move at speed and the golden globe began to shrink. Gwalchmai followed the wizard through, but Victorinus ran back to aid the bowman. Breathing heavily, Prasamaccus hurled himself through the light. Victorinus hesitated. The glow was no bigger than a window, and shrinking fast as the wolves poured into the circle. A hand reached through the golden light, hauling the Roman clear. There was a sensation like ice searing hot flesh and Victorinus opened his eyes to see Gwalchmai still holding him by the robe . . . only now they were standing in Caerlyn wood, overlooking Eboracum.

'Your timing is impeccable, Lord Maedhlyn,' said Victorinus.

'Long practice,' said the Enchanter. 'You must make your report to Aquila, though he already knows that Aurelius is dead.'

'How?' asked Gwalchmai. 'Did someone else escape?'

'He knows because I told him,' snapped Maedhlyn. 'That's why I am an Enchanter and not a cheese-maker, you ignorant moron.'

Gwalchmai's anger flared. 'If you are such an Enchanter, then why is the king dead? Why did your powers not save him?'

'I'll not bandy words with you, mortal,' hissed Maedhlyn, looming over the tribesman. 'The king is dead because he did not listen, but the boy is alive because I led him clear. Where were you, King's Hound?'

Gwalchmai's jaw dropped. 'Thuro?'

'Is alive, no thanks to you. Now begone to the barracks.' Gwalchmai stumbled away and Victorinus approached the Enchanter.

'I am grateful, my lord, for your aid. But you were wrong to berate Gwalchmai. I led him from Deicester; we believed the boy dead.'

Maedhlyn waved his hand as if swatting a fly. 'Wrong, right! What does it matter? The clod made me angry; he was lucky I didn't turn him into a tree.'

'If you had, my lord,' said Victorinus, with a hard smile, 'I'd have slit your throat.' He bowed and followed Gwalchmai towards the barracks.

'And what is your part in this?' Maedhlyn asked Prasamaccus.

'I was hunting deer. This has not been a good day for me.'

*

Prasamaccus hobbled into the barrack square, having lost sight of the swifter men. Some children gathered to mock him, but he was used to this and ignored them. The buildings here were grand, but even Prasamaccus could tell where the old Roman constructions had been repaired or renovated; the craftsmanship was less skilled than the older work.

The roads and alleyways were narrow and Prasamaccus passed through the barracks square and on to the Street of Merchants, pausing to stare into open-fronted shops and examine cloth, or pottery, and even weapons in a large corner building. A fat man wearing a leather apron approached him as he examined a curved hunting-bow.

'A fine weapon,' said the man, smiling broadly. 'But not as fine as the one you are carrying. Are you looking to trade?'

'No.'

'I have bows that could outdistance yours by fifty paces. Good strong yew, well seasoned.'

'Vamera is not for sale,' said Prasamaccus, 'though I could use some shafts.'

'Five denarii each.'

Prasamaccus nodded. It had been two years since he had seen money coin, and even then it had not been his. He smiled at the man and left the shop. The day was bright, the snow absent from the town, though still to be seen decorating the surrounding hills. Prasamaccus thought of his predicament. He was a hunter without a horse, and with only two arrows, in a land that was not his own. He had no coin and no hope of support. And he was hungry. He sighed, and wondered which of the Gods he had angered now. All his life people had told him the Gods did not like him. The injury to his leg was proof of that, they said. The only girl he had ever loved had died of the Red Plague. Not that Prasamaccus had ever told her of his love but even so, as soon as his affection materialised within him, she had been struck down. He turned his pale blue eyes to the heavens. He felt no anger at the Gods. How could he? It was not for him to question their likes and dislikes. But he felt it would be pleasant at least to know which of them held him in such low esteem.

'What's wrong with your leg?' asked a small, fair-haired boy of around six years.

'A dragon breathed on it,' said Prasamaccus.

'Did it hurt?'

'Oh yes. It still does when the weather turns wet.'

'Did you kill the dragon?'

'With a single shaft from my magic bow.'

'Are they not covered with golden scales?'

'You know a great deal about dragons.'

'My father has killed hundreds. He says you

can only strike them behind their long ears; there is a soft spot there that leads to the brain.'

'Exactly right,' said Prasamaccus. 'That's how I killed mine.'

'With your magic bow.'

'Yes. Would you like to touch it?' The boy's eyes sparkled and his small hand reached out to stroke the black, glossy frame.

'Will the magic rub off?'

'Of course. The next time you see a dragon, Vamera will appear in your hand with a golden arrow.'

Without a goodbye the boy raced off shouting his father's name, desperate to tell him of his adventure. Prasamaccus felt better. He hobbled back into the barrack square and followed the smell of cooking meat to a wide building of golden sandstone. Inside was a mess hall with rows of bench tables and at the far end a huge hearth where a bull was spitted. Prasamaccus, ignoring the stares as he passed, moved slowly to the line of men waiting for food and picked up a large wooden platter. The line moved on, each man receiving two thick slabs of meat and a large spoonful of sprouts and carrots. Prasamaccus reached the server, a short man who was sweating profusely. The man watched him for a moment, offering no meat.

'What are you doing here, cripple?'

'I am waiting to eat.'

'This is the Auxiliaries' dining-hall. You are no soldier.'

'The Lord Maedhlyn said I could eat here,' lied Prasamaccus smoothly. 'But if you wish, I

96

will go to him and say you refused. What is your name?'

The man dumped two slabs of meat on his plate. 'Next!' he said. 'Move along now.'

Prasamaccus looked for a nearby empty table. It was important not to sit too closely to other men, for all who saw him knew he was despised by the Gods and none would want that luck rubbing off. He found a table near the window and sat down; taking his thin-bladed hunting-knife from its sheath, he sliced the meat and ate it slowly. It tasted fine, but the fat content was high. He belched and leaned back, content for the first time since the incident with the Atrols. Food was now no longer a problem. The magic name of Maedhlyn cast a powerful spell, it seemed.

A stocky, powerfully built man with a square-cut beard sat opposite him. Prasamaccus looked up into a pair of dark brown eyes. 'I understand the Lord Enchanter told you to eat here,' said the man.

'Yes.'

'I wonder why,' the man went on, his suspicion evident.

'I have just returned from the north with Gwalchmai and . . . the other fellow.'

'You were with the king?'

'No. I met Gwalchmai and came with them.'

'Where is he now?'

'Making a report.' Prasamaccus could not remember the name of the clan leader, used by Maedhlyn.

'What news from the north?' asked the man. 'Is it true the king is dead?'

Prasamaccus remembered the savage joy in his own Brigante village on hearing the news. 'Yes,' he answered. 'I am afraid that it is.'

'You do not seem too concerned.'

Prasamaccus leaned forward. 'I did not know the man. Gwalchmai feels his loss keenly.'

'He would,' said the man, relaxing. 'He was the King's Hound. How was the deed done?'

'I do not know all the facts. You must ask Gwalchmai and . . .'

'Who?'

'I am bad with names – a tall man, dark-haired, curved nose.'

'Victorinus?'

'That was it,' said Prasamaccus, remembering the sibilant calls of the Atrols.

'What happened to the others?'

'What others?'

'The king's retainers?'

'I do not know. Gwalchmai will answer all your questions.'

'I am sure that he will, my Brigante friend, and until he arrives you must consider yourself my guest.' The man stood and called two soldiers over. 'Take this man into custody.'

Prasamaccus sighed. The Gods were surely laughing today.

The two soldiers walked Prasamaccus across the square, keeping out of arm's reach of the cripple. One carried his bow and quiver, the other had taken possession of his hunting-knife. They led him to a small room with a barred door and no window. Inside was a narrow pallet bed. He listened as the bar dropped into place and then lay down on the bed. There was a single blanket and he covered himself. Food had been taken care of and now they had given him a bed. He closed his eyes and fell asleep almost instantly.

His dreams were good ones. He had killed a Mist demon – he, 'Prasamaccus the Cripple'. In his dreams his leg was restored to health and beautiful maidens attended him.

He was not happy to be awakened.

'My friend, please accept my sincere apologies,' said Victorinus as Prasamaccus sat up, rubbing his eyes. 'I had to make my report, and I forgot all about you.'

'They fed me and gave me a place to sleep.'

'Yes, I see that. But I want you to be a guest in my home.'

Prasamaccus swung his legs from the bed. 'Can I have my bow back?'

Victorinus chuckled. 'You can have your bow, as many arrows as you can carry and a fine horse from my stable. Your own choice.'

Prasamaccus nodded sagely. Perhaps he was still dreaming after all.

7

For three weeks now Thuro had followed the instructions of Culain. He had run over mountain trails, chopped and sawed, carried and worked, and been 'killed' on countless occasions by a succession of swordsmen conjured by the Mist Warrior. His greatest moment had been when he finally beat the young Roman. He had noticed during their three previous bouts that his opponent was thick-waisted and unbending, so he had advanced, dropped to his knees and thrust his gladius up into the man's groin. The soldier had vanished instantly. Culain had been well pleased, but had added a cautionary note.

'You won, and should enjoy your triumph. But the move was dangerous. Had he anticipated it, he would have had an easy kill with a neck thrust.'

'But he did not.'

'True. But tell me, what is the principle of sword-fighting?'

'To kill your opponent.'

'No. It is *not* to be killed *by* your opponent. It is rare that a good swordsman leaves an opening. Sometimes it is necessary, especially if you find your enemy is more skilled, but such risks are generally to bc avoided.'

After that Culain had conjured a Macedonian warrior from the army of Alexander. This man, grim-eyed and dark-bearded, had caused Thuro great problems. The boy had tried the winning cut he had used against the Roman, only to feel the hideous sensation of a ghostly sword entering his neck. Shamefaced, he had avoided Culain's eye but the Mist Warrior did not chide him.

'Some people always need to learn lessons the painful way,' was all he said.

One morning Laitha came to watch him, but his limbs would not operate smoothly and he tripped over his apparently enlarged feet. Culain shook his head and sent the laughing Laitha away.

Thuro finally despatched the Macedonian with a move Culain taught him. He blocked the man's sweeping cut from the left, swung on his heel to ram his elbow into the man's face and finished him with a murderous slice to the neck.

'Tell me, do they feel pain?'

'They?'

'The soldiers you conjure.'

'They do not exist, Thuro. They are not ghosts, they are men I knew. I create them from my memories. Illusions if you like.'

'They are very good swordsmen.'

'They were bad swordsmen – that's why they are useful now. But soon you will be ready to tackle adequate warriors.'

When he was not working Culain would walk

him through the woods, pointing out animal tracks and identifying them. Soon Thuro could spot the spoor of the red fox with its five-pointed pads or the cloven hooves of a trotting fallow deer, light and delicate on the trail. Some animals left the most bewildering evidence of their passing; one such they found by a frozen stream, four closely-set imprints in a tight square. Two feet further on there were another four . . . and so on.

'It is a bounding otter,' said Culain. 'It kicks off with its powerful hind legs and comes down on its front paws. The rear paws then land just behind the front and the beast takes off for another bound, leaving four tracks close together. Obviously it was frightened.'

At other times Thuro would walk with Laitha, whose interest was trees and flowers, herbs and fungi. In her cabin she had sketches, richly coloured, of all kinds of plants. Thuro was fascinated.

'Do you like mushrooms?' asked Laitha, one day in early spring.

'Yes, fried in butter.'

'Does this look tasty?' She showed him a beautifully sketched picture of four capped fungi growing from the bole of a tree. They were the colour of summer sunshine.

'Yes, they look delicious.'

'Then you would be wise to remember what they look like. They are Sulphur Tufts and a meal of these would leave you in great pain and probably kill you. What of this one?' It was a foul-looking object in cadaver grey.

'Edible?'

'Yes, and very nutritious. It also tastes pleasant.'

'What is the most dangerous?' he asked.

'You should be interested in the most nutritious, but since you ask it is probably this,' she answered, producing a drawing of a delicate white and yellow-green fungi. 'It is usually found near oak.' she said, 'and is called Death Cap; I leave it to you to guess why.'

'Do you never get lonely up in the mountains?'

'Why should I?' she replied, putting down her drawings. 'I have Culain as my friend, and the animals and birds and trees to study and draw.'

'But do you not miss people, crowds, fairs, banquets?'

'I have never been among crowds – or to a banquet. The thought does not thrill me. Are you unhappy here, Thuro?'

He gazed into her gold-flecked eyes. 'No, I am not lonely – not with you, anyway.' He was aware that his tone was too intense and he flushed deep red. She touched his hand.

'I am something you can never have,' she told him. He nodded and tried to smile.

'You love Culain.'

'Yes. All my life.'

'And yet you cannot have him, as I can never have you.'

She shook her head. 'That has yet to be decided. He still sees me as the child he raised.

It will take time for him to realise I am a woman.'

Thuro closed his mouth, stopping the obvious comment from being voiced. If Culain could not see it now, he would never see it. Added to which, here was a man who had known life since the dawn of history. How many women had he known? How many had he wed? What beauties had lain beside him through the centuries?

'How did he find you?' asked Thuro, seeking to move from the painful subject.

'My parents were Trinovante and they had a village some sixty miles south. One day there was a raid by Brigantes. I cannot remember much of it, for I was only five, but I can still see the burning thatch and hear the screams of the dying. I ran up into the hills and two horsemen pursued me. Then Culain was there with his silver lance; he slew the riders and carried me high into the mountains. Later we returned, but everyone was dead. So he kept me with him; he raised me and he taught me all I know.'

'It is hardly a surprise that you love him. I wish you success . . . and happiness.'

Every morning Culain would put Thuro through two hours of heavy exercise: running, lifting rocks, or making him hang by his arms from the branch of a tree and raise his weight until his chin touched the branch. At first Thuro could only raise himself three times before his arms would tremble and refuse the burden. But now, as spring painted her dazzling colours on the mountainside, he could manage thirty. He could run for an hour with no sign of fatigue, and he had despatched twelve of the ghostly opponents Culain created. The last had proved difficult; he was a Persian from the army of Xerxes and he fought with dagger and sabre. Four times he defeated Thuro before the youth won through. He did it by leaving a fractional opening twice, and covering late; the third time he lured the Persian into a lunge, side-stepped and cut his gladius into his opponent's neck. Culain had clapped him on the back and said nothing. Thuro was sweating hard, for the fight had lasted more than ten minutes.

'Now I think,' said Culain, 'that you are ready for the reasonable swordsmen.'

A movement to Thuro's left and a ghostly sword cut into his shoulder, numbing his left arm. He threw himself from the log on which he sat and rolled to his feet. The man before him was a blond giant over six feet tall, wearing a bronze helm adorned with a bull's horns. He held a longsword and was wearing a chain-mail vest.

Thuro blocked the man's sudden charge, but his opponent's shoulder crashed into him, sending him sprawling to the grass. Thuro rolled as the longsword flashed for his head. With his enemy off-balance, he regained his feet and launched a blistering attack, but his arm was weary and he was beaten back. Three times he almost found a way through, but his opponent – with his longer sword and greater reach – fended him off. Sweat dripped into the youth's eyes and his sword-arm burned. The warrior lunged, Thuro parried, swung on his heel and hammered his elbow into the man's face. The warrior staggered back and Thuro, still moving round, plunged his sword into the man's chest. As his enemy disappeared the young prince fell to his knees, his breath coming in great gasps. After several minutes his angry eyes locked on Culain.

'That was unfair!'

'Life is unfair. Do you think your enemies will sit back and wait until you are fresh? Learn to marshal your strength. Were I to produce another warrior now, you would not last five heartbeats.'

'There is a limit to every man's strength,' observed Thuro.

'Indeed there is – a good point to remember. One day, perhaps, you will lead an army into battle. You will be filled with the urge to draw your sword and fight alongside your men. You will think it heroic but your enemy will rejoice, for it is folly. As the long day wears on, all enemy eyes will be upon you and your weakening body. All their attacks will be aimed at you. So always bear that in mind, young prince. There is a limit to every man's strength.'

'And yet do the men you lead not need to know you will fight alongside them? Will it not raise their morale?' asked Thuro.

'Of course.'

'Then what is the answer to the riddle? Do I fight, or not fight?'

'Only you can decide that. But use your head. At some time in every battle, there is a moment when it can turn. Weaker men blame it on the Gods, but it has more to do with the hearts of the warriors. You must learn to read these moments, that is when you enter the fray, to the bitter dismay of your enemies.'

'How is such a moment recognised?'

'Most men recognise it only in hindsight. The truly great general sees it in an instant. But I cannot teach you that, Thuro. That is a skill you either have or do not have.'

'Do you have it?'

'I thought that I did, but when Paullinus lured me to attack him at Atherstone my talent deserted me. He sensed the moment and attacked, and my brave Britons collapsed around me. We outnumbered him twenty to one. An unpleasant man, Paullinus, but a wily general.'

Often, when not with either Culain or Laitha, Thuro would wander the hillsides, enjoying the freshness of spring in the mountains. Everywhere was colour: white-petalled wood anemone tinged with purple, golden celandine, mauve violets, snow-white wood sorrel, and the tall, glorious purple orchid with its black-spotted leaves and petals shaped like winged helms.

Early one morning, with his chores completed, Thuro wandered alone in the valley below Culain's cabin. His shoulders had widened and he could no longer squeeze into the clothes he had worn a mere two months ago. Now he wore a simple buckskin tunic and woollen leggings over sheepskin boots.

He sat by a stream, watching the fish glide

below the water until he heard a horse moving along the path. Then he stood and saw a single rider. The man spotted him and dismounted. He was tall and slender, with shoulder-length red hair and green eyes, and he wore a longsword at his waist. He walked to Thuro and stood with hands on hips.

'Well, it has been a long chase,' he said, 'and you are much changed.' He smiled. His face was open and handsome and Thuro could detect no malice there.

'My name is Alantric,' said the newcomer, 'I am the King's Champion.' He sat down on a flat rock, tugged free a length of grass and placed it between his teeth. 'Sadly, boy, I have been instructed to find your body and bring your head to the king.' The man sighed. 'I do not like killing children.'

'Then return and say you could not find me.'

'I would like to . . . truly. But I am a man of my word. It is unfortunate that I serve a king whose character is less than saintly. Do you know how to use that sword, boy?'

'That you will find out,' said Thuro, his heart-rate increasing as fear wormed into his heart.

'I will fight you left-handed. It seems more fair.'

'I wish for no advantage,' snapped Thuro, regretting it as he spoke.

'Well said! You are your father's son after all. When you meet him, tell him I had no part in his killing.'

'Tell him yourself,' said Thuro.

Alantric stood and drew his longsword and

Thuro's gladius flashed into the air. Alantric moved out on to open ground, then spun and lunged. Thuro side-stepped and blocked, rolling his gladius over the blade and slicing a thin cut on Alantric's forearm. 'Well done!' said the champion, stepping back, his green eyes blazing. 'You've been taught well.' He advanced once more, with care. Thuro noted the liquid grace of his enemy's style, the perfect balance and the patience he showed. Culain would have been impressed by this man. Thuro attacked not at all, merely blocking his opponent at every turn while studying his technique.

Alantric attacked, his sword flashing and cutting, and the discordant clash of iron on iron echoed in the woods. Suddenly the Brigante faked a cut, twisted his wrist and lunged. Caught by surprise Thuro parried hastily, feeling the razor-sharp blade slide across his right bicep. Blood began to seep through his shirt. A second attack saw Alantric score a similar wound at the top of Thuro's shoulder, close to the throat. The youth moved back and Alantric sprang forward. This time Thuro read the attack, swayed and lanced his gladius into Alantric's side. But the Brigante was fast and he leapt back before the blade had penetrated but an inch.

'You have been taught well,' he said again. He raised his sword to his lips in salute, then attacked once more. Thuro, desperate now, resorted to the move Culain had taught him. He blocked a thrust and spun on his heel, his elbow flashing back – into empty air! Off-balance, the young prince fell to the grass. He rolled swiftly, but felt Alantric's sword resting on his neck.

'A clever move, Prince Thuro, but you tensed before you tried it and I read your intent in your eyes.'

'At least I . . .' In the moment of speaking Thuro kicked Alantric's legs from under him and rolled to his feet. The Briton sat up and smiled.

'You are full of surprises,' he said as he stood and sheathed his sword. 'I think that I could kill you, but the truth is I do not wish to. You are worth ten of Eldared. It seems I must break my word.'

'Not at all,' said Thuro, sheathing his gladius. 'You were sent to look for my corpse. It is true to say that you did not find it.'

Alantric nodded. 'I could serve you, Prince Thuro . . . should you ever be a king.'

'I will remember that,' Thuro told him, 'as I will remember your gallantry.' Alantric bowed and walked to his horse.

'Remember, Prince Thuro, never let your enemy read your eyes. Do not think of an attack – just do it!'

Thuro returned the bow and watched as the warrior mounted and rode from sight.

*

Prasamaccus followed Victorinus to the Alia stables where the young Roman ordered a chestnut gelding with three white fetlocks to be saddled for the Brigante. Having not genuinely

110

believed he would be allowed to pick his own mount, Prasamaccus was therefore not disappointed with the beast. Victorinus mounted a black stallion of some seventeen hands and the two rode west along the wide Roman road outside Caerlyn. They skirted Eboracum and continued west for an hour until they came to the fortress town of Calcaria.

'My villa is beyond the next hill,' said Victorinus. 'We can rest there and bathe.'

Prasamaccus smiled dutifully and wondered what, under the sun, was a villa. Still, the sun was shining, his leg felt almost at ease and he was not yet hungry again. All in all, the Gods must be sleeping. A villa, it turned out, was a Roman name for a palace. White walls covered with vines, a garden, terrace steps and pretty maidens running to take the reins of their horses. Gorgeous young creatures – all with teeth.

He fought to look dignified, copying the solemn expression on Victorinus' swarthy face. Unfortunately he could not slide from the saddle with the Roman's grace, but even so he climbed down sedately and made every effort to keep his limp to the minimum. It surprised him not at all when no one laughed. Who would laugh at the guest of so important a chieftain? They moved inside and Prasamaccus looked around for evidence of a fire, but there was none. The mosaic floor depicted a hunting scene in glorious reds and blues, golds and greens. Beyond this was an arch, and here the two men were helped from their clothes and offered goblets of warmed wine. It seemed bland compared with the Water of Life distilled in the north, but even so Prasamaccus could feel its heat slipping through his veins.

Yet another room contained a deep pool and Prasamaccus gingerly followed the Roman into the warm water. Below the surface there were seats of stone and the Brigante leaned his head against the edge of the bath and closed his eyes. This, he thought, was the closest to paradise he had ever known. After some twenty minutes the Roman climbed from the water and Prasamaccus dutifully followed. They sat together on a long marble bench, saying nothing. Two young girls, one as black as night, came from the archway bearing bowls of oil. If the bath had been paradise, there was little left to describe the sensation that followed as the oil was softly rubbed into their skin and then scraped away with rounded knives of bone.

'Would you feel better for a massage?' asked Victorinus, as the girls moved away.

'Of course,' said Prasamaccus, wondering if one ate it or swam in it.

Victorinus led them through to a side-room where two tables were placed next to each other. The Roman stretched his lean, naked frame out on the first and Prasamaccus took the second. Two more girls entered and began to rub yet more oil into their bodies, but this they did not scrape off. Instead they kneaded the muscles of the upper back, stroking away knots of tension of which Prasamaccus was previously unaware. Slowly their hands moved down, and the men's shoulders were covered with warm white cloths. The Brigante sensed the girl's uncertainty as she reached his ruined leg. Her fingers floated over the skin like moths' wings and then she began, with skilful strokes, to ease the deep ache that was always with him. Her skill was beyond words and Prasamaccus felt himself slipping towards the sleep of the blessed. Finally the girls stepped back and two male servants approached with togas of white. Dressed in one of these Prasamaccus felt faintly ridiculous and not a little over-dressed. Yet another in an apparently interminable series of rooms followed. Here two divans were set alongside a table laden with fruit, cold meats and pastries. Prasamaccus waited while the Roman settled himself on a divan, leaning on his elbow, then the Brigante once more copied the pose.

'You are obviously a man of some breeding,' said Victorinus. 'I hope you will feel at home within my house.'

'Of course.'

'Your bravery in aiding us will not go unrewarded, though I can imagine your distress at being taken from your home and family must be great.'

Prasamaccus spread his hands and hoped his expression conveyed the right emotions – whatever they might be.

'As you no doubt know, there will be a war between the tribes that follow Eldared and our own forces. We will of course win, but the war will hamper our battles in the south against the

113

Saxon and Jute. What I am saying is that it will be difficult to assist you in getting home. But you are welcome to stay.'

'Here in your villa?' asked Prasamaccus.

'Yes – though I don't doubt you would rather risk the perils of the road north. If that is the case, as I said, you must pick your own horse from the stable and I will assist you with supplies and coin.'

'Does Gwalchmai live here?'

'No. He is a soldier and lives in the barracks at Caerlyn. He has a woman there, I believe.'

'Ah, a woman. Yes.'

'How foolish of me!' said Victorinus. 'Any of the slaves who take your fancy, you may feel free to bed. I would recommend the Nubian, who will guarantee a good night's sleep. And now I must leave you. I have a meeting to attend at the castle but I will be back at around midnight. My man, Grephon, will show you to your room.'

Prasamaccus watched the Roman leave and then wolfed into the food. He was not hungry, but he had found it never paid to waste the opportunity to eat.

The servant Grephon approached silently, then cleared his throat. He watched as the Briton gorged himself, but kept his face carefully void of expression. If his master had chosen to bring this savage to the villa there was obviously good reason for it. At the very least the man must be a prince among the northern tribes and therefore, despite his obvious barbarism, would be treated as if he were a senator. Grephon was a life servant to the Quirina family, having served Victorinus' illustrious father for seven years in Rome; he ran the household with iron efficiency. He was a short man, stocky and bald – despite being only twenty-five – with round unblinking eyes, dark as sable. Originally he had come from Thrace, a boy slave brought into the Quirina household as a stable-boy.

His swift mind had brought him to the attention of Marcus Lintus, who had taken him into the household as a playmate for his son, Victorinus. As the years passed, Grephon's reputation grew. He was undeniably loyal, close-mouthed and with an eye for organisation. By the age of nineteen he was organising the household. When Marcus Lintus died four years ago, young Victorinus had asked Grephon to accompany him to Britain. He had not wished to come and could have refused, for he had become a freedman on the death of Marcus. But the Quirina family were rich and Grephon's future was assured with them, so with a heavy heart he had made the long journey through Gaul and across the sea to Dubris and up through the cursed countryside to the villa at Calcaria. Here he had staffed it and run it to perfection while Victorinus followed the High King as Primus Pilus, the first centurion to Aurelius' rag-bag auxiliaries. Grephon could not understand why a high-born Roman could concern himself with such a rabble.

He cleared his throat once more and this time the savage noticed him. Grephon bowed.

'Is there anything you desire, sir?' The man belched loudly.

'A woman?'

'Yes, sir. Do you have a choice in mind?' The Briton's pale blue eyes fixed on Grephon.

'No. You choose.'

'Very well, sir. Let me show you to your room and I will send someone up to you.'

Grephon moved slowly, aware of the guest's disability, and led him up a short stairway to a narrow corridor and an oak door. Beyond it was a wide bed, surrounded by velvet curtains. It was warm, though there was no fire. Prasamaccus sat down on the bed as Grephon bowed and departed. Damned if he would send the Nubian to such as this, he decided. He walked briskly to the kitchen and summoned the German slave girl, Helga. She was short, with hair like flax and pale blue eyes devoid of passion. Her voice was guttural as she struggled with the language, and though she was good enough at heavy work none had so far seen fit to bed her. She was certainly not good enough to catch Victorinus' eye.

He explained her duties and was rewarded by a look close to fear in her eyes. She bowed her head and walked slowly towards the inner house. Grephon poured himself a goblet of fine wine and sipped it slowly, eyes closed, picturing the vineyards beyond the Tiber.

Helga climbed the stairs with a heavy heart. She had known this day would come and had dreaded it. Ever since being captured and raped by men of the Fourth Legion in her native homeland, she had lived with the secret fear of being abused once more. She had almost come to feel safe within this household, for the men were happily indifferent to her. Now she was being used to humour a crippled savage, a man whose deformity would have ensured his death in her own tribe.

She opened the door to the bedroom to see the British prince kneeling by a hot air vent and peering into the dark interior. He looked up and smiled but she did not respond. She walked to the bed and unfastened her simple green dress, a colour that did not match her eyes.

The Briton limped to the bed and sat down. 'What is your name?'

'Helga.'

He nodded. 'I am Prasamaccus.' He gently touched the soft skin of her face, then stood and struggled to free himself from the toga. Once naked, he slipped under the covers and invited her to join him. She did so and lay back across his arm. They stayed motionless for several minutes and then Prasamaccus, feeling her warmth against his body, drifted to sleep.

Helga gently raised herself on one elbow, looking down into his face. It was slender and fine-boned, lacking cruelty. She could still feel the soft touch of his hand on her cheek. She had no idea what to do now. She had been told to make him happy, so that he could rest well. Now that he was resting, she should return to the kitchens. Yet if she did, they would question why she had returned so quickly; they would think he had sent her away and perhaps punish her. She settled down beside him and closed her eyes.

At dawn she awoke to feel a soft hand touching her body. She did not open her eyes and her heart began to hammer within her. The hand slid, so slowly, across her shoulder and down to cup her heavy breast. The thumb circled the nipple, then the touch moved on, up and over the curve of her hip. She opened her eyes and saw the Briton staring at her body, his face lost in a kind of wonderment. He saw that she was awake and flushed deep red, pulling the covers back over her. Then he lay down and moved his body more closely alongside her, softly kissing her brow, then her cheek and finally her lips. Almost without thinking she reached up and curled her arm over his shoulder. He groaned . . . and she knew. In that instant she knew it all, as if she held Prasamaccus' soul under her eyes.

For the first time in her life Helga knew the meaning of power. She could choose; to give, or not to give. The man beside her would accept her choice. Her mind flew back to the brutality of her captors, men she would like to have killed. But they were men unlike this one.

This man left her free to choose, not even understanding that he did so. She looked into his eyes once more and saw that they were wet with tears. Leaning forward she kissed each eye, then drew him to her.

And in giving freely, she received a greater gift.

Her memories of lust and cruelty dissolved and returned to the past devoid of the power ever to haunt her again.

*

For several days Victorinus rose early and returned late, seeing little of his house guest who spent most of the time locked in his room with the kitchen-maid. The Roman had weightier problems on his mind. The Fifth Legion was stationed at Calcaria, auxiliary militia who were allowed home in spring to see to their farms and their families. Now, with Eldared and his Selgovae and Novantae allies ready to invade, and the Saxon King Hengist preparing to ravage the south, there was no way these auxiliaries could be allowed to disband for two months. Tension was running high among the men, many of whom had not seen their wives since the previous September, and Victorinus feared a mutiny.

Aquila had asked him to help build morale by offering coin and salt to the men, but this had not been enough and desertions were increasing daily. The choices were limited. If they allowed the men home, Eboracum and the surrounding countryside would be defended by only one regular legion – five thousand men. Ranged against them would be a possible thirty thousand. Alternatively, they could recall a legion from the south, but the Gods knew how badly the general Ambrosius needed men around Dubris and Londinium.

The third choice was to recruit and train a new militia, but this would be the same as send-

119

ing children out against wolves. The Brigante and their vassal tribes were renowned warriors.

Victorinus dismissed the Nubian slave, Oretia, and climbed from his bed. He dressed and made his way to the central room, where he found Prasamaccus sitting by the far window staring out over the moonlit southern hills.

'Good evening,' said Victorinus. 'How are you faring?'

'Well, thank you. You seem tired?'

'There is much to do. Does Helga please you?'

'Yes, very much.'

Victorinus poured himself a goblet of watered wine. It was almost midnight and his eyes ached for the sleep he knew would evade him. It annoyed him that the Briton was still here after six days. He had only invited him so as to offset the rough treatment he had received in being gaoled, otherwise he would have placed him in the barracks with Gwalchmai. Now it looked as if he had a permanent house guest. The small fortress town was alive with rumours concerning the Brigante – all had him marked as a prince at the very least. Grephon had purchased some new clothes for him and these only added to the image: the softest cream wool edged with braid, leather troos decorated with silver discs, and fine riding-boots of softest doeskin.

'What is your problem?' asked Prasamaccus.

'Would that there were only one.'

'There is always one larger than the others,' said the Brigante.

Victorinus shrugged and explained – though he knew not why – the problems with the militia men. Prasamaccus sat silently as the Roman outlined the choices.

'How much of this coin is available for the men?' he asked.

'It is not a great sum – perhaps a month's extra pay.'

'If you allow some of the men home, the amount for each man left would grow, yes?'

'Of course.'

'Then make known the total mount on offer and tell the men they can go home. But explain that the coin will be distributed amongst those who choose to remain.'

'What will that serve? What if only one man remains? He would be as rich as Crassus.'

'Exactly,' agreed Prasamaccus, though he had no idea who Crassus was.

'I do not follow you.'

'No, that is because you are rich. Most men dream of riches. Myself, I have always wanted two horses. But the men who want to go home will now have to wonder how much they lose by doing so. What if – as you say – only one is left? Or ten?'

'How many do you think will remain?'

'More than half – if they are anything like the Brigantes I have known.'

'It would entail great risk to do as you suggest, but I feel it is wise counsel. We will attempt it. Where did you learn such guile?'

'It is the Earth Mother's gift to lonely men,' answered Prasamaccus.

His advice was proved right when 3,000 men chose to stay, earning an extra two months' pay per man. It eased Victorinus' burden and earned him plaudits from Aquila.

Three days later an unexpected guest arrived at the villa. It was Maedhlyn – hot, dusty and irritable from his ride. An hour later, refreshed by a hot bath and several goblets of warmed wine, he sat talking for some time with Victorinus. Then they summoned Prasamaccus. When the Brigante saw the portly Enchanter his heart sank. He sat quietly, refusing the wine Victorinus offered.

Maedhlyn sat opposite him, fixing him with his hawk-like eyes.

'We have a problem, Prasamaccus, one which we think you will be able to solve. There is a young man trapped in Brigante territory far to the north of the Antonine Wall in the Caledones mountains. He is important to us and we want him brought home. Now, we cannot send our own men, for they do not know the land. But you do, and could travel there without suspicion.'

Prasamaccus said nothing, but now he reached for the wine and took a deep draught. The Gods give, the Gods take away. But this time they had gone too far, they had allowed him to taste a joy he had previously believed to be fable.

'Now,' said Maedhlyn persuasively, 'I can magic you to a circle of stones near Pinnata Castra, some three days' ride from Deicester Castle. All you will need to do is locate the boy, Thuro, and return him to the circle exactly six days later. I will be there – and I will return every night at midnight thereafter in case you are delayed. What do you say?'

'I have no wish to return north,' said Prasamaccus softly. Maedhlyn swallowed hard and glanced at Victorinus as the Roman sat beside the Brigante.

'You would be doing us a great service, and would be well rewarded,' Victorinus told him.

'I will need a copper bracelet edged with gold, a small house, also enough coin to purchase a horse and supply a woman with food and clothing for a year. Added to this, I want the slave Helga freed to live in this house.' As he had been speaking, the colour left his face and he feared he had set the price at an awesome level.

'Is that all?' asked Victorinus and Prasamaccus nodded. 'Then it is agreed. As soon as you return, we will arrange it.'

'No,' said the Brigante sternly. 'It will be arranged tomorrow. I am not a foolish man and know I may not survive this quest. The land of the Caledones is wild and strangers are not welcome. Also the boy, Thuro, is the son of the Roman king. Eldared will wish him dead. It is not meet that you should ask me to undertake your duties, but since you have then you must pay . . . and pay now.'

'We agree,' said Maedhlyn swiftly. 'When do you wish the marriage to take place?'

'Tomorrow.'

'As a Druid of long standing I shall officiate,'

declared Maedhlyn. 'There is an oak tree back along the trail and we shall travel there in time for the birth of the new sun. You had best tell your lady.'

Prasamaccus stood and bowed and, with as much dignity as allowed a limping man, returned to his room.

'What was that about marriage?' asked Victorinus.

'The bracelet is for her. It marks the Ring of Eternity and the never-ending circle of life that springs from the union of love. Touching!'

8

Alantric knew his life would be forfeit should anyone find out about his meeting with the prince, so the only person he told was his wife Frycca, as she stitched the wound in his arm. Frycca loved him dearly and would do nothing to harm him, but she was proud of his gallantry and spoke of it to her sister, Marphia, swearing her to the strictest secrecy. Marphia told her husband, Briccys, who only told his dearest friend on the understanding that the secret was to remain locked within him.

Within two days of his return Alantric was dragged from his hut by three of Eldared's carles. Realising at once that he was doomed, he turned and shouted back to Frycca: 'Your loose tongue has killed me, woman!'

He did not struggle as they pulled him towards the horses, but walked with head down, totally relaxed. The guards relaxed with him and he tore his right arm free and smote the nearest man on the ear. As the guard staggered, Alantric pulled free the man's sword and plunged the blade into the heart of the second soldier. The third stepped back, dragging his own blade into the air and Alantric leapt for the nearest horse, but the beast shied. Now a dozen more guards came running and the King's champion backed away to the picket fence, a wild smile on his features.

'Come then, brothers,' he called. 'Learn a lesson that will last all your lives!'

Two men rushed in. Alantric blocked a blow, sent a backhand cut to the first man's throat and grunted as the second attacker's sword slid into his side. Twisting, he trapped the blade against his ribs and skewered the swordsman.

'Alive! Take him alive!' screamed Cael from the battlements above.

'Come down and do it yourself, whoreson!' shouted Alantric as the guards came in a rush. Alantric's blade wove a web of death and in the mêlée that followed a sword entered his back, tearing open his lungs. He sank to the ground and was hauled into the castle; he died just as Cael ran into the portcullis entrance.

'You stupid fools!' bellowed Cael. 'I'll see you flogged. Get his wife!' But Frycca, in her anguish, had cut her own throat with her husband's hunting-knife and lay in a pool of blood by the hearth.

Eldared's torturer worked long into the night on the others who had shared the secret, emerging with only one indisputable fact. The boy prince was indeed alive, and hiding in an unknown area of the Caledones mountains.

Eldared summoned Cael to him. 'You will go to Goroien and tell her I need the Soul Stealers. We have six people below whose blood should please her, and as many whelps as she needs. But I want the boy!'

Cael said nothing. Of all the dark legends of the mist, the Soul Stealers alone made him shiver. He bowed and left the brooding king to sit alone, staring into the hills of the south.

*

Thuro awoke still feeling the pain of the wound that had killed him, a lightning-fast roll and thrust from the Greek's short-sword. Culain helped him to his feet.

'You did well, better than I could have hoped. Give me another month and there will not be a swordsman to rival you in all of Britain.'

'But I lost,' said Thuro, recalling with a shiver the ice-cold eyes of his young opponent.

'Of course you lost. That was Achilles, the finest warrior of his generation, a demon with sword or lance. A magnificent fighter.'

'What happened to him?'

'He died. All men die.'

'I had already surmised that,' said Thuro. 'I meant how.'

'I killed him,' said Culain. 'I had another name then; I was Aeneas, and Achilles killed a friend of mine during the war against Troy. Not only that but he dragged the body round and round the city behind his chariot. He humiliated a man of great courage, and brought pain to the father.'

'I have heard of Troy. It was taken by a wooden horse with men hidden inside.'

'Do not be misled by Homer, for he was jesting. "Wooden Horse" is slang for a useless object, or for something pretending to be what

127

it is not. It was a man who went to the Trojans pretending to betray his masters, the Greeks. The king, Priam, believed the man. I did not. I left the city with those who would follow me and fought my way to the coast. Later we heard that the man, Odysseus, had opened a side gate to allow Greek soldiers to enter the city.'

'Why did the king believe him?'

'Priam was a romantic who saw the best in everyone. That is how he allowed the war to begin, by seeing the best in Helen. The face that launched a thousand ships was merely a scheming woman with dyed yellow hair. The Trojan War was begun by her husband Menelaus and planned by Helen. She seduced Priam's son, Paris, into taking her to his city. Menelaus then sought the aid of the other Greek kings to get her back.'

'But why go to so much trouble over one woman?'

'They did not do it for a woman, or for honour. Troy controlled the trade routes and levied great taxes on ships bound for Greece. It was – as are all wars – brought for profit.'

'I think I prefer Homer,' said Thuro.

'Read Homer for enjoyment, young prince, but do not confuse it with life.'

'What has made you so gloomy today?' asked Thuro. 'Are you ailing?'

Culain's eyes blazed briefly, and he walked away towards his cabin. Thuro did not follow at first, but noticed the Mist Warrior glance back over his shoulder. The prince grinned, sheathed his gladius and followed to find Culain sitting at the table nursing a goblet of strong spirit.

'It's Gian,' said Culain. 'I have caused her distress; it is not something I intended, but she rather surprised me.'

'She told you she loved you?'

'Do not be too clever, Thuro,' snapped Culain. He waved his hand, as if to wipe away the angry words. 'Yes, you are right. I was a fool not to see it. But she is wrong; she has known no other man and has lifted me to the skies. I should have taken her to a settlement long since.'

'What did you tell her?'

'I told her I saw her as my daughter, and could not love her more than that.'

'Why?'

'What sort of a question is why? Why what?'

'Why could you not take her to wife?'

'There was my second mistake, for she asked the same question. I have already given my heart; there can be no one else for me while my lady lives.' Culain smiled. 'But she will not have me because I choose to be mortal, and I cannot love her while she remains a goddess.'

'And this you told to Laitha?'

'Yes.'

'It was not wise,' said Thuro. 'I think you should have lied. I am not versed in the ways of women, but I think Laitha would forgive you anything except being in love with someone else.'

'I can do many things, Thuro, but I cannot turn back the hours of my life. I would not wish pain on Gian, but it is done. Go to her; help her to understand.'

'Not an easy task, and the more difficult for me because I do love her, and would take her to wife tomorrow.'

'I know that – so does she. So you are the one who should go to her.'

Thuro stood, but Culain waved him to his chair once more. 'Before you go, there is something I want you to see and a gift I wish you to have.' He fetched a bowl of water and placed it before the prince. 'Look deeply into the water, and understand.' Culain took a golden stone from his pocket and held it over the bowl until the water misted. Then he left the cabin, pulling shut the door behind him.

Thuro gazed down to find himself staring into a candle-lit room, where several men stood silently around a wide bed in which lay a slender child with white-blond hair. A man Thuro recognised as Maedhlyn leaned over and placed his hand on the child's head.

'His spirit is not here,' came Maedhlyn's voice, whispering inside Thuro's mind. 'He is in the Void; he will not return.'

'Where is this Void?' came another voice that brought a pang of deep sadness to the boy. It was Aurelius, his father.

'It is a place between Heaven and Hell. No man can fetch him back.'

'I can,' said the king.

'No, sire. It is a place of Mist Demons and darkness. You will be lost, even as the boy is lost.'

'He is my son. Use your magic to send me there. I command it!'

Maedhlyn sighed. 'Take the boy into your arms and wait.'

The water misted once more and Thuro saw the child wandering in a daze on a dark mountainside, his eyes blank and unseeing. Around him stalked black wolves with red eyes and slavering jaws. As they crept towards the child, a shining figure appeared bearing a terrible sword. He smote the wolves and they fled. Then he swept the child into his arms and knelt with him by a black stream where no flowers grew. The child awoke then and cuddled into the chest of the man, who ruffled his hair and told him all was well. Three terrible beasts approached from a sudden mist, but the king's sword shone like fire.

'Back!' he said. 'Or die. The choice is yours.'

The beasts looked at him, gauging his strength, then returned to the mist.

'I will take you home, Thuro,' said the king. 'You will be well again.' His father kissed him then.

Thuro's tears splashed to the bowl, disturbing the scene, but just as it faded a dark shadow flitted across his vision.

Culain entered silently. 'Gian said you regretted having no memory of the scene. I hope it was a gift worth having.'

Thuro cleared his throat and wiped his eyes. 'I am more in your debt now than ever. He came into Hell to find me.'

'For all his faults he was a man of courage.

131

By all the laws of Mystery he should have died there with you, but such men are made to challenge the immutability of such laws. Be proud, Thuro.'

'One more question, Culain. What kind of man has a grey face and opal eyes?'

'Where did you see such a man?'

'Just as the vision faded, I saw a man in black running forward with a sword raised. His face was grey and his eyes clouded, like a blind man – only he was not blind.'

'And you felt he was looking at you?'

'Yes. There was no time to feel fear; it was gone in an instant.'

'Fear is what you should feel, for the man was a Soul Stealer, a drinker of blood. They exist in the Void and none know their origins. It was a source of great interest in the Feragh. Some contend they are the souls of the evil slain, others that they come from a race similar to our own. Whatever the truth they are dangerous, for their speed is like nothing human and their strength is prodigious. They feed on blood and nothing else, and cannot stand strong sunlight; it causes their skin to blister and peel, and eventually can kill them.'

'Why would I see one?'

'Why indeed? But remember you were looking into the Void, and that is their home.'

'Can they be slain?'

'Only with silver, but few men can stand against them even then. They move like shadows and strike before a warrior can parry. Their knives and swords do not cut, they merely numb. Then a man feels their long hollow teeth in his throat, drawing his life-blood. Give me your gladius.'

Thuro offered the weapon hilt first. Culain ran his golden stone along both edges of the blade, then returned it. The prince examined it, but could see no change.

'Let us hope you never do,' said Culain.

*

Thuro found Laitha in the upper mountains, sitting on a flat rock and sketching a purple butterburr. Her eyes were red-rimmed and the sketch was not of her usual high quality.

'May I join you?'

She nodded and placed her parchment and charcoal stick to her left. She was wearing only a light green woollen tunic and her fingers and arms were blue with cold. He removed his own sheepskin jerkin and draped it over her shoulders.

'He told you then,' she said, not looking at him.

'Yes. It is cold here – let us go back to your cabin and light a fire.'

'You must think me very foolish.'

'Of course I do not. You are one of the brightest people I have ever met. The only foolishness is Culain's. Now let's go back.' She smiled wanly and climbed from the rock. The sun was sinking in fire and a bitter wind was whispering through the rocks.

Back at the cabin, with the fire roaring in the hearth, she sat before the flames hugging her knees. He sat opposite her, nursing a goblet of watered wine from a cask in the back room.

'He loves someone else,' she said.

'He has loved her since before you were born – and he is not a fickle man. You would not love him yourself if he were.'

'Did he ask you to speak for him?'

'No,' lied Thuro. 'He merely told me how distressed he was to cause you pain.'

'It was my own fault. I should have waited a year; it was not so long. I am still lean like a boy; I will be more womanly next year. Perhaps by then he will realise his own true feelings.'

'And perhaps not,' warned Thuro softly.

'She is not here – whoever she is. I am here. He will come to me one day.'

'You are already beautiful, Laitha, but I think you underestimate him. What is a year to a man who has tasted eternity? He will never love you in the way you desire. Your passion will hurt you both.'

Her eyes came up and the look hit him like a blow. 'You think I don't know why you are saying this? You want me yourself. I can see it in your moon-dog eyes. Well, you won't have me. Ever! If I can't have Culain, I will have no man.'

'Fifteen is a little young to make such a decision.'

'Thank you for that advice, Uncle.'

'Now you are being foolish, Laitha. I am not your enemy and you gain nothing by hurting me. Yes, I love you. Does that make me a villain? Have I ever pressed my suit upon you?'

She stared into the flames for several minutes, then smiled and reached out to touch his hand. 'I am sorry, Thuro. Truly. I am so hurt inside I just want to strike out.'

'I have something to thank you for,' he said. 'You told Culain about me wanting to recall the day my father held me, and he used his magic Stone to bring it to pass.' He went on to explain about the vision, and how Culain had touched his sword.

'Let me see,' she asked.

'There is nothing to see.' He drew the gladius and the blade shone like a mirror.

'He has turned it to silver,' said Laitha.

A dark shadow flitted by the window and Thuro hurled himself across the room just as the door began to open. His shoulder slammed into the wood and the door closed with a crash. Thuro fumbled for the bar, dropping it into place.

'What is happening?' cried Laitha and Thuro swung round. The window was shuttered and barred against the cold. The door to the back room opened and a dark shadow swept across the hearth. Laitha, half rising, slumped to the floor as a grey blade touched her flesh. Thuro dived to his left, rolled and rose. With preternatural speed the shadow closed on him and his blade flashed up instinctively, slicing through the dark, billowing cloak. There was an unearthly cry, and Thuro saw a corpse-grey face and opal eyes just before the creature vanished in smoke. A stench filled the room that caused Thuro to retch. Dropping to his knees, he crawled to Laitha; her eyes were open, but she was unmoving. He ran into the back room just as a second shadow darkened the window; his sword snaked out and the apparition fled back into the night. He slammed the shutters and barred them.

Returning to Laitha, he stared into her eyes. She blinked. 'If you can hear me, blink twice.' She did so. 'Now blink once for yes, twice for no. Is there any movement at all in your limbs?' Twice she blinked.

A crash came at the window and a sword-blade shattered the wood. Thuro, his own gladius burning with blue fire, ran to the window and waited. A second crash came from the back room, then another unearthly cry rose from outside the cabin and Thuro risked a glance through the shattered window.

Culain was standing alone in the clearing, his silver lance in his hands. Three figures moved towards him with blistering speed. He dropped to his knees, the lance flashing and lunging. Two cloaked assassins fell. Thuro tore open the cabin door and rushed into the night as four others closed on Culain.

'No, Thuro!' bellowed Culain, but it was too late for a Soul Stealer flew at the prince. Thuro blocked a thrust and sliced his silver blade across his enemy's throat and the creature vanished. Two others were on their way. Culain attacked the two facing him, blocking and cutting, despatching one with a thrust to the belly. The second advanced, but Culain pressed a stud in the lance and a sharp silver blade flashed through the air and into the Soul Stealer's chest.

Thuro managed to kill the first of the assassins, but the second sank a cold knife between his ribs. All strength fled from him and his legs gave way. He fell on his back and saw the grey face looming above him, huge hollow teeth descending towards his throat.

Culain ran forward three paces, then threw the heavy lance. It sliced into the creature's back, plunging through to jut from its chest. It vanished, and the lance fell to the ground beside Thuro.

Culain lifted the paralysed prince and carried him into the cabin where Laitha was beginning to stir. 'Get the fire built up and lock the door,' he said.

He moved to her bow and emptied her quiver. There were twenty arrows. He touched his Sipstrassi Stone to the head of each but nothing happened. Culain lifted Thuro's gladius; once more it was iron.

'What were they?' asked Laitha, rubbing limbs that ached with cold.

'Void killers. We are no longer safe here. Come here!' As she approached he lifted her hand. A copper bracelet graced her left wrist and he touched the Stone to it. 'If ever it shines silver, you know what it will mean?'

She nodded. 'I am sorry, Culain. Will you forgive me?'

'There is nothing to forgive, Gian Avur. I should have told you about my lady, but I have not seen her for more than forty years.'

'What is her name?'

'Her name is an old one, meaning Light into Life. She is called Goroien.'

*

Culain sat up through the night, but the Soul Stealers did not return. Thuro awoke in the morning, his head seemingly full of wool, his movements slow and clumsy. Culain took him outside and the crisp air drove the drowsiness from him.

'They will come again,' said Culain. 'There is no end to them. They did not expect you to be armed with silver.'

'I cannot stand against them, they are too fast.'

'I have spoken to you, Thuro, of Eleari-mas, the Emptying. It is something you will need to master. Skill is not enough, speed is insufficient; you must free your instinct, empty your mind.'

'I have tried, Culain. I cannot master it.'

'It took me thirty years, Thuro. Do not expect to excel in a matter of hours.' The sun was shining with golden brilliance and the events of the night seemed of another age. Laitha was still sleeping. The Mist Warrior looked gaunt and jaded, the silver at his temples shining like snow on the distant mountain peaks. Dark rings circled his eyes. 'Eldared has recruited an ally from the Feragh,' he said. 'No one else could open the Void. I thank the Source that you saw the vision, but who knows what will come next? Atrols, serpents, dragons, demons. The perils of the Mist are infinite. I blame myself, for I first used the floating gateways.'

'In what way?' asked Thuro.

'When I led Boudicca's Iceni against the Romans there was an elite Legion, the Ninth. They marched south from Eboracum to catch us and trap us between themselves and Paullinus. But I sent the Mist and they marched onto it and out of history.'

'The legendary Ninth,' whispered Thuro. 'No one has ever known of their fate.'

'Nor will any man. Even I. They died out of sight of their friends, their families and even their land.'

'Five thousand men,' said Thuro. 'That is power indeed.'

'I would not do such a thing again . . . but someone has.'

'Who has the power?'

'Maedhlyn. Myself. Maybe a dozen others. But that pre-supposes the lack of intellect and imagination in any of a hundred thousand worlds within worlds that make up the Mist. Perhaps someone has travelled a new road.'

'What can I do? I cannot just remain here until they find me, and it puts both you and Laitha in peril.'

'You must find your father's sword and your own destiny.'

'Find . . . ? It was taken by a ghostly hand below the surface of the lake. I cannot travel there.'

'Would that it were truly so simple. But the sword is not in the lake – I have searched there.

No, it is in the Mist and we must travel there to find it.'

'You said there were thousands of worlds within the Mist. How will we know where to search?'

'You are joined to the sword. We will take a random path and see where it leads us.'

'You will forgive me for saying that it does not sound very hopeful.'

Culain chuckled. 'I will be with you, Thuro. Though, yes, it will be like searching for one pebble in a rock-slide. But better than waiting here for the demons to strike, yes?'

'When do we leave?'

'Tomorrow. I must prepare the path.'

'And we must spend one more night waiting for the Soul Stealers?'

'Yes, but we have an advantage now. We know they are coming.'

'A slim advantage indeed.'

'Perhaps as slender as the difference between life and death.'

9

Prasamaccus was grateful for the tears Helga shed so publicly as he mounted the huge black stallion, chosen this morning from Victorinus' stable. No warrior should leave on a dangerous hunt without such a display from a loving wife. He had been lucky, for Maedhlyn had been forced to wait five weeks after his magic disclosed to him that the passes into the Caledones mountains were all blocked by heavy snow. Prasamaccus had used the time well, getting to know Helga and she him. Happily they both liked what they found. The house on the outskirts of Calcaria had been bought by Grephon at a fraction of its value, the owner being terrified of the coming war. At the back of the small white building was a ramshackle paddock, and two fields that could be given over to crops.

Now Prasamaccus leaned over his saddle. 'Hush woman!' he said. 'This is not seemly.' But Helga's tears would not cease and it was with a happy heart that Prasamaccus rode alongside the Enchanter towards the remnants of the stone circle above Eboracum.

For his part Maedhlyn was less than happy with the choice of messenger-escort he was sending to Thuro. The slender blond cripple was obviously a man of wit, but hardly a warrior. And could he be trusted?

The Brigante cared nothing for the doubts he saw in Maedhlyn's sullen expression. The Caledones were, in fact, sparsely peopled, and the Vacomagi that did dwell in the foothills were renowned as a friendly tribe. With luck his mission would require no more than a six-day round journey and a swift return to his white palace. He glanced nervously at the sky; he had kept his face blank, but the gods had a way of reading men's eyes.

Only two broken teeth remained of the circle and Prasamaccus stood now where he had appeared six weeks before, overlooking the fortress city.

'You understand? Six days,' said Maedhlyn.

'Yes. I'll notch a stick,' replied Prasamaccus.

'Do not be flippant. You will appear above Pinnata Castra. In the mountains you will meet a man named Culain; he is tall, with eyes the colour of storm-clouds. Do not anger him. He will take you to the prince.'

'Storm eyes. Yes, I'm ready.'

With a muttered curse Maedhlyn produced a yellow-gold Stone and waved it over his head. A golden glow filled the circle. 'Ride west,' said the Enchanter and Prasamaccus mounted and headed the stallion forward. It shied, and came down running, directly at the largest stone. Prasamaccus closed his eyes. A smell like oil burning on cloth smote his nostrils, and his ears ached. He opened his eyes as the horse charged out of the circle where he had killed the Atrol.

He pulled Vamera from his saddle pouch and strung her swiftly. Then, with an angry oath he hung the bow on his pommel.

'Stupid wizard,' he said. 'This is the wrong circle. I am days from the Caledones.'

*

Throughout the day Culain worked to assemble a circle of slender golden wire in the clearing below his cabin. He looped the wire around four birch trees, then marked the earth within the circle in a series of pentangles highlighted with chalk. At the centre of the circle he constructed a perfect square, measuring the distances with great care from the angles of the square to the furthest points of the pentangles.

At noon he stopped and Thuro brought him a goblet of wine, which he refused.

'This needs a clear head, Thuro.'

'What are you doing?'

'I am re-creating the base layout of a minor Circle – creating a gateway, if you like. But if I am more than a hair's breadth out in my calculations, we will end up in a world or a time we do not desire.'

'Where is Laitha?'

'She is watching the valley for sign of Eldared's hunters.'

'Can I fetch you some food?'

'No. I must finish the circle and lay on the lines of magic. It will work only once; we will not be able to return here.'

'I will watch with Laitha.'

'No,' said Culain sharply, 'you are necessary here. This whole circle is geared to you and

143

your Harmony. It is our only hope of finding the sword.'

Towards dusk Laitha came running into the clearing.

'There is a single rider moving up the valley,' she said. 'Shall I kill him?'

Culain looked bone-weary. 'No. No needless slaying. I am almost ready. Thuro, go with Laitha and see the man. Gian, stay hidden and if the rider has hostile intent, shoot him down.'

'I thought you needed me,' said Thuro.

'The work is nearly done, the destination set. We will leave at dawn.'

'Would it not be safer to leave now?' asked Laitha.

'The sun is almost gone, and we need its energies. No, we must survive one more night in the mountains.'

Thuro and Laitha set off to intercept the rider, moving swiftly down the forest trails. As Thuro ran behind the lithe girl he found his mind straying from concern at the horseman to appreciation of the supple, liquid grace of Laitha's movements.

Thuro spotted the rider moving carefully up the mountain trail and squatted down with Laitha behind a thick bush. The man rode a tall black stallion of almost seventeen hands and was dressed in a cream woollen tunic edged with braid and black troos decorated with small silver discs; he carried a dark bow of horn. He was in his early twenties, with fair hair and a straggly blond beard.

Thuro stepped out on to the path as Laitha notched an arrow to her bow.

'Welcome, stranger,' said Thuro.

The man reined in. 'Prince Thuro?'

'Yes.'

'I have been sent to find you.'

'Then step down from your mount and draw your sword.'

Laitha had no intention of allowing Thuro to fight and loosed her shaft. At that moment an owl fluttered from a nearby branch and the stallion shied. Laitha's arrow took the horse in the throat and it fell, throwing the rider into the bushes beside the trail. Thuro was furious. He ran forward and helped the man to his feet, noticing for the first time that the rider was a cripple. Laitha stood with a second arrow notched.

'Damn you!' yelled Thuro. 'Get out of my sight!' He moved to the horse which was writhing on the ground, and opened its jugular with his hunting-knife. 'I am sorry,' he told the man. 'It was none of my doing.'

'It was a fine horse – best I ever owned. I hope you have others?'

'No.'

The man sighed. 'The Gods give, the Gods take away.'

'Where is your sword?' asked Thuro.

'For what should I need a sword?'

'To fight me, of course. Or were you intending to use your bow?'

'Maedhlyn sent me to fetch you home. My

name is Prasamaccus; I have been staying with Victorinus.'

'Thuro!' called Laitha. 'Look!'

Further down the trail some dozen riders were following the tracks left by Prasamaccus.

'Your friends have arrived,' said the prince.

'No friends of mine. What I told you was true.'

'Then you had better follow me,' said Thuro. 'Here, let me carry your bow.'

Prasamaccus handed him the weapon and the trio set off, keeping away from the path. The sun was sinking now and the three faded from sight in the gathering gloom. They moved on for more than a quarter of an hour, forced to walk slowly to allow the limping Prasamaccus to keep up.

They reached the cabin as the moon cleared the clouds and Culain ran forward to meet them.

'Who is he?'

'He says Maedhlyn sent him,' answered Thuro, 'but Eldared's hunters are only minutes behind us.' Culain cursed.

A gasp came from Laitha and the three men swung towards her. She was holding up her arm and staring at the bracelet on her wrist; it had begun to glow faintly.

'The Soul Stealers,' whispered Thuro.

'Would it be possible to have my bow back?' asked Prasamaccus.

Culain drew a silver knife and held it gently to the Brigante's throat, then he took the Sipstrassi Stone from his pocket and touched it to the man's temple. 'Tell me why Maedhlyn sent you?'

'He said to bring the prince to the Circle of Stones near Pinnata Castra. Then he would spirit us both home.'

The knife returned to Culain's sheath. 'Give him his bow, and let me have the arrows.' The Mist Warrior touched his stone to each of the twenty arrow-heads and handed the quiver to Prasamaccus.

He notched an arrow to the string. The head shone with a white-blue light. 'Very pretty,' he said. A dark shadow sped from the trees and before Laitha could react Prasamaccus had drawn and loosed. The shaft took the assassin in the chest; the dark cloak billowed and fell to the ground, the Brigante's arrow beside it.

'Into the circle!' yelled Culain. More dark shapes moved into sight. Prasamaccus and Laitha both loosed shafts while Culain ran forward, sweeping up his lance from the ground beside the golden wire. 'Move to the central square,' said Culain. As Thuro, Laitha and Prasamaccus clambered over the wire, the Mist Warrior swung in time to block the thrust of a grey blade, cutting the lance-head through the assassin's neck. More of the shadows converged towards the circle. Culain leapt the wire, but a cold knife cut into his shoulder. As his limbs lost their power, he shouted one word. A golden light filled the circle, forcing the shadow killers back. Bright as noonday, the glare was blinding. When it faded the circle was empty, the golden wire gone, the earth smouldering.

*

Culain awoke in a broken circle of stones on the side of a high hill overlooking a deserted Roman fortress. He sat up and breathed deeply until the unearthly drowsiness left his limbs. The fortress below had partially collapsed, and several huts nearby had been constructed partly of stone from the ruined building. Culain glanced at the sky; a single moon hung there. The sky was clear and he examined the stars. He was still in Britain. He cursed loudly.

A glow began to his left and he swept up his lance and waited. Maedhlyn appeared.

'Oh, it's you,' said the Enchanter. 'Where is the boy?'

'Gone seeking his father's sword.'

'Alone?'

'No, he has a girl and a cripple with him.'

'Wonderful,' said Maedhlyn.

Culain pushed himself to his feet. 'It is better than him being dead.'

'Marginally,' agreed Maedhlyn. 'What happened?'

'Soul Stealers came upon us. I sent Thuro and the others through a gateway.'

'Which one?'

'I made it.'

'Made? Oh Culain, that was foolhardy indeed.'

'Worse than you know. I had to send them at night.'

'Better and better.' Maedhlyn sniffed loudly and cleared his throat. 'You look older,' he said. 'Do you need a Stone?'

'I have one, and I look older because I choose

148

to. It is time to die, Maedhlyn. I have lived too long.'

'Die?' whispered Maedhlyn, his eyes widening. 'What nonsense is this? We are immortal.'

'Only because we choose to be. I choose not to be.'

'What does Athena say about this?'

'Her name is Goroien. We left that Greek nonsense behind centuries ago – and I have not seen her in forty years.'

'It is cold here. Let us return to my palace; we'll talk there.'

Culain followed him within the glow and the two walked down the long hill to Eboracum and the converted villa Maedhlyn owned near the southern wall. Inside a fire burned brightly in an ornate stone hearth. The Enchanter had always heartily disliked Roman central heating, claiming it made his head thick and disturbed his concentration.

'You used not to think it nonsense,' said the Enchanter, as they sat together drinking mulled wine by the fire. 'You made a wonderful Ares, a fine god of war. And we did help the Greeks after a fashion; we gave them philosophy and algebra.'

'You always were a capricious meddler, Maedhlyn. How do you maintain your appetite for it?'

'People are wonderful creatures,' said the Enchanter. 'So inventive. I never tire of them and their gloriously petty wars.'

'Have I mentioned before that I dislike you intensely?'

'Once or twice, Culain, now I come to recall – though I cannot understand why. You know I would have given my life to save Alaida . . .'

'Do not speak of her!'

Maedhlyn settled back in his deep leather chair. 'Getting old does not suit you,' he said. Culain chuckled, but there was little humour in the sound.

'Getting old? I *am* old – as old as time. We should have died with the waves that destroyed Balacris.'

'But we did not, thank the Source! Why did you leave Goroien?'

'She could not understand my decision to become mortal.'

'That's understandable. If you remember, she fell in love with the hero Gilgamesh and watched him age; some problem with his blood that the Stone could not overcome. But I can see how she would not want to watch such an event again.'

'I liked him,' said Culain.

'Even though he took Goroien from you? You are a strange man.'

'It was a passing fancy, and it is truly ancient history. What are your plans now, my Lord Enhancer? Now that someone else is playing your game?'

'Enchanter, if you please. And I am unconcerned. Whoever it is can never play as well as I. You should know that, Culain; you have witnessed my genius through the ages. Did I not inspire the building of Troy? Did I not take Alexander to the brink of domination? To name but two small achievements. You think Eldared's petty sorcerer can oppose me?'

'As always, your arrogance is a joy to behold. You seem to forget how it has humbled you in the past. Troy fell, despite your attempts to save it. Alexander took a fever and died. And as for Caligula . . . what on earth did you see in that boy?'

'He was bright as a button – much maligned. But I take your point. So who do you think is behind Eldared?'

'I have no idea. Pendarric has the power, but he tired of mortals long ago. Brigamartis, perhaps.'

'She took to playing the Gods' game with the Norse, but she's gone now. I haven't heard of her in a century or more. What of Goroien?'

'She would never use the Soul Stealers.'

'I think you forget how ruthless she could be.'

'Not at all. But not for someone else – not a petty king like Eldared. He couldn't pay enough. However, that is your problem now, Enchanter. I want nothing more to do with it.'

'You surprise me. If Eldared has the power to summon the Soul Stealers and open a gate on your mountain, then he has the power to send assassins after the boy wherever he is. I take it you left nothing belonging to the prince on the mountain?'

Culain closed his eyes. 'I left his old clothes in a chest.'

'Then they can find him. Unless you stop them.'

'What are you suggesting?'

'Find the power behind Eldared and slay it. Or slay the king.'

'And what will you be doing while I am scouring the countryside?'

'I will use this,' said the Enchanter, lifting a yellowed leather-covered wedge of parchment. 'It is the most valuable possession Thuro had. The works of Plutarch. Much of his Harmony remains in it. I shall follow him through the Mist.'

*

Prasamaccus gazed around him. The landscape had changed; it was more rugged and open, the mountains stretching out into the distance beyond an immediate wooded valley. And it was bright . . . he looked up, and his heart sank. Two moons hung in the sky, one huge and silver-purple, the other small and white. The Brigante feared he knew what such phenomena might mean, and it was not good news. There was no sign of the warrior with the storm-cloud eyes.

'Where is Culain?' screamed Laitha.

'He did not manage to reach the central square,' said Thuro softly. His eyes met those of Prasamaccus, who understood the unspoken thought. Culain had fallen among the Soul Stealers; both had seen it. Laitha began to search beyond the circle of white stones, calling Culain's name. Thuro sat down alongside Prasamaccus.

'I did not think anything could kill him,' said Thuro. 'He was an amazing man.'

'I regret not having known him,' said Prasamaccus, with as much sincerity as he could muster. 'Tell me, how do we get home?'

'I have no idea.'

'Strange, I thought you were going to say that. Do you know where we are?'

'I am afraid not.'

'I should have been a fortune-teller. I am beginning to know the answers to these questions before you speak. One last question. Does that second moon mean what I think it means?'

'I am afraid so.'

Prasamaccus sighed and opened his pouch, producing a small seed cake. Thuro smiled; he was beginning to like the crippled archer.

How did you meet Victorinus?'

Prasamaccus swallowed the last of the seed cake. 'I was out hunting . . .' He told Thuro the tale of seeing the Atrols and fleeing to a stone circle, and of the journey with Maedhlyn back to Eboracum. He did not mention Helga; the thought of never seeing her again was too painful. Meanwhile Laitha wandered back into the circle and sat down, saying nothing. Prasamaccus offered her his last seed cake, but she refused.

'It's your fault, cripple,' she snapped. 'If we had not had to wait for you, we could have escaped with Culain.'

Prasamaccus merely nodded. It did not pay to argue with women.

'Nonsense!' stormed Thuro. 'If you had not killed the poor man's horse, we would have arrived the sooner.'

'You are saying it is my fault he is dead?'

'You are the one who introduced the question of fault, not I. Now if you cannot be civil, hold your tongue!'

'How dare you? You are not my kinsman, nor my prince. I owe you nothing.'

'If I might . . .' began Prasamaccus.

'Be quiet!' snarled Thuro. 'I may not be your prince, but you are my responsibility. It is what Culain would have wanted.'

'How would you know what he wanted? You are a boy; he was a man.' She stood and stalked off into the darkness.

'Arguing with women offers no reward,' said Prasamaccus softly. 'They are always right; I saw that in my village. You'll only have to apologise to her.'

'For what?'

'For pointing out that she was wrong. What are your plans, prince?'

Thuro sat back. 'Are you not angry with her for accusing you?'

'Why should I be? She was right; I slowed you down.'

'But . . .'

'I know, she killed my horse. But how far can we take this back? Had I not been riding into the mountains you would not have been delayed at all. Had you not been missing, I would not have been riding. Is it your fault? Arguing about it will not light us a fire, or find food.'

'You are very philosophical.'

'Of course,' agreed Prasamaccus, wondering

154

what it meant. He stood and limped out beyond the circle, seeking twigs for a fire, but there were none. 'I think we should camp in those woods until morning,' he said.

'I'll fetch Laitha.'

'I'll do it,' said Prasamaccus swiftly, limping out to where she sat.

The trio found a sheltered hollow and lit a camp-fire against a fallen trunk. Without blankets or food they sat silently, each lost in thought. Laitha grappled with grief and ill-understood anger. Thuro wondered what plan Culain might have conceived following their arrival. Would he have known this land? And if he had not, what would he have done? Set off north? South? Prasamaccus lay down beside the fire and thought of Helga. Five weeks of bliss. He hoped she would not have to wait for him too long.

When Thuro awoke Prasamaccus had already started a fire and four clay spheres were sitting in the flames. The prince stretched his cramped muscles. Laitha still slept.

'You are up early,' said Thuro, glancing at the dawn sky.

'Best to catch pigeons while they sleep. Are you hungry?'

'Ravenous.' Prasamaccus hooked a ball from the fire with a short stick, then cracked a rock to it. The clay split cleanly, taking all feathers from the bird. The meat was dark and similar to beef and Thuro devoured it swiftly, sucking clean the fragile bones.

'I found a high hill,' said Prasamaccus, 'and

from there studied the land. I could see no sign of building, but there is some evidence of tilled fields to the west.'

He rolled another ball from the fire and split it; then he moved to where Laitha lay and gently pushed her shoulder. She awoke and he smiled at her. 'There is breakfast cooking. Come eat.' She did so in silence, careful to avoid even looking at Thuro.

'Why did Storm-eyes send you here?' asked the Brigante.

'To find my father's sword, the Sword of Cunobelin. But I do not know where to look, and I am not even sure that this is the world we were meant to enter. Culain said we needed the power of the sun, and we certainly left without that.'

Prasamaccus cracked another clay sphere and sat back quietly. He had Vamera and therefore a constant supply of food. When they found people, he could trade skins and meat and perhaps buy a horse eventually. He would not starve, but what of his wards? What skills could the young prince bring to bear on this new world, where he was not even a prince? The girl was not a concern, for she was young and pretty and her hips looked good for childbirth. She would not go hungry. Suddenly an unpleasant thought struck him. This was another world. Supposing it was the world of the Atrols, or other demons? He remembered the tilled fields and was partially relieved. Demons tilling fields were somehow less demonic.

'We will go west,' said Thuro, 'and find the owners of the field.'

Prasamaccus was relieved that Thuro had decided to be the leader; he was much more content to follow and advise and that way little blame could attach should matters go awry. The trio set off through the woods, following obvious game trails and coming across the spoor of deer and goat. The tracks were somewhat larger than Prasamaccus had known, but not so large that they gave cause for concern. By mid-morning they spotted the first deer. It was almost six feet high at the shoulders, which were humped, and it had a flap of skin hanging on its throat. Its antlers were sharp, flat and many-pointed.

'It would need a fine strike to kill that beast,' said Prasamaccus. He said no more, for his ruined leg was beginning to ache from the long walk. Thuro noticed his limp growing more pronounced and suggested a halt.

'We have only come about three miles,' protested Laitha.

'And I am tired,' snapped Thuro, sitting down against a tree. The Brigante sank gratefully to the grass. The boy would make a fine leader if he lived long enough, he thought.

After a short rest it was Prasamaccus who suggested they move on, smiling his thanks to Thuro, and towards late afternoon they emerged from the wood into a rolling land of gentle hills and dales. The distant mountains reared white and blue against the horizon, and in their shadow – some two miles further west

– was a walled stockade around a small village. Cattle and goats could be seen grazing on a hillside.

Thuro gazed long at the village, wondering at the wisdom of walking in. Yet what choice did he have? They could not spend their lives hiding in the woods. The path widened and they followed it until they heard the sound of horsemen. Thuro stood in the centre of the road; Prasamaccus moved to the left, Laitha to the right.

There were four men in the party, all heavily armoured and wearing high plumed helms of shining brass. The leader halted his mount and spoke in a language Thuro had never heard. The prince swallowed hard, for this was a consideration that had not occurred to him. Whatever it was that the man said, he repeated it – this time more forcefully. Instinctively Thuro's hand curved around the hilt of his gladius.

'I asked what you were doing here,' said the rider.

'We are travellers,' answered Thuro, 'seeking rest for the night.'

'There is an inn yonder. Tell me, have you seen a young woman, heavily pregnant?'

'No, we have just come from the woods. Is she lost?'

'She is a runaway.' The warrior turned to his men, lifted his arm and the four horsemen thundered by. Thuro took a deep, calming breath. Prasamaccus limped towards him and spoke. The words were unintelligible, a seemingly rhythmless series of random sounds.

'What are you talking about?' asked the prince. Prasamaccus looked startled and swung towards Laitha, whose words were equally strange, though almost musical. Thuro clapped his hands and they both turned towards him. He slowly pulled clear his gladius, offering the hilt to Prasamaccus; the Brigante reached out and touched it. 'Now do you understand me?'

'Yes. How do you come by this magic?'

Laitha interrupted them with an incomprehensible question.

'Might be best to leave her like that,' said Prasamaccus. Laitha was becoming angry and she shook her fist at Thuro. As she did so, the copper bracelet on her arm slid down over her tunic sleeve and touched the skin of her wrist.

'Thuro, you miserable whoreson? Do not leave me like this.'

'I will not,' said Thuro. Her eyes closed in relief, then they flared open.

'What happened to us?'

'Culain touched my sword and your bracelet with his magic Stone. I suspect we are now speaking whatever language is common to this world.'

'What did the riders want?' asked Laitha, dismissing the previous problem from her thoughts.

'They were seeking a runaway woman – heavily pregnant.'

'She is hiding in those rocks,' Prasamaccus told them. 'I saw her just as we heard the soldiers.'

'Then let us leave her be,' declared Thuro. 'We want no trouble.'

'She is hurt,' said Prasamaccus. 'I think she's been whipped.'

'No! We have problems enough.'

Prasamaccus nodded, but Laitha walked away from the path and up the short climb to the rocks. There she found a young girl, no older than herself. The girl's eyes widened in terror and she bit her lip, her slender hand moving protectively across her swollen stomach.

'I shall not hurt you,' said Laitha, kneeling beside her. The girl's shoulders were bleeding and it was obvious a whip had been laid there with considerable force. 'Why are you hunted?'

The girl touched her belly. 'I am one of the Seven,' she said, as if that answered the question.

'How can we help you?'

'Take me to Mareen-sa.'

'Where is that?' The girl seemed surprised, but she pointed up into the hills where a shallow wood opened beyond a group of marble boulders. 'Come, then,' said Laitha, holding out her hand. The girl rose, and with Laitha's support began the climb.

Below them Prasamaccus sighed and Thuro fought to control his anger.

'Easier to tame a wild pony than a wild woman,' muttered the Brigante. 'Said to be worth the effort, though.'

Thuro felt the anger seep from him in the face of the man's mildness.

'Does nothing disturb you, my friend?'

'Of course,' said Prasamaccus, hobbling off in the wake of the woman.

Thuro followed, his eyes sweeping the hills for sign of the horsemen.

10

The vanguard of the Brigante army – some seven thousand fighting men – crossed the Wall of Hadrian at Cilurnum, moving on in a ragged line to the fortress town of Corstopitum. The force was led by Cael and spearheaded by seven hundred riders of the Novontae, skilled horsemen and ferocious swordsmen.

Corstopitum was a small town of fewer than four hundred people, and the council leaders sent messages of support to Eldared, promising supplies of food to the army on its arrival. They also ordered the withdrawal of the British garrison and the hundred soldiers marched to Vindomara twelve miles south-east. The town leaders in this larger settlement had studied the omens and followed the example of their northern neighbours. Once more, the garrison was expelled.

Eldared was winning the war even before the first battle lines had been drawn.

Now, kneeling behind a screen of bushes in the woods above Corstopitum, Victorinus studied the camp below. The Brigantes had pitched their tents in three fields outside the city, the Novontae riders further to the west beside a swift-flowing stream.

Gwalchmai moved silently alongside the swarthy Roman. 'At least two thousand more than we expected, and the main force still to come,' said the Cantii.

'Eldared is hoping his show of force will cow Aquila.'

'That is not unreasonable. The cities do not relish a war.'

Behind the two men waited a full cohort of Alia, four hundred and eighty hand-picked fighting men, trained for battle as either foot soldiers or *cohors equitana*, mounted warriors. Victorinus moved back from the bushes and summoned the troop commanders to him. As with the old Roman army the cavalry was split into turma – or troops – of thirty-two men each, with sixteen turmae to a cohort.

The commanders gathered around Victorinus in a tight circle as he outlined the night's plan of action. Each commander was given a specific target and the various counter-options open to him depending on the fortunes of the battle. Within such a ferocious skirmish the best-laid plans could come to nothing and Victorinus knew there would be no opportunity for tactical changes once the fight began. Each turma would accomplish its own task and then withdraw. Under no circumstances would one group go to the aid of another.

For more than an hour they discussed the options, then Victorinus walked among the soldiers checking weapons and horses and talking to the men. He wore, as did they, a leather-ringed breastplate and wooden helm covered with lacquered cow-hide, with scimitar shaped ear-guards tied under the chin. His thighs were protected by a leather kilt, split into five sections above copper-reinforced boots which had replaced the more traditional greaves. The men were nervous, yet anxious to inflict punishment on the proud Brigantes.

At one hour after midnight, with the Brigante camp silent, three hundred horsemen thundered down the hill. Four turmae rode to the Brigante supply wagons, overturning them and putting them to the torch. Another troop galloped to the Novontae picket line, killing the guards and driving the horses up and into the hills. Brigante warriors streamed from their tents, but a hundred veteran lancers led by Gwalchmai hammered into them, driving them back. Behind the lancers two turmae galloped around the tents, hurling flaming brands to the canvas. The camp was in an uproar.

High above Corstopitum, Victorinus watched with concern as the flames grew and the pandemonium increased.

'Now, Gwalchmai! Now!' whispered the Roman. But still the battle raged, and the Brigante leaders began to restore order. As Victorinus verged on the edge of rage, he saw Gwalchmai's lancers wheel into the 'flying arrow' formation and charge. The wedge, with Gwalchmai at the point of the arrow, sundered the gathering Brigante, and the other turmae galloped in behind the wings of the lancers as they broke clear into the fields. Several horses went down, but the main force escaped into the hills.

In their wake Victorinus viewed with pleasure the burning wagons and tents and the scores of Brigante bodies that littered the fields.

The days of blood had begun . . .

*

Bitterness was so much part of Korrin Rogeur's life that he was hard pressed to remember a time when different emotions had fuelled his spirit. He stood now on the outskirts of the forest of Mareen-sa, watching the small group make its way down the hill towards the trees. He recognised Erulda and was pleased at her escape – though not for her sake, but for the chagrin it would cause the Magistrate. In Korrin Rogeur's world, the only moments of pleasure came when his enemies were discomfited.

He was a tall man, wand-slim, and wearing hunting garb of browns and dark greens which allowed him to merge with the forest. By his side was a longsword, and across his back a longbow of yew and a quiver of black-feathered arrows. His eyes were dark and a permanent scowl had etched deep lines into his brow and cheeks, making him seem older than his twenty-four years.

As the group grew closer he studied the woman helping Erulda. She was young, tall and lithe, long-legged and proud as a colt. Behind her came a fair-haired young man, and behind him a cripple.

Korrin scanned the skyline for sign of soldiers lying in wait, aware that the arrival of Erulda could herald a trap. He signalled the men hiding in the bushes then moved out on to open ground. Erulda saw him first and waved; he ignored her.

'And where do you think you are going, Pretty?' he asked Laitha.

Laitha said nothing. Her upbringing with Culain had lacked some of the finer points of communication. She drew her hunting-knife and stepped forward.

'My, my,' said Korrin, 'a ferocious colt! Do you plan to stick me with your pin?'

'State your business, Ugly, and be done with it,' she told him.

Korrin ignored her and turned to Thuro. 'Your women fight for you, do they? How pleasant.'

Thuro advanced to stand before the taller woodsman. 'Firstly, she is not my woman. Secondly, I do not like your tone. That may seem a small matter, especially as you have five men in the bushes even now, with shafts aimed. However, believe me when I tell you I can kill you before they can aid you.'

Korrin grinned and walked beyond Thuro to where Prasamaccus had seated himself on the grass. 'Your turn to offer me violence, I believe?'

'This is a foolish and foolhardy game,' said the Brigante, rubbing at his aching leg. 'There are soldiers hunting this girl, who could come riding over the rise at any moment. I take it from her reaction when she saw you that you are a friend, so why not act like one?'

'I like you, cripple. You are the first of your group to make sense. Follow me.'

'No,' said Thuro softly. 'We are looking for no trouble with the soldiers. You have the girl; we will leave.'

Korrin lifted his arm and five men stepped from the trees, arrows notched to taut bowstrings. 'I fear not,' he said. 'I must insist you join us for a midday meal. It is the least I can offer.'

Thuro shrugged, pulled Prasamaccus to his feet and followed the woodsman into the forest. Erulda ran forward to walk beside Korrin, linking her arm in his.

The pace was too swift for Prasamaccus, despite the fist that kept prodding his back, and on a slippery patch where the path rose he fell. As Thuro leaned to assist him, a dark-bearded woodsman kicked Prasamaccus in the back, hurling him to the ground once more. Thuro hit the man backhanded across the face, spinning him to the grass. A second man leapt forward, but Thuro spun and hammered his elbow into his attacker's throat. Prasamaccus scrambled to his feet as the others swarmed in to tackle the prince.

'Stop!' bellowed Korrin and the men froze. 'What is going on?'

'He struck me,' stormed the first woodsman, pointing at Thuro.

'You are a troublesome boy,' said Korrin.

'Ceorl kicked the cripple,' said another man. 'He got what he asked for.'

Ceorl swore and rounded on the speaker, but Korrin stepped between them.

'You fight when I tell you, never before. And

you will not strike a brother, Ceorl. *Ever*. All we have is our bond, one to the other. Break it and I'll kill you.' He swung on Thuro. 'I will say this once: You are at present a guest, albeit a reluctant one. So curb your temper, lest you truly wish to be treated like an enemy.'

'There is a difference between the two?'

'Yes. We kill our enemies. Bear that in mind.'

They walked on at a reduced pace, and Prasamaccus was pleased to note the absence of the fist in his back. Still his leg was raging by the time they reached the camp-site, a honeycomb of caves in a rocky outcrop. He, Thuro and Laitha were left to sit in the open under the eyes of four guards while Korrin and Erulda vanished into a wide cave-mouth.

'You must learn not to be so hot-headed,' said Prasamaccus. 'You could have been killed.'

'You are right, my friend, but it was a reaction. How is your leg?'

'It hardly troubles me at all.'

'She did not even thank me,' said Laitha suddenly. Thuro took a deep breath, but Prasamaccus tapped his arm sharply.

'It was a fine gesture nonetheless,' said the Brigante.

Laitha dipped her head. 'I am sorry I said what I did, Prasamaccus. You did not cause Culain's death. Will you forgive me?'

'I rarely recall words said in anger or grief. There is nothing to forgive. What we must decide is how to deal with our current situation. We appear to be sitting at the heart of a war.'

'Surely not,' said Laitha. 'This is just an outlaw band.'

'No,' put in Thuro, 'the girl was some kind of hostage. And if these men were truly outlaws, they would have searched us for coin. They appear to be a brotherhood.'

'And a small one,' said the Brigante, 'which probably makes them the losing side.'

'Why does that affect us?' asked Laitha. 'We mean them no harm.'

'What we may intend is not the point,' said Thuro. 'This looks to be a more or less permanent camp and now we know how to find it. If the soldiers question us, we could betray the brotherhood.'

'So? What are you suggesting?'

'Simply that we will either be slain out of hand or offered a place among them. The latter is more likely since we were not killed back in the hills.'

Prasamaccus merely nodded.

'So what should we do?' asked Laitha.

'We join them – and escape when we can.'

Korrin emerged from the cave and summoned Thuro. 'Leave your sword and knife with your friends, and follow me.' The prince did as he was bid and walked behind the woodsman deep into the torchlit maze of caves, arriving at last at a wide doorway cut into the sandstone. Korrin halted. 'Go inside,' he said softly. From within the entrance came a deep, throaty growl and Thuro froze.

169

'What is in there?'
'Life or death.'

*

The prince stepped into the shadow-haunted interior. Only one flickering candle lit the room beyond and Thuro waited as his eyes grew accustomed to the dark. In the corner sat a hunched figure, seemingly immense in the shadows. The prince approached and the figure turned and rose, towering over him. The head was grotesque, bulging-eyed and savagely marked, while the face was a mixture of man and bear. Saliva dripped from the jaws and though the figure was robed in white like a man, the huge paws that extended from the sleeves were clawed and bestial.

'Welcome to Mareen-sa,' said the creature, its voice deep and rolling, its words slurred almost beyond recognition. 'Tell me of yourself.'

'I am Thuro. A traveller.'

'A servant of whom?'

'I am no man's servant.'

'Each man is a servant. From where have you travelled?'

'I have walked the Mist. My world is far away.'

'The Mist!' whispered the creature, moving closer, its claws resting on Thuro's shoulder close to his throat. 'Then you serve the Witch Queen?'

'I have not heard of her. I am a stranger here.'

'You know, do you not, that I am ready to slay you.'

'So I understand,' replied Thuro.

'I do not wish to. I am not as you see me, boy. Once I was tall and fair, like my brother Korrin. But it does not pay to fall into the clutches of Astarte. Worse it is to love her, as I loved her. For then she does not kill you. No matter . . . go away, I am tired.'

'Do we live or die?'

'You live . . . today. Tomorrow? We will talk again tomorrow.'

The prince backed from the chamber as the hunched figure settled down in the corner. Korrin was waiting.

'How did you enjoy your meeting?' asked the woodsman. Thuro looked deeply into his eyes, sensing the pain hidden there.

'Can we talk somewhere?' The man shrugged and walked back towards the light. In a side chamber containing a cot and two chairs Korrin sat down, beckoning Thuro to join him.

'What would you like to talk about?'

'This may seem hard to believe, but I and my companions know nothing of your lands or your troubles. Who is Astarte?'

'Hard to believe? No. Impossible. You cannot travel anywhere on the face of this world without knowing Astarte.'

'Even so, bear with me. Who is she?'

'I have no time for games,' said Korrin, rising.

'This is not a game. My name is Thuro and

I have travelled the Mist. Your land, your world, is new to me.'

'You are a sorcerer? I find that hard to take. Or are you really hundreds of years old and only pretending to be a beardless boy?'

'I came here – was sent here – by a man of magic. He did it to enable us to escape being murdered. That is the simple truth – question my friends. Now, who is Astarte?'

Korrin returned to his seat. 'I do not believe you, Thuro, but you gain nothing by hearing me speak of her, so I will tell you. She is the Dark Queen of Pinrae. She rules from ocean to ocean, and if sailors can be believed she controls lands even beyond the waters. And she is evil beyond any dream of man. Her foulness is such that if you truly have not heard of her you will not believe her depravity. The girl you helped was one of the Seven. Her fate was to be taken to Perdita, the castle of iron, and there to see her babe devoured by the Witch Queen. Think on that! Seven babes every season!'

'Eaten?' said Thuro.

'Devoured, I said, by the Bloodstone.'

'But why?'

'How can you ask a sane man why? Why does she destroy rather than heal? Why did she take a man like Pallin and turn him into the beast that he is becoming? You know why she did that? Because he loved her. Now do you understand evil? Every day that good man becomes more of a beast. One day he will turn on us and rend and slay, and we will have to

172

kill him. Such is the legacy of the Witch Queen, may the Ghosts disembowel her!'

'I take it she has an army?'

'Ten thousand strong, though she has disbanded twice that number following her conquests of the Six Nations. But she has other weapons – dread beasts she can summon to rip a man to bloody ribbons. Have you heard enough?'

'How is it that you survive against such a foe?'

'How indeed? If she killed us now, how would we suffer? Allowing us to live and watch Pallin go mad, that is wondrously venomous. When we have been forced to kill him and our hearts are broken, then they will come.'

'She sounds vile indeed,' said Thuro. 'Now I understand what you meant about the bond of brotherhood. But tell me, why do the people stand for such evil? Why do they not rise up in their thousands?'

Korrin leaned back, fixing his dark eyes on Thuro as if seeing him for the first time. 'Why should they? I did not – until my wife's name was drawn from the list. Until they dragged her screaming from our home, carrying a babe I would never see. Life is not unpleasant in Pinrae. There is enough food and work and there are no enemies any longer across the borders. Now the only danger is to pregnant women – and only twenty-eight of those a year from a nation of who knows how many thousand? No, why should a man seek to overthrow such a benign ruler? Unless his wife and child are slain . . . unless his brother is turned into a foul monster, doomed to be killed by his own kin.'

'How long has Astarte ruled Pinrae?'

Korrin shrugged. 'That is a matter for historians. She has always been Queen. And yet to look at her . . . My brother journeyed to the castle of iron to plead for Ishtura, my wife. The Queen took him to her bosom and he fell for her golden beauty. What a price he paid to bed her!'

'Why do you not flee the land?' asked the prince.

'To where? Across the oceans? Who knows what evil dwells there? No, I shall stay and attempt all in my power to destroy her, and all who serve her. What a burning there will be on that glad day!'

Thuro rose. 'Oil never killed a fire,' he said softly. 'I think I will return to my friends.'

'The fire I shall light will never be put out,' said Korrin, his eyes gleaming in the torchlight. 'I have the names on a scroll of life. And when she is dead others will be named, and they can follow her screaming into darkness.'

'The names of people who did not fight her?'

'Exactly.'

'Names like yours – before they took your wife?'

'You do not understand. How could you?'

'I hope I never do,' said Thuro, walking out into the corridor and on into the warmth of the afternoon sun.

*

Thuro and the others were not called to see the man-beast Pallin during the next four days, and Korrin Rogeur all but ignored them. Prasamaccus was infuriated at the lack of skill shown by the brotherhood's hunters, who returned empty-handed at dusk each day, complaining that the deer were too fast, too canny, or that their bows were not strong enough, their shafts not straight enough. On the fourth day they brought back a doe whose meat was so tough as to be indigestible. Prasamaccus sought out Korrin as the woodsman was setting off to scout in the north.

'What is it, cripple' I have little time.'

'And little food . . . and even less skill.'

'Make your meaning plain.'

'You do not have a huntsman in your tiny army who could hit a barn wall from the inside – and I am tired of chewing on roots or meat unfit for a hunter. Let me take my bow and bring some fresh meat to the caves.'

'Alone?'

'No. Give me someone who has a little patience and will do as he is told.'

'You are arrogant, Prasamaccus,' said Korrin, using the Brigante's name for the first time.

'Not arrogant, merely tired of being surrounded by incompetents.'

Korrin's eyebrows rose. 'Very well. Do you have anyone in mind?'

'The quiet one who spoke out against Ceorl.'

'Hogun is a good choice. I'll tell him to kill

you if you so much as appear to be trying to escape.'

'Tell him what you wish – but tell him now!'

Thuro watched as the two men left the clearing, Prasamaccus limping behind the taller Hogun. Korrin Rogeur approached him. 'Can he use that bow?'

'Time will tell,' said Thuro. Korrin shook his head and departed with four other men. Laitha sat beside the prince.

'They brought in three other pregnant women last night, she told him. 'I heard them talking. It seems Korrin raided a convoy they were with: four soldiers killed and several others wounded.'

Thuro nodded. 'It is his only chance to hurt Astarte – rob her of her sacrifices. But he is doomed, poor man, just like his brother.'

'While he lives, there is hope – so Culain used to say.'

Thuro nodded. 'There is truth in that, I suppose. But there are not more than fifty men here – against an army of ten thousand. They cannot win. And have you noticed the lack of organisation? It is not just that they lack skill as huntsmen, but they do nothing but sit and wait for Pallin to go mad. There are not enough scouts out to adequately protect the camp; they have no meetings to discuss strategy; they do not even practise with their weapons. A more disorganised band of rebels I have never heard of; they wear defeat like a cloak.'

'Perhaps they were just waiting for a prince with your battle experience,' snapped Laitha.

'Perhaps they were!' Thuro pushed himself to his feet and approached the nearest guard, a hulking youngster armed with a longbow. 'What is your name?' asked Thuro.

'Rhiall.'

'Tell me, Rhiall, if I were to walk from this camp what would you do?'

'I would kill you. Would you expect me to wave?' This brought a chuckle from the other three guards who had gathered around.

'I do not think you could kill me with that bow – not were I ten feet tall, six feet wide and riding a giant tortoise.' The other men grinned at Rhiall's discomfort. 'What is there for the rest of you to smile about? You!' hissed Thuro, pointing at a lean man with a dark beard and green eyes. 'Your bow is not even strung. Were I to run yonder into the trees you would be useless.'

'It doesn't pay to be insulting boy,' said the huntsman.

'Wrong,' Thuro told him. 'It does not pay to insult *men*. What are you, runaway servants? Clerics? Bakers? There is not a warrior amongst you.'

'That does it!' said the lean man. 'It is time someone taught you a lesson in manners, boy.' Thuro stepped back, allowing the man to draw his longsword, then the prince's gladius snaked into the sunlight.

'You are right about lessons, forester.' The prince leapt lithely back as the huntsman raised his sword and charged, slashing the weapon in a vicious arc towards Thuro's left side. The prince blocked the sweep with ease, pivoted on his heel and hammered the man from his feet. The huntsman's sword flew through the air to clatter against the trunk of a nearby tree. 'Lesson One,' said Thuro. 'Rage is no brother to skill.'

A second man came forward, more carefully. Thuro engaged him and their blades whispered together. He was more skilful than his comrade, but he had not been trained by Culain lach Feragh. Thuro stepped forward, rolled his sword over his opponent's blade, then flicked his wrist. The huntsman's sword followed that of his comrade and the man backed away, but Thuro sheathed his gladius. 'Laitha, come over here!'

Scowling, the forest girl obeyed. Thuro turned to the guards. 'I will not lower myself to best you with the bow, but I'll wager my sword against your bows that even this woman can outshoot you.'

'I'll take that wager,' said the lean man.

'I'll not play your games,' stormed Laitha. Thuro swung on her, lashing his open hand across her face; she staggered back, shocked and hurt.

'This time you will do exactly as I say,' snapped Thuro, his eyes blazing. 'I have had enough of your childish outbursts. We are here because of your stupidity. Act your age, woman! And think of Culain!'

At the mention off his name Laitha's anger flowed from her and she walked to the nearest man. 'Name a target,' she whispered.

178

'The tree yonder,' said Rhiall.

'I said a target, not a monument of nature!'

'Then you name one.'

'Very well.' Leaning forward, she deftly scooped Rhiall's dark cap from his head and walked to the tree he had indicated. There she drew her hunting-knife and plunged it through the hat, pinning it to the trunk. Then she paced out thirty steps and waited for the men to join her.

Rhiall strung his bow and notched an arrow. 'That was a good hat,' he grumbled as he pulled back the string, aimed and loosed. The shaft glanced from the trunk and vanished into the forest. The second man's shot missed the hat by a foot; the third man clipped the rim, bringing applause from the others. Lastly the lean huntsman took aim; his shaft hit the handle of Laitha's knife and failed to pierce the target.

'Shoot again,' said Laitha. He did so and scored a full hit in the crown of the hat. Laitha took Rhiall's bow and paced off another ten steps. She turned, drew back the string, froze, released her breath and loosed. The shaft slammed through the crown of the hat alongside the lean-man's arrow.

He sniffed loudly and walked to her mark, then took aim and released the string. The arrow creased the rim. Laitha moved back another ten paces and pierced the hat again. Then she approached Thuro, dropped the bow at his feet and leaned in close.

'Touch me again,' she whispered, 'and I'll kill you.' Turning her back, she returned to her place near the circle of rocks. The lean huntsman stepped forward.

'My name is Baldric. Perhaps you would teach me the move that disarmed me?'

'Gladly,' said Thuro. 'And if you wish to live beyond the spring you should practise your skills. One day soon the soldiers will come.'

'It's not the soldiers we fear,' said Baldric, 'It's the Vores.'

'Vores? I have not heard the name.'

'Great cats. They can crush an ox-skull in their jaws. Astarte uses them for sport – hunting the likes of us. Once they are loosed in the forest, we are truly lost.'

'If the beast is mortal, it can be slain. If one can be slain, ten can die – or a hundred. What you need is to plan for the moment the Vores are loosed.'

'How can you plan to fight a creature that runs faster than a horse and kills with either paw or fang? There used to be Vore hunts when I was a boy: twenty men with bows, another ten on horseback with long lances. And still men would die in the hunt. And here we are talking of twenty Vores, or thirty. And we have no hunting horses and no lances.'

'You are a pitiful bunch, to be sure. The Vores eat meat?'

'Of course.'

'Then set traps. Dig pits, with sharpened stakes at the foot. A man is never beaten until the last drop of his blood drips from the wound. And if you haven't the heart to fight, then leave the forest. But do not dither in the shadows.'

'What is your interest?' asked the hulking Rhiall. 'You are not one of us.'

'Happily true. But I am here and you need me.'

'How so?' asked Baldric.

'To teach you to win. Savour the word. *Win*.'

A terrifying roar came from the cave-mouth and the men swung towards it. There, stark against the rock-face, was a towering bear with no semblance of humanity. It saw the men gathered around Thuro, dropped on all fours . . .

. . . and charged.

*

The beast which had been Pallin moved at ferocious speed, hammering into the group before they could run. Rhiall, the slowest to move, was hurled ten feet in the air to land unconscious by a tall rock. The others were thrown to the ground, where they scrambled to their feet to sprint for the relative safety of the trees. Thuro dived to his left, rolling on his shoulder and rising as the beast reared up on its hind legs, its great talons raking the air. The prince drew his gladius and backed away. The bear advanced, dropped to all fours and charged again. This time Thuro leapt high, coming down on the beast's back with sword raised; but he could not plunge it into the creature's neck, knowing what it once had been. The bear began to thrash around, seeking to dislodge the young warrior. In his efforts to hold on Thuro dropped his sword; it fell to the beast's back and a blinding white light blazed from the blade. The bear dropped without a sound and

Thuro jumped clear of the falling body. The bestial features softened and the young Briton watched as the fur shrank back to reveal the half-human face he recalled from the first meeting deep in the caves. He retrieved his sword, noting the heat emanating from the blade – and the answer came to him.

'Laitha!' he shouted. 'Come quickly!' She ran to him and gazed in horror at Pallin's deformed features.

'Kill it quickly before it recovers.'

'Give me your bracelet. Now!' Swiftly she pulled the copper band clear and Thuro took it and held it to the twisted face. Once more light blazed and Pallin's features softened still further.

'What about the arrows?' whispered Laitha. 'Culain touched those also.'

Thuro nodded and she raced across the clearing to fetch her quiver. One by one Thuro touched the arrow-heads to the stricken half-beast – and each time more of the man emerged. At last the magic was exhausted and Pallin's face was clearly more human than before, but the taloned paws remained and the huge sloping, fur-covered shoulders. His eyes opened.

'Why am I not dead?' he asked, his anguish terrible to hear.

The guards ran forward and knelt before him.

'This young man restored you, Lord,' said Baldric. 'He touched you with his magic sword. Your face . . .' Baldric swept off his brass helm and held it before Pallin's eyes. The man-monster gazed at his distorted reflection, then turned his sad blue eyes on Thuro.

'You have only delayed the inevitable, but I thank you.'

'My friend Prasamaccus has another twenty arrows that were touched by magic. When he returns I will bring them to you.'

'No! Against Astarte we have no magic. Keep them safe. I am doomed, though your aid should grant me another month of life as a man.' He looked down at his terrible hands. 'As a man? Sweet gods of earth and water! What kind of man am I?'

'A good man, I think,' said Thuro. 'Have faith. What magic can do, magic can undo. Are there no Enchanters in this world?'

'You mean the Dream Shapers?' answered the man Baldric.

'If they work magic, yes.'

'There used to be one in the Etrusces – mountains west of here.'

'Do you know where in the mountains he lived?'

'Yes; I could take you.'

'No!' said Pallin. 'I want no one to risk danger for me.'

'You think there is less danger in these woods?' asked Thuro. 'How long before the Vores or the soldiers rip your brotherhood to pieces, or drag your people before Astarte to suffer your fate?'

'You do not understand: this is all a game to the Witch Queen,' said Pallin. 'She told me she could see my every movement, and would watch me slain by my brethren. Even now she has heard your plans and therefore has negated it. The Dark Lady watches us at this moment.'

The guards eased back from the stricken monster, glancing fearfully at the sky. Thuro himself felt a cold shiver on his back, but he forced a laugh and stood.

'Do you think she is the only power in the world?' he scoffed. 'If she is so invincible, why are you not dead? Can you hear me, Witch Queen? Why is he not dead? Come Baldric, lead me to the Dream Shaper.'

Two hundred miles away the silvered mirror shimmered as Astarte passed an ivory hand before it.

'You interest me, sweet boy. Come to me. Come to Goroien!'

11

At sunset Prasamaccus limped into the camp
as Thuro and Baldric were preparing for their
journey. Behind him came the red-faced
Hogun, staggering under the weight of the deer
the crippled Brigante had killed two hours
before. Prasamaccus sank to the ground beside
Laitha.

'What is going on?'

'The noble prince has decided to take on the
Witch Queen,' she answered. 'He is heading
off to some mountain range to find a wizard.'

'Why are you angry? He has obviously
earned their confidence.'

'He is a boy,' she said dismissively.

Tired as he was, Prasamaccus rose and
limped to the group where Thuro outlined the
events of the day. The Brigante said nothing,
but he sensed the growing excitement among
the men. The man-beast Pallin had returned to
the caves.

'How will you find the Dream Shaper?' asked
Thuro.

As Baldric was about to answer Prasamaccus
interrupted sharply: 'A word with you, young
prince?'

Thuro followed the Brigante to a sturdy oak.

'You obviously disbelieve that the Witch Queen overlooks us, but that is an assumption and therefore unwise. Let the man lead us, but do not discuss the exact location.'

'She cannot be everywhere, she is not a goddess.'

'We do not know that. But she must have known the length of her spell on Pallin and she could have been watching for his death. Give me your sword.'

Thuro did so and Prasamaccus took three arrows from his quiver and ran them down the blade. 'I do not know if the magic can be transferred in this way, but I see no reason why not.' He returned the sword to the prince. 'Now let us find this Enchanter.'

'No, my friend. Pallin says that you and Laitha must remain. They will not allow all of us to leave the forest. Look after her and I will see you soon.'

Prasamaccus sighed and shook his head, but he said nothing and watched silently as the two men walked away into the shadows of the trees. Helga seemed so far away. The camp women gathered around the deer, quartering it expertly, and the Brigante lay down beside Laitha, covering himself with a borrowed blanket.

'He did not even say goodbye,' said Laitha.

Prasamaccus closed his eyes and slept.

Two hours later he was awakened by the point of a boot nudging his side. He sat up to see Korrin Rogeur squatting down beside him.

'If your friend does not return, I will cut your throat.'

'You woke me to tell me what I already know?'

Korrin sat down and rubbed at tired eyes. 'Thank you for the deer,' he said, as if the words were torn from him under duress, 'and I am grateful that your friend helped my brother.'

'Was your scouting mission successful?'

'Yes and no. There is an army camped now at the northern border – a thousand men. At first we thought they would enter the forest, but then they were ordered to dismount and return to their camp. It would seem this was around the time that the boy used his magic on Pallin.'

'Then he saved not only your brother, but your people as well,' said Prasamaccus.

'That is how it seems,' admitted Korrin. 'We are doomed here, and it galls me. When I was a child my father told me wonderful stories of heroes who could overcome impossible odds. But that is not life is it? There are thirty-four fighting men here. *Thirty-four*. Not exactly an army.'

'Look at it from Astarte's point of view,' said the Brigante. 'You are important enough to merit the attention of one-tenth of her army. She must fear you, for some reason.'

'We have nothing she should fear.'

'You have a flame here, Korrin. Admittedly it is a small flame, but I once saw an entire forest consumed from the glowing coals of a carelessly lit camp-fire. That is what she fears: that your flame will grow.'

187

'I am tired, Prasamaccus. I will see you in the morning.'

'Come hunting with me.'

'Perhaps.' Korrin stood and moved away towards the caves.

'You are a wise man,' said Laitha, pushing back her blanket and joining Prasamaccus. He smiled.

'I wish that were true. But were it the case I would be back in the Land Between Walls, or in Calcaria with my wife.'

'You are married? You have not mentioned her.'

'Memory is sometimes painful and I try not to think of her. Wherever she is now, she is not seeing the same stars as I. Good night, Laitha.'

'Good night, Prasamaccus.' For a few minutes there was silence, then Laitha whispered, 'I am glad you are here.'

He smiled, but did not answer. This was not a time for conversation . . . not when Helga was waiting within his dreams.

*

Thuro and Baldric walked through most of the night in a forest lit by the bright light of two moons – a silvered, almost enchanted woodland that Thuro found bordering on the beautiful. They slept for two hours and at dawn were at the western edge of the forest, facing the open valleys before the white-blue mountains.

'Now the danger begins,' said Baldric. 'May the Ghosts preserve us!'

The two men strode out into the open. Baldric strung his bow and walked with an arrow ready. Thuro scanned the skyline, but there was no sign of soldiers. Small huts and larger houses dotted the land and there were cattle grazing on the hillsides.

'Who are these Ghosts you pray to?' he asked Baldric.

'The Army of the Dead,' answered the lean huntsman.

At noon they stopped at a farmhouse and Baldric was offered a loaf of dark bread. The inhabitants, a young man and woman, seemed fearful and all too anxious for the travellers to move on. Baldric thanked them for the food and they vanished within the house.

'You knew them?' asked the prince.

'My sister and her husband.'

'They were not very friendly.'

'To speak to me is death since the warrant went out.'

'What was your crime?'

'I killed a soldier who came for my neighbour's wife. She was one of the Winter Seven.'

'What happened to the woman?'

'Her husband handed her over two hours later and named me as the killer. I ran and joined Korrin.'

'I would have thought there would be more rebels?'

'There were,' said the huntsman. 'An army of two thousand rose in the north, but they were taken and crucified on the trees of Caliptha-sa. Astarte wove a spell about them so that even when the crows had torn the flesh from their bones they were still alive. Their screams

189

came from the forest for more than two years before she relented and released their souls. Now there are not many rebels.'

The two travellers came to the foothills of the Etrusces by mid-afternoon of the following day. The mountains reared above them, gaunt giants against the gathering storm-clouds. 'There is a cabin,' said Baldric, 'about a mile ahead, in a narrow valley. We will stay the night there.'

The building was deserted, the windows hanging open and their leather hinges rotted. But the night was not cold and the two men sat before a fire, saying little. Baldric seemed an insular, introverted man.

Towards midnight the storm broke above the mountains, rain lashing the sides of the cabin and driven through the open windows by a shrieking wind. Thuro wedged the broken windows into place and watched as lightning speared the sky. He was tired and hungry, and his mind drifted to thoughts of Culain. He had not realised how fond he had grown of the Mist Warrior. That he had died at the hands of the Soul Stealers was more than a travesty. At least Aurelius had had the small satisfaction of taking some of his killers with him on the dark road. At the thought of his father, Thuro's mood mellowed to the point of melancholy. He could remember only four long conversations with the king; all of them had concerned his studies. But they never spoke as father and son . . .

A shadow moved across the clearing before

the cabin and Thuro jerked upright, blinking rapidly to clear his vision; he could see nothing. He drew his sword; the blade was shining like dull silver.

The door exploded inwards, but Thuro was already moving. The shadow swept towards him even as Baldric awoke, reaching for his bow. Thuro's mind emptied as his gladius blocked a grey blade and slashed through the dark cape and up into the corpse-grey face. The demon vanished in an instant, cape fluttering to the floor. Thuro ran to Baldric, touching his sword to the man's arrow-head. They waited, but nothing moved in the storm. Thuro glanced down at his sword. Was it still silver, or iron grey? He could not tell, and a tense hour followed. Taking a risk he moved to the door, lifting it back into place and wedging it shut.

Baldric's face was white, his eyes fearful. 'What was that thing?'

'A creature from the Void. It is dead.'

'From its face it was dead before it came in. How did you match it? I have never seen anything as swift.'

'I used a trick taught me by a master. It is called Eleari-mas – the Emptying.' Thuro gave a silent prayer of thanks to the departed Culain and allowed his body to relax. He thrust the gladius into the wooden floor. 'If the blade glows silver, it means they have returned,' he told the huntsman.

'You are more than you seem, boy. A goodly deal more.'

'I think I have passed from youth to manhood

in but a few days. Do not call me boy. My name is . . .' He stopped and smiled. 'I carry a boy's name still. My naming was due to have been conducted at Camulodunum in the summer, but I shall not be there. No matter. I need no druid nor Enchanter to tell me that I am a man.' He dragged the sword from the wood and held it aloft. 'Thuro is now the memory the man carries, a memory of youth and lesser days. This sword is mine. It is the sword of Uther Pendragon, the man.'

Baldric stood and offered his hand. Uther took it in the warrior's grip, wrist to wrist. 'More than a man,' said Baldric. 'You are a brother.'

*

Gwalchmai sat with head bowed, the bandage on his arm dripping blood to the grass. His turma had been cut to pieces in a raid three miles from the merchant town of Longovicium. Twenty-seven men were dead or captured; the remaining four sat with Gwalchmai in a small wood thinking of their comrades: men who awoke to a bright sun and this afternoon stared sightlessly at a darkening sky.

Summer had arrived in northern Britain, but it had brought no joy to the beleaguered army of Lucius Aquila. The Brigantes, under Eldared and Cael, had conquered Corstopitum, Vindomara, Longovicium, Voreda and Brocavum. Now they besieged the fortress city of Cataractonium, pinning down six cohorts of fighting men from the Fifth Legion. News from the south was scarcely better; Ambrosius had been forced to retreat against Hengist and the Saxon king had taken Durobrivae in the south-east.

A Jute named Cerdic had raided the south-west and sacked the town of Lindinis, destroying two cohorts of auxiliaries. No one talked of victory now, for the British army was running short of men, and hope, and the early victory at Corstopitum no longer boosted morale. Rather it was the reverse, for it had raised expectations which had not been realised.

Gwalchmai sat, watching the blood on his arm thicken and dry. He made a fist and felt the pain in his bicep. It would heal – given time. But how much time did he have?

'If the king were still alive . . .' muttered a short, balding warrior named Casmaris, not needing to finish the sentence.

'He is not,' snapped Gwalchmai, torn between agreement with the unspoken sentiment and loyalty to Aquila. 'What is the point of this endless hankering for things past? *If* the king were alive. *If* Eldared could have been trusted. *If* we had ten more legions.'

'Well, I am tired of running and holding,' said Casmaris. 'Why can we not bring up the Fourth and take them on in one bloody battle?'

'All or nothing?' queried Gwalchmai.

'And why not? Nothing is what we will have anyway. This is the slow death we are suffering.'

Gwalchmai turned away; he could not argue. He was a Cantii tribesman, a Briton by birth and temperament, and he did not understand the endless strategies. His desire was simple:

193

meet your enemy head on and fight until someone lost. But Aquila was a Roman of infinite
patience, who would not risk an empire on one
throw of the dice. Deep inside him, Gwalchmai
could feel that they were both wrong. Perhaps
there was a time for patience, but there was
also a time for raw courage and a defiance of
the odds.

He pushed himself to his feet. 'Time to ride,'
he said.

'Time to die,' muttered Casmaris.

*

Uther awoke with his heart thumping errati-
cally, fear making him roll and rise, groping for
his sword. He had fallen asleep while on watch.

'Have no fear,' said Baldric, who was honing
the blade of his hunting-knife as the dawn sunlight streamed through the open window. The
storm had passed and the morning was bright
and clear under a blue sky.

Uther smiled ruefully. Baldric offered him
the last of the black bread, which the prince
was forced to dampen with water from his companion's canteen before it became edible. They
set off minutes later, heading higher into the
timber-line of the mountains, following a
narrow trail dotted with the spoor of mountain
goats and big-horn sheep. At last, as the sun
neared noon, they came to a high valley where
a small granite-built house nestled in the hollow
of a hill. The roof had been thatched, but was
now black and ruined by fire.

The two men waited in the tree-line, scanning
the countryside for signs of soldiers. Satisfied

they were alone, they descended to the house, stopping at a huge oak. Crucified upon the trunk was the near skeleton of a man.

'This would be Andiacus,' said Baldric, 'and I do not think he can help us.' The leg bones were missing, obviously ripped away by wolves or wild dogs, and the skull had fallen to the earth by the tree-roots. Uther wandered to the house, which was well-built around a central room with a stone hearth. Everywhere was chaos – books and scrolls littering the floor, drawers pulled from chests, tables overturned, rugs pulled up. The three back rooms were in similar condition. Uther righted a cane chair and sat, lost in thought.

'Time to be leaving,' said Baldric from the doorway.

'Not yet. Whoever did this was searching for the source of the Enchanter's power. They did not find it.'

'How can you say that? They have torn the place apart.'

'Exactly, Baldric. There is no evidence of an end to the search. It follows that either they found the source at the very last, or they did not find it. The latter is more probable.'

'If they did not find it, how can we?'

'We know where not to look. Help me clear the mess.'

'Why? No one lives here.'

'Trust me.' Together the two men righted all the furniture, then Uther sat down once more staring at the walls of the main room. After a while he stood and moved to the bedroom. The quantity of books and scrolls showed Andiacus to be a studious man. Some of the manuscripts were still tied and Uther studied them. They were carefully indexed.

'What are we looking for?' asked the huntsman.

'A Stone. A golden Stone, black-veined, possibly the size of a pebble.'

'You think he hid it before they killed him?'

'No. I think he hid it as a matter of course, probably every night. And he did not have it with him when they captured him, which could mean they took him in his sleep.'

'If he hid it, they would have found it.'

'No. If *you* hid it, they would have found it. We are talking of an Enchanter and a magic Stone. He hid it in plain sight, but he changed it. Now all we must do is think of what it might have been.'

Baldric sat down. 'I am hungry, I am tired, and I do not understand any of this. But last night a creature of darkness tried to kill us, and I would like to be gone from these mountains before nightfall.'

Uther nodded. He had been thinking of the Soul Stealer and wondering whether it had been sent by Eldared or Astarte, or was merely a random factor associated with neither. He pushed his fears from his mind and returned to the problem at hand. Maedhlyn had often told him not to waste his energies on matters beyond his knowledge.

The murdered Enchanter either hid the Stone or transformed it. Had it been hidden, the searchers would have found it. Therefore it was transformed. Uther rose from the bed. Any one of the scattered objects on the floor could be Sipstrassi. Think, Uther, he told himself. Use your mind. Why would the Enchanter disguise the Stone? To safeguard it, so that no one would steal it. Around the room were ornate goblets, gold-tipped quills, items of clothing, blankets, candle-holders, even a lantern. There were scrolls, books and charms of silver, bronze or gold. All would be worth something to a thief and therefore useless as a disguise for a magic Stone. Uther eliminated them from his thoughts, his eyes scanning the room – seeking an object that was functional and yet worthless. There was a desk by the window, the drawers ripped out and smashed. Beside it lay piles of scattered papers . . . and there in the corner, nestling against the wall, an oblong paperweight of ordinary granite.

Uther pushed himself from the bed and moved to the rock. It was heavy, and ideal for the purpose it served. He held it over the desktop and concentrated hard. After several seconds his hand grew warm and there appeared two platters of freshly roasted beef. The granite in his hand disappeared, to be replaced by a thumbnail-sized Sipstrassi Stone with thick black veins interweaving on the golden surface.

'You did it!' whispered Baldric. 'The Dream Shaper's magic.'

Uther smiled, holding his elation in check, savouring the feeling of triumph – the triumph of mind. 'Yes,' he said at last, 'but the power of the Stone is not great. As the magic is exhausted, these black veins swell. When the gold is used up, the power is gone. Enjoy the meat. We cannot afford to waste any more enchantment; we must heal Pallin.'

The food was as close to divine as either man had tasted. Then gathering their weapons, Uther and Baldric left the house, the younger man carrying the Sipstrassi Stone in his hand. As they passed the skeleton the Stone grew warmer and Uther paused. A whisper like a breeze through dry leaves echoed inside his head and a single word formed.

'Peace.' It was a plea born of immense suffering. Uther remembered Baldric's word about the army of rebels who had been crucified and yet not allowed to die. Stooping he lifted the skull, touching the Stone to its temple. White light blazed and the voice inside Uther's head grew in power.

'I thank you, my friend. Take the Stone to Erin Plateau. Bring the Ghosts home.' The whisper faded and was gone, and the black threads on the Stone had swelled still further.

'Why did you do that?' asked Baldric.

'He was not dead,' answered Uther. 'Let us go.'

*

Maedhlyn hurled the black pebble to the table-top where Culain swept it up. Neither man said anything as Maedhlyn poured a full goblet of pale golden spirit and drained it at a swallow. The Enchanter looked in a dreadful condition, his face sallow, the skin sagging beneath his beard. His eyes were bloodshot, his movements sluggish. For seven days he had tried to follow Thuro, but the Standing Stones above Eboracum merely drained the power from his Sipstrassi. The two men had travelled to another circle to the west, outside Cambodunum. The same mysterious circumstances applied. Maedhlyn worked for days on his calculations, snatching only an hour's sleep in mid-afternoons. Finally he attempted to travel back to Eboracum, but even that could not be achieved.

The companions had returned to the capital on horseback where Maedhlyn searched through his massive library, seeking inspiration and finding none.

'I am beaten,' he whispered, pouring another goblet of spirit.

'How can it be that the Standing Stones no longer operate?' asked Culain.

'What do you think I have been working on this past fortnight? The rising price of apples?'

'Be calm, Enhancer. I am not seeking answers, I am searching for inspiration. There is no reason for the Stones to fail. They are not machines, they merely resonate compatibly with Sipstrassi. Have you ever known a circle to fail?'

'No, not fail. And how can I be calm? The immutable laws of Mystery have been overturned. Magic no longer works.' Maedhlyn's eyes took on a fearful look. He sat bolt upright and fished in the pocket of his dark blue robe, producing a second Sipstrassi Stone. He held it over the table and a fresh jug of spirit materialised; he relaxed. 'I have used up the power of two Stones that should have lasted decades, but at least I can still make wine.'

'Have you ever been unable to travel?'

'Of course. No one can travel where they already are, you know that. Law number one. Each time scale sets up its own opposing forces. It pushes us on – makes us accept, in the main, linear time. At first I thought I could not follow Thuro because I was already there. No Circle would accept my journey on that score. Wherever he is, and in whatever time, then I am there also. But that is not the case. It would not affect a journey from Cambodunum to Eboracum in the same time scale. The Circles have failed and I do not understand why.'

Culain stretched out his lean frame on the leather-covered divan. 'I think it is time to contact Pendarric.'

'I wish I could offer an argument,' said Maedhlyn. 'He is so dour.'

'He is also considerably more wise than both of us, your arrogance notwithstanding.'

'Can we not wait until tomorrow?'

'No, Thuro is in danger somewhere. Do it, Maedhlyn!'

'Dour is not the word for Pendarric,' grumbled the Enchanter. Taking his Stone he held his fist over the table and whispered the words of Family, the Oath of Balacris. The air above the table crackled and Maedhlyn hastily withdrew the two jugs of spirit. A fresh breeze filled the room with the scent of roses and a window

200

appeared on to a garden, wherein sat a powerful figure in a white toga. His beard was golden and freshly curled, his eyes a piercing blue. He turned, laying down a basket of perfect blooms.

'Well?' he said and Maedhlyn swallowed his anger. There was a wealth of meaning in that single word, and the Enchanter remembered his father using the same tone when young Maedhlyn had been found with the maidservant in the hay wagon. He pushed the humiliating memory from his thoughts.

'We seek your advice, Lord,' muttered Maedhlyn, afraid that the words would choke him. Pendarric chuckled.

'How that must pain you, Taliesan. Or should I call you Zeus? Or Aristotle? Or Loki?'

'Maedhlyn, Lord. The Circles have failed.' If Maedhlyn had expected Pendarric to be ruffled by the announcement, he was doomed to disappointment. The once-king of Atlantis merely nodded.

'Not failed, Maedhlyn. They are closed. Should they remain closed, then yes, they will fail. The resonance will alter.'

'How can this be? Who has closed them?'

'I have. Do you wish to dispute my right?'

'No, Lord,' said Maedhlyn hastily, 'but might I enquire the reason?'

'You may. I did not mind the more capricious of my people becoming gods to the savages – it amused them and did little real harm – but I will not tolerate the same lunacy we suffered before. And before you remind me, Maedhlyn, yes, it was my lunacy. But the world toppled.

The tidal waves, the volcanoes and the earth-quakes almost ripped the world asunder.'

'Why should it happen again?'

'One of our number has decided it is not enough to play at being a goddess; she has decided to *become* one. She has built a castle spanning four gateways and she is ready to unleash the Void upon all the worlds that are. So I have closed the pathways.'

Maedhlyn spotted a hesitation in Pendarric's comment and leapt on it: 'But not *all* of them?'

The king's face showed a momentary flash of annoyance. 'No. You were always swift, Talie-san. I cannot close her world . . . not yet. But then I did not believe any immortal would be foolish enough to repeat my error.'

Culain leaned forward. 'May I speak, Lord?'

'Of course, Culain. Are you standing by your decision to become mortal?'

'I am. When you say your error, you do not mean the Bloodstone?'

'I do.'

'And who is the traitor?' asked Culain, fear-ing the answer.

'Goroien.'

'Why would she do it? It is inconceivable.'

Pendarric smiled. 'You remember Gilga-mesh, the mortal who could not accept Sip-strassi immortality? It seems he had a disease of the blood and he gave it to Goroien. She began to age, Culain. You, of all of us, know what that must have meant to her. She now drains the life force from pregnant women into her Bloodstone. It will not be enough; she will

202

need more souls, and more again. In the end a nation's blood will not satisfy her, nor a world's. She is doomed and will doom us all.'

'I cannot accept it,' said Culain. 'Yes, she is ruthless. Are we not all ruthless? But I have seen her nurse a sick faun; help in childbirth.'

'But what you have not seen is the effect of the Bloodstones. They eat like cancers at the soul. I know, Culain. You were too young, but ask Maedhlyn what Pendarric was like when the Bloodstone ruled Atlantis. I ripped the hearts from my enemies. Once I had ten thousand rebels impaled. Only the end of the world saved me. Nothing will save Goroien.'

'My grandson is lost in the Mist. I must find him.'

'He is in Goroien's world, and she is seeking him.'

'Then let me go there. Let me aid him. She will hate him, for he is Alaida's son – and you know Goroien's feelings for Alaida.'

'Sadly, Culain, I know more than that. So does Maedhlyn. And, no the gates stay closed – unless, of course, you promise to destroy her.'

'I cannot!'

'She is not the woman you loved; there is nothing but evil left in her.'

'I have said no. Do you know me not at all, Pendarric?'

The king sat silent for a moment. 'Know you? Of course I know you. More, I like you, Culain. You have honour. If you should reconsider, journey to Skitis. One gateway remains. But you will have to slay her.'

Storm-clouds swirled in Culain's eyes and his face was white. 'You survived the Bloodstone, Pendarric, though many would have liked to slay you. Widows and orphans in their thousands would have sought your blood.'

The king nodded agreement. 'Yet I was not diseased, Culain. Goroien must die. Not for punishment – though some would argue she deserves it – but because her disease is destroying her. At the moment she sacrifices two hundred and eighty women a year from ten nations under her control. Two years ago she needed only seven women. Next year, by my calculations, she will need a thousand. What does that tell you?'

Culain's fist rammed to the table. 'Then why do you not hunt her? You were a warrior once. Or Brigamartis?'

'This would make you happy, Culain? Bring you contentment? No, Goroien is a part of you and you alone can come close to her. Her power is grown. If it is left to me to destroy her, I will have to shatter the world in which she dwells. Then thousands will die with her, for I will raise the oceans. Your choice, Culain. And now I must go.'

The window disappeared. Maedhlyn poured another goblet of spirit and passed it to Culain but the Mist Warrior ignored it.

'How much of this did you know?' he asked Maedhlyn. The Enchanter sipped his own drink, his green eyes hooded.

'Not as much as you think. And I would urge you to follow your own advice and be calm.'

Their eyes met and Maedhlyn swallowed hard, aware that his life hung by a gossamer thread. 'I did not know of Goroien's illness, only that she had taken to playing goddess once more. That I swear.'

'But there is something else, Enhancer – something Pendarric is aware of. So out with it!'

'First you must promise not to kill me.'

'I'll kill you if you do not!' stormed Culain, rising from his chair.

'Sit down!' snapped Maedhlyn, his fear giving way to anger. 'What good does it do you to threaten me? Am I your enemy? Have I ever been your enemy? Think back, Culain. You and Goroien went your separate ways. You took Shaleat to wife and she gave you Alaida. But Shaleat died, bitten by a venomous snake. You knew – and do not deny it – that Goroien killed her. Or if you did not know, you at least suspected. That is why you allowed Aurelius to take Alaida from the Feragh. You thought that Goroien's hatred would be nullified if Alaida chose mortality. You did not even allow her a Stone.'

'I do not want to hear this!' shouted Culain, fear shining in his eyes.

'Goroien killed Alaida. She came to her in Aurelius' castle and gave her poison. The babe took it in and it changed Alaida's blood. When she gave birth, the bleeding would not stop.'

'No!' whispered Culain, but Maedhlyn was in full flow now.

'As for Thuro, he had no will to live and I

used up a complete Stone to save him. But Goroien was always close through those early years, and I could not allow Thuro to grow strong. I gave him the weakness in his chest. I robbed him of his strength. Goroien saw the king's suffering and let the boy live. She was always a vindictive witch, only you were too blind to see it. At last she decided the time had come to wreak her full vengeance. She it was who went to Eldared, lifting him with dreams of glory. Not to kill the king, but Alaida's child – your grandson.

'You blamed me for Alaida's death. I said nothing. But when I left her on that fateful morning her pulse was strong, her body fit, her mind happy. She did not have the disease of kings at that time, Culain.'

The Mist Warrior lifted his goblet and drained the spirit, feeling its warmth cut through him. 'Have you ever loved anyone, Maedhlyn?'

'No,' replied the Enchanter, realising as he said it the regret he carried.

'You are right. I knew she killed Shaleat, yet I could not hate her for it. It was why I decided on mortality.' Culain laughed without humour. 'What a weak response for a warrior. I would die to punish Goroien.'

'It is ironic, Culain. You are dying when you do not have to, and she is dying when she does not wish to. What will you do?'

'What choice do I have? My grandson is lost in her world, along with another I love dearly.

To save them I must kill the woman I have loved for two thousand years.'

'I will come with you to Skitis Island.'

'No, Maedhlyn. Stay here and aid the Roman, Aquila. Hold the land for Thuro.'

'We cannot hold. I was thinking of taking up my travels once more.'

'What is left for you?' asked Culain. 'You have enjoyed the glories of Assyria, Greece and Rome. Where will you go?'

'There are other worlds, Culain.'

'Give it a little time. We have both given a great deal to this insignificant island. I would rather Eldared did not inherit it – or the barbarian Hengist.'

Maedhlyn smiled wistfully. 'As you say, we have given a great deal. I will stay awhile. But I feel we are holding back the sea with a barrier of ice . . . and summer is coming.'

12

Prasamaccus sat with Korrin Rogeur behind a screen of bushes on the eastern hills of Mareensa, watching a herd of flat-antlered deer grazing three hundred paces away.

'How do we approach them?' asked Korrin.

'We do not. We wait for them to approach us.'

'And if they do not?'

'Then we go home hungry. Hunting is a question of patience. The tracks show the deer follow this trail to drink. We sit here and we let the hours flow over us. Your friend Hogun chose to sleep the time away, which is as good a way as any – so long as someone stays on watch.'

'You are a calm man, Prasamaccus. I envy you.'

'I am calm because I do not understand hate.'

'Has no one ever wronged you?'

'Of course. When I was a babe a drunken hunter rode his horse over me. All my life since I have known pain – the agony of a twisted limb, the hurt of being alone. Hatred would not have sustained me.'

The dark huntsman smiled. 'I cannot be like

you, but being *with* you calms me. Why are you here in Pinrae?'

'I understand we are seeking a sword. Or rather that Thuro is seeking a sword. He is the son of a king – a great king by all accounts – who was murdered a few months ago.'

'From which land across the water do you come?'

Prasamaccus sat back and stretched his leg. 'It is a land of magic and mist. It is called Britain by the Romans, but in reality is many lands. My tribe is the Brigante, possibly the finest hunters of the world – certainly the most ferocious warriors.'

Korrin grinned broadly. 'Ferocious? They are not all like you then?'

Before Prasamaccus could reply the deer stampeded in a mad run towards the west. The Brigante pushed himself to his feet. 'Quickly,' he said. 'Follow me!' He limped towards an ancient oak and Korrin joined him.

'What are you doing?'

'Help me up.' Korrin linked his lands and levered the Brigante high enough to grab an overhanging branch and haul his body across it.

'Swiftly now, climb!' urged Prasamaccus. The Brigante moved aside and strung Vamera, notching a long shaft to the string. A terrible roar reverberated through the forest and Korrin leapt for the branch, pulling himself up just as the first Vore bounded into the clearing. Prasamaccus' arrow flashed into its throat, but its run continued unchecked.

A second shaft bounced from its skull as it sprang towards the hunters. Its claws scrabbled at the branch but Korrin kicked out, his boot smashing into the gaping jaws. The beast fell back and two others joined it, pacing round the tree. Prasamaccus sat very still, a third arrow ready, and stared at the great cats. They were each some eight feet long, with huge flat faces, oval yellow eyes and fangs as long as a man's fingers. The first beast sat down and worried at the arrow in its throat, snapping it with his paw. He then continued to prowl the tree. The beasts' backs were ridged with muscle and the Brigante could see no easy way to kill them.

'Shoot at them!' urged Korrin. At the sound of his voice the beasts began to roar and leap for the branch, but none could get a hold. Prasamaccus lifted his finger to his lips and mouthed a single word.

'Patience!'

He swung his quiver to the front and began to examine his arrows. Some were single-barbed, others double. Some had smooth heads for easy withdrawal; some were light, others heavy. Finally he chose a double-barbed shaft with a strongly weighted head. He notched it. It seemed to the Brigante that the only weak spot the Vore had was behind the front leg at the back of the ribs. If he could angle a shot correctly . . .

He waited for several minutes, occasionally drawing back the string, but hesitating. The watching Korrin grew ever more tense - but he held his tongue. A Vore paced away from the tree, presenting his back and Prasamaccus whistled softly. The beast stopped and turned. In that instant the arrow flashed through the air, slicing into the Vore's back and through to its heart. It slumped to the ground without a sound.

Selecting a fresh arrow, the Brigante waited. A second Vore approached the dead beast and began to push at the corpse with its snout, trying to raise it. Another arrow sang through the clearing and the Vore reared and fell to its back, its hind legs kicking. Then it was still. The third beast was confused; it approached its comrades and then backed away, smelling blood. It roared its anger to the skies.

A single bugle call echoed through the forest and the Vore turned towards the sound, then padded away swiftly. For some minutes the two men remained where they were, then Korrin made to climb down.

'Where are you going?'

'The beast is gone.'

'There may be others further west. Let us wait awhile.'

'Good advice, my friend. How did you know the Vores were loose?'

'The deer did not just run, they fled in panic. A man's smell would not do that, nor would a wolf. Since the wind was coming from behind and to the right of us, I reasoned the beasts must be close.'

'You are a canny man to have around, Prasamaccus. Perhaps our luck has changed.'

As if to evidence his words, a large Vore

raced across the clearing before them, oblivious to their presence and leapt the corpses in a headlong rush towards the bugle call.

'You think it is safe now?' asked Korrin.

'A few more minutes.' Prasamaccus could feel sadness riding him. Korrin had not yet stopped to consider the full meaning of the attack, and the Brigante hesitated to voice his fears. If four Vores had been loosed, why not all of them? And if that were the case, what had befallen the brotherhood at the caves? 'I think it is safe now,' he said at last.

Korrin sprang to the ground and waited to aid the slower Prasamaccus.

'I owe you my life. I shall not forget it.'

He began to walk back towards the camp, but Prasamaccus' slender hand fell on his shoulder. 'A moment, Korrin.' The taller man swung towards him, his face paling as he saw the look of concern in Prasamaccus' eyes. Then realisation struck.

'No!' he screamed and tore himself from the Brigante's grip to race away through the trees. Prasamaccus notched an arrow and followed at his own halting pace. He did not hurry, having no wish to arrive too soon. When at last he did come in sight of the caves, his worst fears were realised. Bodies scattered the clearing and in his path was a leg dripping blood to the grass. It was a scene of carnage. In the cave-mouth knelt Korrin alongside the giant body of his brother. Prasamaccus approached. The man-beast lay beside the bodies of three Vores and his talons were red with their blood. Beyond

Korrin, cowering in the darkness, were three children and Laitha. Part of his burden lifted as he saw that she was safe. Korrin was weeping openly, holding a blood-stained paw in his lap. The man-beast's eyes opened.

Prasamaccus touched Korrin's shoulder. 'He lives,' he whispered.

'Korrin?'

'I am here.'

'I stopped them, Korrin. The Witch Queen did me a service after all. She gave me the strength to stop her own hunting cats.' He took a deep shuddering breath and Prasamaccus watched as his life-blood continued to flow from the dreadful wounds.

'Four of the Seven are safe within the caves. Some of the men ran into the forest; I do not know if they survived. Get them away from here, Korrin.'

'I will, brother. Rest. Be at peace.' The body shimmered as if in a heat haze, then shrank to that of a normal man, slender and fine-boned, the face handsome and gentle. 'Oh, sweet Gods,' whispered Korrin.

'Very touching,' came a woman's voice and Prasamaccus and Korrin turned. Sitting on a nearby rock was a golden-haired woman in a dress of spun silver that looped over one ivory-skinned shoulder.

Korrin lunged to his feet, dragging his sword clear. He ran at the woman, who lifted a hand and waved her fingers as if casually swatting a fly. Korrin flew from his feet to land against the rocks ten feet away.

'I said I would watch him die . . . and I have. Bring my women to the camp in the north. Perhaps then I will allow the rest of you to live.'

Prasamaccus laid down his bow, feeling her eyes upon him.

'Why do you not attempt to kill me?' she asked.

'To what purpose, lady? You are not here.'

'How perceptive of you.'

'It takes no great perception to see that you cast no shadow.'

'You are disrespectful,' she chided. 'Come to me.' Her hand pointed and Prasamaccus felt a pull at his chest, hauling him to his feet. He stumbled on his bad leg and heard her soft lilting, mocking laughter. 'A cripple? How delicious! I was going to play a game with you, little man – make you suffer as Pallin suffered. But I see there is no need. Fate has perhaps dealt with you more unkindly than I could. And yet, you should suffer some pain for your insolent glances.' Her eyes shone.

Prasamaccus was still holding the arrow he had notched earlier and as her hand came up once more he raised the arrow-head before him. A blaze of white light came from her fingers, touched the arrow and returned to smite her in the chest. She screamed and stood . . . and in that moment Prasamaccus saw the golden hair show silver at the temples. Her hand shot to her aging face and panic replaced the malevolent smile. She disappeared in an instant.

Korrin stumbled to the Brigante's side. 'What did you do?'

Prasamaccus looked down at the arrow; the shaft was black and useless, the head a misshapen lump of metal. He hurled it aside. 'We must get the women from here before the soldiers come, as surely they will. Is there another hiding place in the forest?'

'Where can we hide from her?'

'One step at a time, Korrin. Is there a place?'

'Perhaps.'

'Then let us gather what is useful and go.' As he spoke, five men emerged from the trees. Prasamaccus recognised the tall Hogun and the hulking Rhiall.

'So,' said the Brigante, 'the brotherhood still lives.'

*

Laitha strode from the cave to the body of a dead warrior and unbuckled the man's sword-belt. Swinging it round her lean hips she drew the blade, hefting it for weight. The hilt was long and tightly covered with dark leather, and she could grip it double-handed for the cut or sweep. Yet the blade was not so long or heavy that she was unable to use it one-handed. She found a suitable whetstone and began to hone the edge. Prasamaccus joined her.

'I am sorry you had to suffer such an ordeal.'

'I did not suffer; Pallin kept the Vores from me. But the screams of the dying . . .'

'I know.'

'That woman radiated evil – and yet she was so lovely.'

215

'There is no mystery in that, Laitha. Pallin was a good man, yet sight of him would cause sleepless nights. All that is good is not always handsome.'

'I do not like to admit this, but she frightened me. All the way down to my bones. Before we left Culain I saw a Soul Stealer from the Void. Its face was the grey of death, yet it inspired less fear in me than the Witch Queen. How was it that you were able to speak so to her?'

'I do not follow you.'

'There was no fear in your voice.'

'It was in my heart, but all I saw was an evil woman. All she could do was kill me. Is that so terrible? In fifty years no one will remember my name. I will be merely the dust of history. If I am lucky, I will grow old and rot. If not, I will die young. Whatever, I will still die.'

'I never want to die – or grow old. I want to live for ever,' said Laitha. 'Just as Culain had the chance to do. I want to see the world in a hundred years, or a thousand. I never want the sun to shine without it shining on me.'

'I can see how that would be . . . pleasant,' said the Brigante, 'but for myself I think I would rather not be immortal. If you are ready, we should be on our way.'

Laitha looked deeply into his sad blue eyes, not understanding his melancholy mood. She smiled, rose smoothly and pulled him to his feet. 'Your wife is a lucky woman.'

'In what way?'

'She has found a gentle man who is not weak. And yes, I am ready.'

The small group, joined by four other survivors, numbered nineteen people as they headed high into the hills at the centre of Mareen-sa. There were four pregnant women, three children and, counting Laitha, twelve warriors.

Due to the advanced stage of one of the pregnancies the pace was slow, and it was dusk when Korrin led them up a long hill to a circle of black stones each some thirty feet high. The circle was more than a hundred yards in diameter and several – now deserted - buildings had been constructed around the eight-foot altar. Korrin dragged open a rotted door and pushed his way into the largest building. Prasamaccus followed him. Inside was one vast room over eighty feet long. Ancient dust-covered tables were set at right-angles to the walls, with bench seats alongside.

Korrin made his way to a large hearth, where a fire had been neatly laid. A huge cobweb stretched from the logs to the chimney-breast. Korrin ignored it and sparked the tinder. Flames rose hungrily at the centre of the dead wood, and a warm red light bathed the central hall.

'What is this place?' asked Prasamaccus.

'The Eagle sect once dwelt here – seventy men who sought to commune with the Ghosts.'

'What happened to them?'

'Astarte had them slain. Now no one comes here.'

'I cannot bring myself to blame them,' said the Brigante, listening to the wind howling across the hilltop. One of the women began to moan and sank to the floor. It was Erulda.

'The babe is due,' said Hogun. 'We'd best leave her to the women.' Korrin led the men outside to a smaller building where a dozen rotted cot-beds lined the walls. A rats' nest had been built against the far wall and the room stank of vermin. Once more a fire had been laid and Korrin ignited it.

Prasamaccus tested several beds, then gingerly laid himself down. There was no conversation and the Brigante found himself thinking of Thuro, and wondering if the Vores had killed him. He awoke an hour before dawn, half-convinced he had heard the sound of drums and marching feet. He stretched and sat up. Korrin and the other men were still sleeping around the dying fire. He swung his legs from the cot and stood, suppressing a groan as the weight came down on his twisted limb. Taking up his bow and quiver, he stepped out into the pre-dawn light. The door of the main building opened and Laitha moved into sight. She smiled a greeting, then ran across to him. 'I have been waiting for you for a full hour.'

'Did you hear the drums?'

'No. What drums?'

'I must have been dreaming. Come, we'll find some meat.' The two of them, both armed with bows, set off down the hill.

On this day Prasamaccus could do no wrong. He killed two deer and Laitha slew a big-horn sheep. Unable to carry the meat home, they quartered the beasts, hanging the carcases from three high tree branches.

With Prasamaccus carrying the succulent loin section of the deer, Laitha stopped to gather several pounds of mushrooms which she carried inside her tunic blouse; the two hunters were greeted with smiles on their return. After a fine breakfast Korrin sent Hogun, Rhiall and a man called Logay to scout for the soldiers, while Prasamaccus told them where he had hidden the rest of the meat. Somehow the terrifying events of yesterday seemed less hideous in the wake of Erulda delivering a fine baby son. His lusty cries were greeted with smiles among the women, and Prasamaccus marvelled anew at the ability of man to cope with terror. Even Korrin seemed less tense.

There was a stream at the bottom of the hill, near a basin of clay. The three remaining women spent the day creating pitchers and firing them in a kiln built some thirty feet from the stream. It made little smoke. Prasamaccus watched them work and thought of Helga back in Calcaria. Had the war reached her? How was she faring? Did she miss his presence as much as he missed hers, or had she even now found a fit husband with two good legs? He would not blame her if she had. She had given him a gift beyond price, and had he believed in benevolent Gods he would have prayed for her happiness.

He glanced down at his leather leggings. They were filthy and torn and several of the silver discs had come loose. His fine woollen tunic was grimy and the gold braid at the cuffs was frayed. He hobbled to the stream and removed his tunic, dipping it in the cool water and cleaning it against a rock. On impulse he stripped his troos and sat in the water, splashing it to his pale chest. The women nearby giggled and waved; he bowed gravely and continued to wash. Laitha wandered down the hill and one of the women approached her, offering her something Prasamaccus could not make out. The forest girl smiled her thanks and removed her boots, wading out to where Prasamaccus sat.

'What did she want?'

'She had a gift for the hunter,' answered Laitha, showing him a small phial stoppered with wax. 'It is a cleansing oil for the hair.' So saying she tugged him backwards, submerging him. He came up spluttering and she broke the wax seal, pouring half the contents over his head. Tucking the phial into her belt, she began to massage his hair, which was an experience to rival the ministrations of Victorinus' slaves. She spoiled it by ducking him again when she was done. He sat up to hear the chuckling of the working women and the rich, rolling laughter of the men who sat at the top of the hill.

The good humour lasted until Hogun and the others returned at dusk. Prasamaccus knew something was wrong, for they had not bothered to gather the meat. He limped across to Korrin and the dark huntsman looked up from his seat.

'The soldiers are coming,' he said simply.

*

The small amphitheatre was bare of spectators, bar the queen who sat at the centre on a fur-covered divan. Below her on the sand stood four warriors, their swords raised in salute. She leaned forward.

'You are each the finest gladiators of your lands. None of you has tasted defeat, and all have killed more than a score of opponents. Today you have the opportunity of carrying from Perdita your own weight in gems and gold. Does that excite you?' As she spoke her right hand caressed the skin of her throat and neck, enjoying the smooth silky feel of young flesh. Her blue eyes raked the warriors: strong men, lean and wolf-like, their eyes confident as they looked upon one another, each feeling he was destined to be the victor. Goroien smiled.

'Do not seek to gauge the men around you. Today you fight as a team, against the champion of my choosing. Kill him and all the rewards you have been promised will be yours.'

'We are all to fight one man, lady?' asked a tall warrior with jet-black beard.

'Just one,' she whispered, her voice growing hoarse with excitement. 'Behold!'

The men turned. At the far end of the arena stood a tall figure, a black helm covering his face. His shoulders were wide, his hips lean and supple. He wore a cut-away mailshirt and a loincloth and carried a shortsword and a dagger.

'Behold,' said the queen once more. 'This is the queen's champion, the greatest warrior of this or any age. He too has never known defeat. Tackle him singly, or all at once.'

The four men looked at one another. The riches were there, so why take risks? They advanced on the tall helmed warrior, forming a half-circle. As they approached he moved with dazzling swiftness, seeming to dance through them. But in his wake two men fell, disembowelled. The others circled warily. He dived forward, rolling on his shoulder, the dagger slicing the air to plunge home in Blackbeard's throat. Continuing his roll he came alongside the last man, blocked his lunge and sent a dazzling riposte through his enemy's jugular. He walked forward and bowed to the queen.

'Always the best,' she said, the colour high on her cheeks. She held out her hand and he rose through the air to stand before her. She stood and ran her hands over his shoulders and down his glistening flanks.

'Do you love me?' she whispered.

'I love you. I have always loved you.' The voice was soft and distant.

'You do not hate me for bringing you back?'

'Not if you do as you promised, Goroien.' His hand circled her back, pulling her to him. 'Then I will love you until the stars die.'

'Why must you think of him?'

'I must be the Lord of Battle. I have nothing else. I never had. I am faster now – more deadly. And still he haunts me. Until I kill him I will never be that which I desire.'

'But he is no longer a match for you. He has

chosen mortality and grows older. He is not what he was.'

'He must die, Goroien. You promised him to me.'

'What is the point? He could not have beaten you at his best. What will you prove by slaying a middle-aged man.'

'I will know that I am what I always was, that I am a warrior.' His hands roved her body: 'I will know that I am still a man.'

'You are, my love. The greatest warrior who ever lived.'

'You will bring him to me then?'

'I will. Truly I will.'

Slowly he removed the helm. She did not look at his eyes . . . could not. Ever since the day she had brought him back from the grave, they had defeated her.

Glazed as they had been in death, the eyes of Gilgamesh remained to torment her.

*

Uther and Baldric entered the forest of Mareen-sa just after dawn following a perilous journey from the Etrusces mountains. Three times they had hidden from soldiers, and once had been pursued by four mounted warriors, escaping by wading through a narrow stream and climbing an almost sheer rock-face. They were tired now, but Uther's spirits were high with the thought that they were almost home. He would lift the spell from the man-beast Pallin, and then continue his search for his father's sword.

He was mildly ashamed of himself as he contemplated the jubilant scenes when Pallin was restored, the cheers and the congratulations, and his modest reactions to their compliments on his heroism. He pictured Laitha, seeing the admiration in her eyes and her acceptance of his manhood. He grew almost dizzy with the fantasy and wrenched his thoughts back to the narrow trail they were following. As he did so, his eyes lit on a massive track beside the path. He stopped and stared; it was the pad of a giant cat.

Baldric, walking ahead, swung and saw the prince kneeling by the wayside. He strolled back, froze as he saw the print and pulled an arrow from his quiver.

'The Vores are loose,' he whispered, his eyes scanning the trail.

Uther stood, his grey eyes narrowed in concentration. There was a stream nearby and the prince walked to it and began to dig a narrow channel in the bank.

'What are you doing?' asked Baldric but Uther ignored him. He widened the channel into a circle and watched as the water slowly filled it. When it was still, he lay full-length and stared into it, raising the Sipstrassi Stone above the water, whispering the words of power Culain had used. The surface shimmered and he saw the caves and the bodies. Two foxes were tugging at the flesh of a severed leg. He stood.

'They have attacked the camp. Many are dead, but there is no sign of Korrin, Prasamaccus or Laitha.'

'You think they have been taken?'

'I do not know, Baldric. Where else could they be?'

The man shrugged. 'We are lost.' He sat down and buried his face in his hands. Uther saw a shadow flash across the ground and glanced up to see a huge eagle circling high overhead. The prince gripped the Stone and focused on the bird. His head swam and his mind merged. The forest was far below him and he could see as he never had before: a rabbit in the long grass, a fawn hidden in the undergrowth. And soldiers moving towards a high hill, on which stood a circle of jutting black stones. There were some three hundred fighting men on foot, but walking ahead of them was a line of Vores, held in check by forty dark-garbed woodsmen. Uther returned to his body, stumbled and almost fell.

Taking a deep breath to steady himself he began to run, ignoring the slumped Baldric. Up over the narrow trail and down into a muddy glen he slipped and slithered.

A huge stag bounded into his path. He lifted the Stone and the creature froze. Swiftly Uther clambered to its back; the deer turned and ran towards the hill. Several times Uther was almost dislodged, but his legs gripped firmly on the barrel of the creature's body. It leapt into the open and raced up the flanks of the hill, swerving to stand before the Vores. Behind him Uther had seen Prasamaccus, Laitha and several others waiting with arrows ready. Ahead of him the soldiers came into view, dark-eyed men in helms of bronze, black cloaks billowing.

The stag stood statue-still.

'Withdraw or die!' called Uther. After the initial shock of seeing a blond youth riding a wild deer, there had been silence among the soldiers. Now laughter greeted his words. A command rang out and the dark-garbed woodsmen released the chains on the forty Vores. They leapt forward, their roars washing over Uther like thunder. He lifted the Stone, his grey eyes cold as Arctic ice.

The Vores stopped their charge and turned, raging down into the massed ranks of the soldiers. Claws raked flesh, fangs closed on skull and bone. Horses reared and whinnied in terror as the mighty beasts ripped into the startled fighting men. Within seconds the savage carnage gave way to a mass panic and the soldiers fled in all directions as the Vores continued their destruction. Uther turned the stag and slowly rode up the hill. At the top he slid from the creature's back, patting its neck. The deer bounded away.

From the forest the awful screams of the dying filled the air. Korrin approached Uther.

'Are you a God?'

Uther glanced down at the Stone. It was no longer gold with black threads, but black with golden threads. There was little magic left.

'No, Korrin, I am not a God. I am just a man who arrived too late. Yesterday I could have saved Pallin and the others.'

'It is good to see you, Thuro,' said Prasamaccus.

'Not Thuro, my friend. The child is dead. The man walks. I am Uther Pendragon, son of Aurelius. And I am the king, by right and by destiny.'

Prasamaccus said nothing, but he bowed low. The other men, still shocked after their escape, followed suit. Uther accepted the honour without comment and walked away to sit alone on a broken rock overlooking the stream, where Prasamaccus joined him.

'May I sit with you, lord?' he asked, with no hint of sarcasm.

'Do not think me arrogant, Prasamaccus. I am not. But I have killed the Undead and flown on the wings of an eagle. I have ridden the forest prince and destroyed an army. I know who I am. More, I know *what* I am.'

'And what are you, Prince Uther?'

Uther turned and smiled softly. 'I am a young man, barely of age, who needs wise counsel from trusted friends. But I am also the King of all Britain, and I will reclaim my father's throne. No force of this world, or any other, will deter me.'

'It is said,' offered Prasamaccus, 'that blood runs true. I have seen the reverse at times – the sons of brave fathers becoming cowards. But in your case, Prince Uther, I think it is true. You have the blood of a great king in your veins, and also the spirit of the warrior Culain. I think I will follow you, though never blindly. And I will offer you counsel whenever you ask for it. Do I need to kneel?'

Uther chuckled. 'My first command to you is that you never kneel in my presence. My second is that you must always tell me when you feel that arrogance is surfacing in my nature. I have studied well, Prasamaccus, and I know that power has many counterpoints. My father had a tendency to believe himself right at all times, merely because he was the king. He dismissed from his service a warrior-friend who had grown up alongside him. The man disagreed with him on a matter of strategy and my father had him branded disloyal. Yet Aurelius was not a bad man. I have studied the lives of the great, and all become afflicted with pride. You are my champion against such excesses.'

'A heavy burden,' said Prasamaccus, 'but a burden for another day. Today you are not a king; you are a hunted man in the forest of another world. I take it from the manner of your arrival that you found the Dream Shaper?'

'I did. He was dead, but I have the source of his magic.'

'Is it strong enough to get us back home?'

'I do not think so. It is almost gone.'

'Then what do you plan?'

'The spirit of the Dream Shaper came to me, and told me to bring the Ghosts home. Baldric says the Ghosts are an army of the dead. I will try to raise them against the queen.'

The Brigante shivered. 'You will raise the dead?'

'I will if I can find Erin Plateau.'

Prasamaccus sighed. 'Well, that should not prove too arduous. You are sitting on Erin Plateau – and that is the sort of luck I have come to expect.'

'I have little choice, Prasamaccus. I have no intention of dying here – not with my father's murderers tearing at the heart of my kingdom. If I could, I would summon the Demon King himself.'

The Brigante nodded and rose, 'I will leave you to your plans,' he said sadly.

Two hours later Laitha sat shrouded in misery at the edge of the hill beneath the light of the two moons. Since Thuro's return he had not spoken to her or acknowledged her existence. At first she had been angry enough to ignore this, but as the day passed her fury had melted, leaving her feeling lonely and rejected. He was the one link she had to the wonderful world of her childhood. He had known Culain, and knew of her love for him. With him she should have been able to share her grief and, perhaps, exorcize it. Now he was lost to her, as much as she was lost to Culain and the Caledones mountains.

And he had struck her! Before all those men. In retrospect she had been shrewish, but it had been only to bolster her confidence. Her life with Culain had taught her self-sufficiency, but she had always had the Mist Warrior close when real fear pervaded their world. She had felt Thuro was a true friend and had grown to love him in those early weeks, when his gentle nature had shown itself. His lack of skill with weapons made her feel protective. As he had grown in stature under Culain's tutelage, she had grown jealous of the time he spent with her man. All nonsense now.

A chill wind blew and she hugged her shoulders, wishing she had brought out a blanket but not desiring to return inside to fetch one. She wondered if the pain of Culain's passing would ever leave her. Something warm draped her shoulders and she looked up to see Prasamaccus standing by her. He had brought a blanket warmed by the fire. She gathered it around her, then burst into tears. He sat beside her, pulling her to him, saying nothing.

'I feel so alone,' she said at last.

'You are not alone,' he whispered. 'I am here. Uther is here.

'He despises me.'

'I think that he does not.'

'Uther!' she hissed. 'Who does he think he is? A new name every day perhaps?'

'Oh, Laitha! You cannot see, can you? The boy has flown. You have told me of the weakly child he was when you found him, but that is not him any more. Look at his strength when he stood alone against the Vores. He could not be sure he had the strength or the power to turn those cats, yet he did it. That was the work of a man. He says the power is almost gone and many men would flee. But not Uther. Other men would use the remaining magic to find the sword. Not Uther. He seeks to aid the people he has befriended. Do not judge him by yesterday's memories.'

'He does not speak to me.'

'All paths run in two directions.'

'He once said he loved me.'

'Then he loves you still, for he is not a fickle man.'

'I cannot go to him. Why should I? Why should a man alone be allowed the virtue of pride?'

'I am not sure it is a virtue. However, I am here to be a friend. And friends are sometimes helpless between lovers.'

'We are not lovers. I loved Culain . . .'

'Who is dead. But no matter – lovers or friends, there is really very little difference that I can see. You do not need me to tell you how perilous is our situation. None of us can expect to survive long against the Witch Queen. Tomorrow she may return with a thousand men – ten thousand. Then we will be dead and your misery will seem even less important. Go to Uther and apologise . . .'

'I will not. I have nothing to apologise for.'

'Listen to me. Go to him and apologise. He will then tell you what you want to hear. Trust me . . . even if it means lying.'

'And if he laughs in my face?'

'You have lived too long in the forest, Laitha; you do not understand the world. Men like to think they control it but this is nonsense. Women rule, as they always have. They tell a man he is god-like. The man believes them and is in their thrall. For without them to tell him, he becomes merely a man. Go to him.'

She shook her head, but stood. 'I will take

your advice, friend. But in future call be Gian. It is special to me, it is the language of the Feragh: Gian Avur, fawn of the forest.' Then she smiled and wandered to the main building. She opened the door and stepped inside. Uther was sitting with the other men, and they were listening intently to his words. He looked up and saw her. Conversation ceased as he rose smoothly and came to her, stepping out into the night. Prasamaccus was nowhere to be seen.

'You wanted me?' he asked, his chin held high, his tone haughty.

'I wanted to congratulate you, and . . . and to apologise.'

He relaxed and his face softened, breaking into the self-conscious grin she remembered from their first day.

'You have nothing to apologise for. It has been hard for me to become a man. Culain taught me to fight and Maedhlyn, to think. Bringing the two together was left to me. But you have suffered greatly and I have been of little help. Forgive me?' He opened his arms and she stepped into his embrace.

In the background, crouched behind the rocks, Prasamaccus sighed and hoped they would not stand too long in the cold. His leg was aching and he yearned for sleep.

*

Uther returned to the building, gathered his blankets and took Laitha to the west of the hill-top, where a great stone had fallen – making a windbreak. He gathered wood for a small fire and spread the blankets on the ground. All this

232

was done in silence, amid a growing tension of their bodies that did not affect the communion of their eyes. With the fire glowing they sat together and did not notice the limping Prasamaccus returning to his bed.

Uther dipped his head and kissed Laitha's hair, pulling her more closely to him. She lifted her face. He smelt the musky perfume of her skin and brushed his lips against her cheek. His head swam and a dreamlike sensation swept over him. He, the night and Laitha were one. He could almost hear the whispering memories of the giant stones, feel the pulsing distance of the stars. She lay back, her arms curling around his shoulders, drawing him to her. His hand moved slowly down the curve of her back, feeling the flesh beneath her tunic. He was torn between the urge to tear her clothes from her, and yet to savour this moment of moments. He kissed her and groaned. She tugged gently away from him and removed her tunic and leggings. He watched as her skin emerged from the clothing; it gleamed and glistened in the firelight. Stripping himself naked, he hesitated to pull her to him, his eyes drinking in her beauty. His hands were trembling as he reached for her. Laitha's body melted against him and everywhere she touched him seemed to burn. She pushed herself under him, but he resisted. Her eyes opened wide in surprise, but he smiled softly.

'Not swiftly,' he whispered. 'Never swiftly!'

She understood. His head lowered to kiss her once more, his hand moving over her skin as gentle and warm as morning sunlight – touching, stroking, exploring. Finally, his head pounding, he rose above her. Her legs snaked over his hips and he entered her. Thoughts and emotions raged and swirled inside his mind, and he was surprised to find regret swimming amidst the joy. This was a moment he had dreamed of, yet now could never come again. He opened his eyes, looking down on her face, desperate to remember every precious second.

Her eyes opened and she smiled. Reaching up she cupped his face, pulling him closer, kissing him with surprising tenderness. Passion swallowed his regret and he passed into ecstasy.

For Laitha the sensation was different. She too had dreamed of the day she would surrender her virginity to the man she loved. And in a way she had. For Uther was all that was left of Culain and she could see the Mist Warrior in Uther's storm-cloud eyes. And Prasamaccus was right. The weakly youth in the forest had gone for ever, replaced by this powerful, confident young man. She knew she could grow to love him, but never with the wild, wonderful passion she had felt for Culain. As she thought of him, her mind blended her memories with the slow, rhythmic contact at the centre of her being and she felt it was the Lance Lord moving so powerfully above her. Her body convulsed in a searing sea of pleasure that bordered on pain. And in her ecstasy she whispered his name.

Uther heard it, and knew he had lost her in the moment of gaining her . . .

13

Baldric returned to Erin Plateau early the following morning. When the Vores had turned on the soldiers the lean huntsman had swiftly scaled a tree and watched as the carnage continued. The beasts had killed scores of men and horses, driving the army from the forest. Baldric had followed them for some distance and now reported that Mareen-sa was free of threat. Korrin sent out scouts to watch for the enemy's return, glancing at Uther for approval. Uther nodded.

'The enemy will return,' said the prince, 'but we must make the delay work for us.' Uther summoned Prasamaccus, sending him and Hogun to hunt for fresh meat. Laitha went with them to gather mushrooms, herbs and other edible roots. Rhiall and Ceorl were sent to the city of Callia to see what effect the news of the soldiers' defeat would have.

Finally Uther called Korrin to him and the two men walked to the edge of the stone circle, looking out over the vast forest and the sweeping hills of Mareen-sa.

'Tell me about the Ghosts,' said Uther. The woodsman shrugged.

'I have only seen them once – and that from a distance.'

'Then tell me the legend.'

'Is it wise to raise an army of the dead?'

'Is it wise for nineteen people to rebel against a Witch Queen?' responded Uther.

'I take your point. Well, the legend says that the Ghosts were soldiers of an ancient king, and when he died they marched into the underworld to fetch him back. But they became lost and now march for ever through the wilderness of the Void.'

'How many are there?'

'I have no idea. When I saw them I only took one swift glance, and that was over my shoulder while running.'

'Where did you see them?'

'Here,' said Korrin, 'on Erin.'

'Then why have we not seen them?'

'It is the moons – but then you would not know that. On certain nights of the year the light of Apricus, the large moon, cannot be seen. Only Sennicus shines. On those nights the Ghosts walk and the circle is shrouded in mist.'

'How soon before Sennicus shines alone?'

Korrin shrugged. 'I am sorry, Uther, I do not know. It happens about four times a year, sometimes six. Rhiall would know. His father studied the stars and he must have learned something. When he gets back I will ask him.'

Uther spent the day exploring the woodland around the hill, seeking out hiding places and trails the rebels might be forced to take when the soldiers returned. His frustration was great as he walked, for all the warriors whose lives had been researched by Plutarch had one thing in common. They each, at some time in their lives, ruled armies. There was little Uther could achieve with ten woodsmen, a crippled hunter and a forest girl skilled with the bow. And even should he be able to raise a force from amongst the population, how long would it take to train them? How much time would Astarte allow?

He shared the concern of both Prasamaccus and Korrin about using an army of corpses. Yet an army was an army. Without it they were lost.

Hungry and tired, he sat down by a shallow stream and allowed his thoughts to return to the subject he had forced from his mind. At the height of his passion, Laitha had whispered the name of Culain and this caused a terrible split in his emotions. He had worshipped Culain and was now jealous of him – even as he loved Laitha and was now angry with her. His mind told him it was not her fault that she still loved Culain, but his heart and his pride could not accept second place.

'Greetings,' said a voice and Uther leapt to his feet, sword in hand. A young woman sat close by, dressed in a simple tunic of shining white cloth. Her hair was gold, her eyes blue.

'I am sorry,' he said. 'You startled me.'

'Then it is I who am sorry. You seem lost in thought.'

She was quite the most beautiful woman Uther had ever seen. She rose and walked to stand beside him, reaching out to touch his arm.

As she looked into his eyes, he saw a strange look come into hers.

'Is something wrong, lady?'

'Not at all,' she said swiftly. 'Sit with me for a while.' The songs of the forest birds faded into what was almost a melody of soft-stringed lyres. The sun bathed them both, and all the colours of the forest shone with ethereal beauty. He sat.

'You remind me of someone I once knew,' she said, her face close to his, the perfume of her breath sweet and arousing.

'I hope it was someone you liked?'

'Indeed I did. Your eyes, like his, are the colours of the Mist.'

'Who are you?' he whispered, his voice husky.

'I am a dream, perhaps. Or a wood nymph. Or a lover?' Her lips brushed his face and she lifted his hand, pressing it to her breast.

'Who are you?' he repeated. 'Tell me.'

'I am Athena.'

'The Greek goddess?' She drew back from him then, surprised.

'How is it that you know of me? This world is far from Greece.'

'I am far from home, lady.'

'Are you of the Mist?'

'No. What other names have you?'

'You know of the Feragh, I see. I am also called Goroien.'

Now it was Uther's turn to show surprise. 'You are Culain's lady; he spoke of you often.'

She moved subtly away from him. 'And what did he say?'

'He said that he had loved you since the dawn of history. I hope you will forgive me for saying that I can see why?'

She acknowledged his compliment with a slight smile. 'His love was not so great as you think. He left me and chose to become mortal. How would you explain that?'

'I cannot, lady. But I knew Culain and he thought of you always.'

'You say "knew" and "thought". Have you lost touch with him?'

Uther licked his lips, suddenly nervous. 'He is dead, lady. I am sorry.'

'Dead? How?'

'My enemies destroyed him: Soul Stealers from the void.'

'You saw him die?'

'No, but I saw him fall – just before the Circle brought us to Pinrae.'

'And who are you?' she asked, smiling sweetly, her left hand on his back. As she spoke the nails of the hidden hand grew long and silver and hovered over his heart.

'I am Uther.' The talons vanished.

'I do not know the name,' she said, rising and moving to the centre of the clearing.

'Will you help us?' he asked.

'With what?'

'This world is ruled by a Witch Queen and I seek to overthrow her.'

Goroien laughed and shook her head. 'Foolish boy! Sweet, foolish boy. I *am* the Witch Queen. This is my world.'

Uther rose. 'I cannot believe that!'

'Believe it, Prince Uther,' said Prasamaccus, stepping from the shadow of the trees.

'Ah, the cripple,' said Goroien, 'with the magic arrows.'

'Shall I kill her?'asked the Brigante, a shaft aimed at her heart. Goroien turned to Uther, her eyebrows raised.

'No!'

'A wise choice, sweet boy, for now I will let you both live . . . for a little while. Tell me, how long has your name been Uther?'

'Not long, lady.'

'I thought not. You are the boy Thuro, the son of Alaida. Know this, Uther. I slew your mother; I planned your father's death; and I sent the Soul Stealers into the Caledones mountains.'

'Why?'

'Because it pleased me.' She turned on Prasamaccus. 'Loose your arrow, fool!'

'No!' shouted Uther, but the Brigante had already released the string. The shaft flashed in the sunlight, only to be caught in a slender hand and snapped in two.

'You said sweet words to me, Uther. I will not kill you today. Leave this place, hide in the world of Pinrae. I shall not seek you. But in four days I will send an army into this forest, with orders to kill all they find. Do not be here.' She raised her hand in a cutting motion and the air beside her parted like a curtain. Beyond her, in a room adorned with shields, swords and weapons of war, Uther saw a tall man wearing a dark helm. And then they were both gone.

'She came to kill you,' said Prasamaccus.

'But she did not.'

'She is capricious. Let us fetch Laitha and leave this place.'

'I must wait for the one moon.'

'You asked me to be a wise counsellor . . .'

'This is not a time for wisdom,' snapped Uther. 'This is a time for courage.'

*

Under a bright moon a lone figure scaled the outer wall of Deicester Castle, strong fingers finding the tiniest cracks and crevices. Culain moved slowly and with great care. His horse and lance had been hidden in the woods two miles away, and his only weapon was a long hunting-knife in a scabbard at the back of his belt.

The climb would not have been difficult in daylight, for the castle was over two hundred years old and the outer walls were pitted and scarred. But at night he was forced to test every hand- and toe-hold. He reached the battlements just after midnight and was not surprised to find no sentries. For who did Eldared fear in the Caledones? What army could penetrate this far into his territory? He swung his body over the wall and crouched in the moon shadows below the parapet. He wore dark leggings of dyed wool and a close-fitting leather shirt as soft as cloth. He stayed motionless, listening to the sounds of the night. In the barracks below and to the right were only a dozen soldiers. He had counted them from his hiding place during the day; now he could hear some of them playing at dice. To his left the gate sentry was asleep, his feet planted on a chair, a blanket round his shoulders. Culain moved silently to the stairwell. The steps were wooden and he moved down them keeping close to the wall, away from the centre of the slats where the movement and therefore the noise would be greatest. Earlier he had noted the flickering lights at the highest western window of the keep, the rest of the upper living quarters dark and silent.

He crossed the courtyard at a run, halting before the door beside the locked gates of the keep. It was open. Once inside he waited until his eyes grew accustomed to the darkness within, then found the stairs and climbed to the upper levels. A dog growled close by and Culain opened the pouch at his side and pulled clear a fresh-cut slice of rabbit meat. He walked boldly into the corridor. The dog, a grey warhound, rose threateningly, its lips drawn back to reveal long fangs. Culain crouched down and offered his hand. The dog, smelling the meat, padded forward to snatch it from Culain's fingers. He patted the hound's wide head and moved on.

At the furthest door he stopped. A light still showed faintly in the cracks around the frame. He drew his hunting-knife and stepped inside. A candle was guttering by the bedside and in the broad bed lay a man and a woman. Both were young – the woman no more than sixteen, the man a few years older. They were asleep in each other's arms like children, and Culain felt a pang of regret. The woman's face was oval and yet strong even in sleep. The man was fair-haired and fine-boned. Culain touched the cold knife-blade to the man's throat. His eyes flared open and he jerked, cutting the skin alongside his jugular.

'Do not hurt her!' he pleaded. Culain was touched, despite himself, for the man's first thought had been for the woman beside him. He gestured Moret to rise and, gathering the candle, led him through the bedroom into a side chamber, pushing shut the door behind him.

'What do you want?'

'I want to know how you contacted the Witch Queen.'

Moret moved to stand beside a high window overlooking the Caledones mountains. 'Why do you wish to see her?'

'That is my concern, boy. Answer me and you may live.'

'No,' said Moret softly. 'I need to know.'

Culain hesitated, considering killing the man and questioning the woman. But then if she knew nothing his mission would be ruined, for Cael and Eldared were away at war.

'I plan to destroy her,' he said at last.

Moret smiled. 'Go from here to the Lake of Earn. You know it?' Culain nodded. 'There is a circle of stones and a small hut. Before the hut is a tiny cairn of rounded rocks. Build a fire there when the wind is to the north. The smoke enters the hut and Goroien comes forth.'

'Have you seen her?'

'No, my brother travels there.'

Culain returned his knife to his scabbard. 'It is against my better judgement to allow you to live, but I shall. Do not make me regret the decision, for I am not an enemy you would desire.'

'No man who seeks to destroy Goroien could be an enemy of mine,' answered Moret. Culain backed to the door and was gone within seconds. Moret stood for a while by the window, then returned to his bed. Outside the door, Culain heard the bed creak and returned his knife once more to its scabbard.

*

Rhiall and Ceorl returned from Callia in high spirits. Behind them was a convoy of three wagons, sixty-eight men and twelve women, two of them pregnant. The huge youth bounded up the hill, grabbing Korrin's arm.

'The soldiers ransacked the town. They took twenty pregnant women and burnt the shrine to Berec. Two council leaders were hanged. The place is in an uproar.'

'What are they all doing here?' asked Korrin, staring down at the crowd forming a half-circle below the hill.

'They've come to see Berec reborn. The story is spreading like a grass fire that Berec has returned to earth, riding a forest stag and ready to overthrow the Witch Queen.'

'And you let them believe it?'

Rhiall's face took on a sullen look. 'Who is to say it is not true? He did ride a stag, just like Berec, and his magic vanquished the soldiers.'

'What is in the wagons?'

Rhiall's good humour returned. 'Food, Korrin. Flour, salt, dried fruit, oats, wine, honey. And there are blankets, clothes, weapons.'

Uther approached and stared down at the gathering, which grew hushed and silent. The sun was behind him and he appeared to the crowd to be bathed in golden light. Many in the group fell to their knees.

Rhiall and Korrin joined him. 'How many fighting men?' asked Uther.

'Sixty-eight.'

Uther grinned and laid his hand on Rhiall's shoulder. 'That is a good omen. In my land the men fight in Centuries of eighty warriors each. With our own people and these we now have a Century.'

Korrin grinned. 'Your arithmetic is not as strong as your magic. Surely a century is one hundred?'

'True, but with cooks, quartermasters and camp followers the fighting strength is eighty. Our army is formed by such units. Six Centuries equal four hundred and eighty men, or one Cohort, and ten Cohorts make a Legion. It is a small beginning, but a promising one. Korrin, go down among them and find out who the leaders are. Get the men in groups of ten. Add one of your own men to each group, two to the last. Find the groups work to make them feel

245

part of the brotherhood – and weed out the weak in heart, for they will need to fight within four days.'

'One small problem, Uther,' said Korrin. 'They think you are a god. When they find out you are a man we could lose them all.'

'Tell me about the god – everything you can remember.'

'You will play the part then?' asked Rhiall.

'I will not risk losing sixty-eight fighting men. And it is not necessary for me to lie, or to use any deceit. If they believe it, let them continue. In four days we will either have an army or be dead on this forest floor.'

'Does that not depend,' put in Korrin, 'on when Sennicus shines alone?'

'Yes.' Both men turned to Rhiall. 'When will such an event happen again?' asked Uther.

'In about a month,' said the youngster. Uther said nothing, his face without expression. Korrin cursed softly.

'Get the men in groups,' said the prince, walking away to the edge of the stone circle, holding the bitter edge of his anger in check. In four days a terrible enemy would descend on the forest. His one hope was the army of the dead, and they could not be seen for a month. He needed to think, to plan, yet how could he devise a strategy with such limited forces at his disposal? All his life he had studied war and the making of war, seen the plans of generals from Xerxes to Alexander, Ptolemy to Caesar, Paullinus to Aurelius. But never had they been in such a position as his. The unfairness of his situation struck him like a coward's blow. But then why should life be fair, he reasoned? A man could do only his best with the favours the Gods bestowed.

Prasamaccus joined him, sensing his unease.

'Are the Gods being kind?' asked the Brigante.

'Perhaps,' replied Uther, remembering that he had not yet learned of the life of Berec.

'The burden of responsibility is not light.'

Uther smiled. 'It would be lighter if I had Victorinus and several legions behind me. Where is Laitha?'

'She is helping unload the wagons. Is all well between you?'

Uther closed his mouth, cutting off an angry retort, then looked into the Brigante's cool understanding eyes.

'I love her, and she is now mine.'

'But?'

'How do you know there is a but?'

Prasamaccus shrugged. 'Is there not?'

'Where did you learn so much of life?'

'On a hillside between the walls. What is wrong?'

'She loved Culain and it chains her still. I could not compete with him in life – nor in death, it seems.'

Prasamaccus sat silently for a moment, marshalling his thoughts. 'It must be exceptionally hard for her. All her life she has lived with this hero, worshipping him as a father, loving him as a brother, needing him as a friend. It is not difficult to see how she came to believe she wanted him as a lover. And you are right, Prince Uther, you cannot compete. But in time Culain will fade.'

'I know it is arrogance,' said Uther, 'but I do not want a woman who sees me as the shadow of someone else. I made love to her and it was beautiful . . . and then she whispered Culain's name. She lay beneath me and in her mind I was not there.'

There was nothing for the Brigante to say and he had the wisdom to know it. Laitha was a foolish undisciplined child. It would not have mattered if she had screamed his name inside her mind, but to speak it at such a time showed a stupidity beyond comparison. It was with some surprise that Prasamaccus realised he was angry with her; it was not an emotion he usually carried. He sat in silence with the prince for some time and then, when Uther was lost in thought, he rose and limped back to where Korrin waited with a group of strangers.

'These are the leaders of the Callia men,' said the woodsman. 'Is . . . the God ready to receive them?'

'No, he is communing with the spirits,' answered Prasamaccus. Some of the men backed away. The Brigante ignored them and wandered away to the long hall.

Uther the man stared out over the forest, while Thuro the boy sat inside his skull. Only a few short months ago the boy had been weeping in his room, frightened of the dark and the noises of the night. Now he was acting the man, but the torments of adolescence were still with

him. As summer was beginning outside Eboracum, the boy Thuro had wandered into the
woods and played a game where he was a hero,
slaying demons and dragons. Now, with the
summer here once more, he sat on a lonely hill
and all the demons were real. Only there was
no Maedhlyn. No Aurelius with his invincible
legions. No Culain lach Feragh. Only the pretend man, Uther. 'I am the king, by right and
by destiny.' Oh how the words haunted him
now in his despair!

A frightened child sat among the stones of
another world, playing a game of death. His
melancholy deepened and he realised he would
give his left arm if Maedhlyn or Culain could
appear at this moment. More, he would offer
ten years of his life. But the wind blew over the
hill-top and he was alone. He turned and gazed
on the group waiting silently some thirty paces
away. Young men, old men, standing patiently
waiting for the 'God' to acknowledge them and
their fealty. Turning his face from them, he
thought of Culain and smiled. Culain really had
been a God: Ares, the God of War to the
Greeks, who became Mars for the Romans.
Immortal Culain!

Well, thought Uther, if my grandfather was
a God, then why not me? If the fates have
decided I shall die in this deadly game, then let
me play it to the full.

Without looking back he raised his hand,
beckoning the group forward. There were
twelve of them and they shuffled hesitantly to

249

stand before him. He spread his arms, gesturing at the ground and they sat obediently.

'Speak!' he said and Korrin introduced each of the men, though Uther made no effort to remember their names. At the end he leaned forward and looked deeply into each man's eyes. All looked away the moment his gaze locked on theirs. 'You!' said Uther, gazing directly at the oldest man, grey-bearded and lean as a hunting wolf. 'Who am I?'

'It is said you are the God, Berec.'

'And what do you say?'

The man reddened. 'Lord, what I said last night was said in ignorance.' He swallowed hard. 'I merely voiced the doubts we all carried.'

Uther smiled. 'And rightly so,' he said. 'I have not come to guarantee victory, only to teach you how to fight. The Gods give, the Gods take away. All that is of worth is what a man earns with his sweat, with his courage and with his life. Know this: you may not win. I shall not rise to the sky and destroy the Witch with spears of fire. I am here because Korrin called me. I shall leave when I please. Do you have the heart to fight alone?'

The bearded man's head rose, his eyes proud. 'I do. It has taken me time to know it, but I know it now.'

'Then you have learned something greater than a God-gift. Leave me – all but Korrin.'

The men almost scrambled from his presence, some backing away, others bowing low.

Uther ignored them all and when they were out of earshot Korrin moved forward.

'How did you know what that man said?' he asked.

'What do you think of them?' The woodsman shrugged.

'You picked the right man to speak to. He is Maggrig, the armourer. Once he was the most feared swordsman in Pinrae. If he stands, they all will. Do you wish me to tell you of Berec?'

'No.'

'Are you well, Uther? Your eyes are distant.'

'I am well, Korrin,' answered the prince, forcing a smile, 'but I need to think.' The green-eyed huntsman nodded his understanding.

'I shall have food brought to you.'

After he had gone Uther ran his mind back over the meeting. It was no mystery how he had focused on Maggrig; the man's stance showed him to be a warrior and he was the first to come forward, the others crowding around him. It had been a pleasant surprise when Maggrig had misinterpreted Uther's question. But then, as Maedhlyn always said, the prince had a swift mind.

Somehow the meeting left Uther feeling less melancholy. Was it so easy to be a God?

The answer would come within four days.

And it would be written in blood.

14

Culain lach Feragh sat before the cairn of stones watching the smoke from his small fire wafting in through the shattered windows of the derelict house. The Mist Warrior laid his silver lance by his side and pulled on two leather gauntlets edged with silver. His long hair was bound at the nape of the neck and over his shoulders he wore a silver-ringed protector, expertly sewn to a short cape of soft leather. A thick silver-inlaid belt was buckled to his waist and his legs were protected by thigh-length boots, reinforced by silver strips to the fronts and sides. A flickering blue light began inside the dwelling and Culain rose smoothly, placing a silver-winged helm upon his head, tying the scimitar-shaped ear-guards under his chin.

A slender figure came forward through the smoke which billowed and died, the fire quenched in an instant. As he saw her, his mouth went dry and he longed to step forward and pull her into his arms. She in turn stopped in her tracks as she recognised him, her hand flying to her mouth.

'You are alive!' she whispered.

'Thus far, lady.' She was wearing a simple

dress of silver thread, her golden hair held in place by a black band at the brow.

'Tell me that you have come back to be with me.'

'I cannot.'

'Then why do you summon me?' she snapped, her blue eyes bright with anger.

'Pendarric says there is naught but evil in you and he asked me to destroy you. But I cannot until I am convinced he is right.'

'He was always an old woman. He had the world and he lost it. Now it is the turn of others. He is finished, Culain. Come with me; I have a world to myself. Soon it will be four worlds. I have power undreamt of since the fall of Atlantis.'

'And yet you are dying,' he said, the words cutting him like knife wounds.

'Who says that I am?' she hissed. 'Look at me! Am I any different? Is there a single sign of age or decay?'

'Not on the surface, Goroien. But how many have died . . . how many will die to keep you so?'

She moved towards him and the music began in his mind. The air was still and all the world was silent. Her arms came up around his neck and he smelt the perfume of her skin, felt the warmth of her touch. Reaching up he pulled her arms clear of him, pushing her away.

'What will you prove?' he asked. 'That I love you still? I do. That I want you? That too. But I will never have you. You killed Shaleat, you killed Alaida – and now you will destroy a world.'

'What are these savages to you, with their ten-second lives. There will always be more to replace those who die. They are unimportant, Culain. They always were, only you were too obsessed to see it. What does it matter now that Troy fell, or your friend Hector was slain by Achilles? What does it matter that the Romans conquered Britain? Life moves on. These people are as shadows to you and me. They exist to serve their betters.'

'I am one of them now, Goroien,' he said. 'My ten-second life is a joy. I never understood winter before, or truly felt the joy of spring. Come with me. Live out a life unto death, and we will see together what comes after.'

'Never!' she screamed. 'I will never die. You speak of pleasure. I see your decaying face and it makes me want to vomit: lines by your eyes, and I don't doubt that under that helm the silver is spreading like a cancer through your hair. In human terms what are you now, thirty? Forty? Soon you will begin to wither. Your teeth will rot. Young men will push you aside and mock you. And then you will fall and the worms will eat your eyes. How could you do this?'

'All things die, my love. Even worlds.'

'Do not speak to me of love, you never loved me. Only one man ever loved me and I have brought him back from the grave. That is what power is, Culain. Gilgamesh is with me once more.'

He stepped back from the glare of triumph in her eyes. 'That is not possible!'

'I kept his body throughout the centuries, surrounded by the glow of five Stones. I worked and I studied. And one day I succeeded. Go away and die somewhere, Culain, and I shall find your body and bring it back. Then you will be mine.'

'I am coming to Skitis, Goroien,' he said softly. 'I shall destroy your power.'

She laughed then, a rich mocking laughter that caused the colour to flood his cheeks. '*You* are coming? Once that would have put terror into my heart, but not now. A middle-aged man, soft and decaying, is coming to challenge Gilgamesh? You have no idea how often he speaks of you, dreams of killing you. You think to stand against him? I will show you how your arrogance has betrayed you. You always liked the Shade games – play this one.' She gestured with her right hand and the air shimmered. Before Culain stood a tall warrior with golden hair and bright blue-green eyes. He carried a curved sword and a dagger. 'Here is Gilgamesh as he was.' The warrior leapt forward and Culain swept up the lance, twisted the handle and pulled clear the hidden sword. He was just in time to block a savage cut. Then another . . . and another. Culain fought with all the skill of the centuries, but Goroien was right; his aging body was no longer equipped to tackle the whirlwind that was Gilgamesh, the Lord of Battle. Culain, growing desperate, took a risk, spinning on his heel in the move he had taught

Thuro. His opponent leapt to the left, avoiding Culain's raised elbow, and a cold sword slid beneath the Mist Warrior's ribs.

He crumpled, hitting the hard clay ground on his face and dislodging the silver helm. He fought to stay conscious, but his mind fell into darkness. When he awoke Goroien was still there, sitting by the cairn of stones.

'Go away, Culain,' she said. 'What you fought was Gilgamesh as he was. Now he is stronger and faster; he would kill you within seconds. Either that or use this.' She dropped a yellow pebble on the ground before him; it was pure Sipstrassi, with virtually no sign of black veins. 'Become immortal again. Become what you were . . . what you should be. Then you have a chance.'

He pushed himself to his feet. 'It is not usual to give your enemy a chance at life, lady.'

'How could you be my enemy? I have loved you since before the Fall. I will love you on the day the universe ends in fire.'

'We will never be lovers again, lady,' he said. 'I will see you on Skitis Island.'

She stood. 'You fool! You will not see me. You will see your death coming towards you in every stride Gilgamesh takes.'

She walked into the derelict house without a backward glance and Culain slumped to the ground, tears in his eyes. It had taken all his strength to tell her their love was ended. He stared down at the Sipstrassi Stone and lifted it. She was right, he was in no condition to face

Gilgamesh. Her voice drifted back to him, as if from a great distance.

'Your grandson is a handsome boy. I think I will take him. Do you remember my time as Circe?' Her laughter echoed into silence.

Culain sat with head bowed. After the Trojan war Goroien had wreaked her vengeance on the Greeks, causing the bloody deaths of Agammemnon the warlord and Menelaus the Spartan king. But by far the most hideous of her vengeful acts was the shipwreck of Odysseus. For Goroien, as Circe the witch, turned some of the survivors into swine, tricking the others into cooking and eating them.

He picked up his sword and brushed the dirt from the blade.

Walking to his horse, he touched the Sipstrassi Stone to its temple and stepped back. The beast's body collapsed, then swelled and stretched, its smooth flanks growing silveredged scales of deep rust-red. Its head shimmered, its eyes becoming slanted like a great cat's, its snout stretching, fangs erupting from a cavernous mouth. Huge wings unfolded from its ribs and its hoofs erupted into taloned claws. Its long neck arched back and a terrible cry filled the air. Culain looked down at the black pebble in his hand and tossed it to the ground. Sliding his sword back into the haft of his lance, he climbed to the saddle on the dragon's back, whispering the word of command. The beast rose on its powerful legs, the wings spreading wide, then it soared into the night air heading north-west to Skitis.

*

On the third night a fearsome storm broke over Erin Plateau, shafts of lightning spearing the sky. Uther remained where he had stayed for three days now, sitting at the edge of the circle. Prasamaccus and Korrin gathered food and blankets for the prince and stepped out into the driving rain. At that moment lightning streaked the sky and both men saw Uther stand and raise his arms over his head, his blond hair billowing in the shrieking wind. Then he vanished. Korrin ran to the stones, Prasamaccus hobbling behind, but there was no sign of the prince.

The storm broke, the rain easing to a fine drizzle. Korrin sank to a rock.

'It is over,' he said, bitterness returning to his voice for the first time since the Vores turned on the soldiers. Korrin began to curse and swear and the Brigante moved away from him; he too felt demoralised and beaten, and he sat on the fallen stone overlooking the forest.

'What will we tell them?' said Korrin. The Brigante gathered his cloak tightly around his slender frame. His leg ached, as it always did when the weather turned damp, and his heart told him he would never see Helga again. He could offer Korrin no advice. Just then the two moons appeared from behind the breaking clouds and a third man joined them.

'Where is Berec?' asked Maggrig but neither man answered. 'So, we are alone, as he said we might be.' He scratched his greying beard and sat beside Korrin. 'We've set some snares and dug a few pits, which should slow them a little. And there are some five good ambush points.'

Korrin glanced up, surprised. The news of Berec's departure seemed to affect Maggrig not at all. 'We should hit them first at the Elm Hollow. The horsemen will not be able to charge up the rise and we'll have some hundred feet of killing ground. Even our archers should be unable to miss at that distance. We could down perhaps a hundred men.'

'You are talking of eighty men against an army,' said Korrin. 'Are you mad?'

'Eighty men is all we had yesterday. Gods, man, no one lives for ever.'

'Except the Witch Queen,' said Korrin, adding a savage curse.

'Take some advice from an old warrior: tell no one Berec has gone for good. Just say he has . . . who knows? . . . journeyed back to his castle in the clouds. In the meantime, let us hit them hard.'

'Good advice,' said Prasamaccus. 'We do not know how many soldiers are coming, and the forest is immense. We should be able to lead them a merry chase.'

Below, in the tiny village of tents that had sprung up by the stream, a young woman wandered out into the forest to be alone for a while. As she entered the darkness she caught sight of the moonlight reflecting from metal in the distance. She climbed a stout oak and peered to the west.

Moving silently through the trees came the army of Goroien.

*

For more than thirty hours Uther had been

259

awake and worrying at the problem of the Void, searching every angle, exploring all the facts at his disposal. His reasoning and his training hold him that he had overlooked a salient point, but try as he could there seemed no way to home in on it.

And then, just as the storm broke, the answer sailed effortlessly into his mind. Just because the Ghost Army could not be *seen* did not necessarily mean they were not *there*.

It was so simple. The freezing rain was forgotten. Prasamaccus had told him that he had dreamt of drums and marching feet on his first night on Erin Plateau, and Uther should have leapt on that thought like a striking falcon.

All that was left now was to enter the Void – the home of Atrols and Soul Stealers. Yes, he thought, that is all. Do not stop to think, Uther, he told himself. Just do it! He stood, raised his arms above his head, gripped the Stone tightly and wished for the Void.

His head spun and he fell. Around him the Mist swirled. Pushing himself to his knees, he drew his gladius. The Sipstrassi Stone was almost black. He risked touching his sword-blade; it shone with a white light and in the Mist he could see dark shadows and grey, cold faces. A long time ago, Thuro the child had wandered here in a fever dream and Aurelius had brought him back. The fear of that time returned to haunt him, and as his fear grew the shadow-shapes moved closer. Uther the man stood and steadied himself, lifting his sword high above his head. The light shone from the blade, pushing back both the Mist and the shadows within it.

As the Mist rolled away Uther saw the desolate landscape of the Void, a place of ash-grey hills and long-dead trees beneath a slate-dark sky. He shivered. It was no place for a man to die. Far off to his right, he caught the faint sound of drums. Holding his sword high like a lantern, he walked towards the sound. The shadows followed him and he could hear whispering voices calling his name. The prince ignored them. He climbed a low hill and stopped in wonder. There, in a dusty valley, was a defensive enclosure made up of mounds of grey earth thrown up from a huge square ditch. Sharpcncd stakes had been set into the banks. Within the enclosure were scores of tents and at the centre of the square stood a staff bearing a golden eagle, its wings spread. Uther stood for several minutes staring at the camp, unable to accept the vision before his eyes. Yet all the clues had been before him. Korrin had spoken of the Eagle sect who had tried to commune with the Ghosts. The soldiers marched to the drum in perfect order.

And Culain had talked of his greatest regret, when he had consigned an army to the Mist.

Uther stood on the lonely hill-top and gazed in wonder at the Eagle of the Ninth Legion.

The prince walked slowly down the hill to stand before the wide opening to the enclosure. Two legionaries stepped into his path – their eyes tired, their spears sharp. He was commanded to halt. The language was recognisable, but lacked the later British additions. He thought back to his training under Maedhlyn and Decianus, and answered them in their own archaic tongue.

'Who is your Legate?'

The legionaries glanced at one another and the taller man stepped forward.

'Are you Roman?'

'I am.'

'Are we close to home?' The voice quavered.

'I am here to bring you home. Who is your Legate?'

'Severinus Albinus. Wait here.' The soldier raced away and Uther stood, still holding the shining sword. Ten men returned some minutes later and the prince was ushered into the enclosure, an honour guard of five legionaries on either side of him. Men rushed from their tents to see the stranger, their faces ashen, their eyes dull. The guard halted before a wide tent. Uther surrendered his weapons to the centurion at the entrance and ducked inside. A young man of maybe twenty-five, dressed in polished bronze breastplate, was seated on a low stool.

'Your name?' he asked.

'You are Severinus Albinus?' responded Uther, aware that the success of his mission depended on maintaining the initiative.

'I am.'

'The Legate of Legio IX?'

'No. Our Legate is Petillius Cerialis; he did not accompany us. Who are you?' Uther sensed the young man, like all the men he had seen, was on the edge of desperation.

262

'I am Uther.'

'Where is this place?' asked Severinus, rising. 'We have marched here for months. No food. No water. Yet no thirst, nor hunger. There are creatures within the accursed Mist who drink blood. There are beasts the like of which I have never dreamt of. Are we all dead?'

'I can return you to Eboracum,' said Uther, 'but first there is much you should know.' He walked past the young soldier and seated himself on a divan at the back of the tent. Severinus Albinus joined him. 'Firstly, you marched from Eboracum to aid Paullinus against the Iceni uprising. You entered the Mist – a world of the dead.'

'I know all this,' said Severinus. 'How do we get home?'

Uther raised his hand. 'Gently. Listen to every word. Paullinus defeated Boudicca more than four hundred years ago.'

'Then we are dead. Sweet Jupiter, I cannot march any longer!'

'You are not dead, believe me. What I am attempting to tell you is that the world you knew is dead. The Roman Empire is fading. Britain no longer boasts a single Roman legion.'

'I have a wife . . . a daughter.'

'No,' said Uther sadly. 'They have been dead for four centuries. I can take you to Eboracum. The world is much changed, but the sun still shines and the grapes make wine, and the streams flow clear and the water is good to drink.'

'Who rules in Britain now?' asked Severinus.

'The land is at war. The Brigantes have risen and the Saxons and Jutes have invaded. The Romano-Britons led by Aquila, a pure-blood Roman of noble family, are fighting for their lives. There was a king named Aurelius, but he was murdered. I am his son. And I have journeyed beyond the borders of death to bring you home.'

'To fight for you?'

'To fight for me,' said Uther, 'and for yourselves.'

'And you will take us to Eboracum?'

'Not immediately,' said Uther, and told the Roman of the war in Pinrae and the rule of the Witch Queen. Severinus listened in silence.

'There was a time,' he said, when Uther fell silent, 'that I would have mocked your tale. But not here, in this ashen wilderness. You want us to fight for you, Uther? I would sell my soul for one day in the sunshine. No, for a single hour. Just take us away from here.'

*

Fear had brought Uther to the edge of panic. With the four thousand six hundred men of the Ninth Legion marching behind him, he returned to the hill he had first encountered upon entering the Void. Now, after an hour, still he could not open the pathway between the worlds. He had willed himself back, the Stone had glowed and for a moment only he had seen the giant stones of Erin, misty shadows shimmering just out of reach. He heard Severinus Albinus behind him and waved the man back, fighting for calm. He glanced

264

at the Stone; only the thinnest thread of gold remained.

He knew now for certain that the power of the Stone was insufficient to open a gateway large enough to allow the Legion through. He was not even sure whether he himself could return, and his agile mind once more began the long slow examination of all the possibilities.

At last he decided on one supreme effort. He closed his eyes and pictured himself back in Pinrae, but all the while holding the image of the Ninth Legion in his mind. Behind him, Severinus saw Uther grow less tangible, almost wraith-like, but then he was back as before. The prince stared down at the black pebble in his hand and could not find the courage to turn and face the expectant soldiers.

Beyond the Void the army of Goroien had circled the base of the hill, waiting for the order to attack. Maggrig and Korrin had placed archers all around the stones, but there was no way they could repel the armoured soldiers. At best they would wound a score or so, and it seemed to Korrin that more than two thousand men were assembled below.

'Why do they not attack?' he asked the lean wolf-like Maggrig.

'They are afraid of Berec's magic. But they will come soon.'

Twenty paces to their left, kneeling behind a fallen stone, Laitha waited with an arrow notched, her eyes fixed on a tall warrior with a purple plume to his helm. She had already decided he would be her target, for no other reason than that she disliked the arrogant way he strode amongst the men below, issuing orders. It made her feel somehow better to know that the strutting peacock would die before she did.

A hand touched her shoulder and she turned to see a tall broad-shouldered man with a golden beard. She could not remember having seen him before.

'Follow me,' he said, his manner showing he was obviously used to being obeyed. He did not look back as Laitha followed him to the centre of the plateau.

'Who are you?' she asked.

'Hold fast to your questions and climb the altar.' She moved up on the broken central stones, clambering over the scarred and pitted runes worked into the surfaces.

The bearded man spoke just as she reached the highest point and stood precariously on the top stone, some six feet from the ground.

'Now lift your hand above your head.'

'For what purpose?'

'You feel there is time for debate? Obey me.'

Biting back her anger, she raised her right arm. 'Higher!' he said. As she did so her fingers touched something cold and clinging and she withdrew her hand instinctively. 'It is only water,' he assured her. 'Push high and open your fingers. Grasp what is there and draw it down.'

Suddenly a great cry went up, a battle roar that chilled the blood, and the soldiers of Goroien swept up the hill. Arrows sang down to meet them, some glancing from armoured breastplates or helms, others wedging in the flesh of bare legs and arms.

'Reach up!' ordered the tall stranger. 'Swiftly, if you value your life.'

Laitha pushed her hand through the invisible barrier of water and opened her fingers. She felt the cold touch of metal and the yielding warmth of leather. Grasping the object tightly, she drew it down. In her hand was a great sword with an upswept hilt of burnished gold and a silver blade, double-edged, engraved with runes she could not recognise.

'Follow me,' said the man, running towards the rocks where Uther had last been seen. Halting, he pulled Laitha forward. 'When I finish speaking, smite the air before you.' The words which followed meant nothing to Laitha, but the air around him hissed and crackled as if a storm was due. '*Now*!' he shouted. The sword slashed forward and a great wind blew up. Lightning flashed towards the sky and the Mist billowed from where she struck. Laitha was hurled backwards to the ground.

Uther leapt from the Mist, glancing around him. At the far end of the plateau the rebels began to stream back and the prince could see the plumed helms of Goroien's soldiers. Just then, Severinus Albinus stepped into the sunshine with the Ninth Legion following him. Some of the men fell to their knees as the sunshine touched them, others began to weep in their joy and relief. Severinus, though young, was a seasoned campaigner and he took in the situation in an instant.

'Alba formation!' he yelled and Roman discipline was restored. Legionaries bearing their embossed rectangular bronze shields drew their swords and formed a fighting line, pushing forward and spreading out to allow the spearmen through. As the rebels ran back, the line opened before them.

Goroien's soldiers had an opportunity then to rush the line, but they did not. They were mostly men of Pinrae and they knew the legend of the Ghost Army. They stood transfixed as the Legion formed a square and advanced with shields locked, long spears protruding. The soldiers of Pinrae were not cowards – they would face, and had faced, overwhelming odds – but they had already seen the coming of the God, Berec. Now more and more spirits of the dead were issuing from the Mist, and this they could not bear. Slowly they backed away, returning to the base of the hill. The Legion halted at the circle of stones, awaiting orders.

In the safety of the square Uther helped Laitha to her feet. 'How did you do that? I thought I was fin . . .' He stumbled to a halt as he saw the great sword lying on the ground at Laitha's feet. He dropped to his knees, his hand curling round the hilt. 'My father's sword!' he whispered. 'The Sword of Cunobelin.' He rose. 'How?'

Laitha swung around, seeking the man with the golden beard, but he was nowhere in sight.

She explained swiftly as Severinus Albinus approached.

'What are your orders, Prince Uther? Shall we attack?'

Uther shook his head and, carrying the longsword, strode to the edge of the square. The legionaries stepped aside and he walked down the hill, halting some thirty feet from the enemy line. A bowman notched an arrow.

'Draw the string and I'll turn your eyes to maggot balls,' said the prince. The man dropped both bow and arrow instantly.

'Let your leader step forward!'

A short, stocky middle-aged man in a silver breastplate walked from the line. He licked his lips as he came but held his shoulders back, pride preventing him from a display of fear.

'You know who I am,' said Uther, 'and you can see that the Ghosts have come home. I gauge you are now outnumbered two to one, and I can see that your men are in no condition for battle.'

'I cannot surrender,' said the man.

'I see that, but neither would the queen desire you to throw away the lives of your men needlessly. Take your army from Mareen-sa and report to Astarte.'

The man nodded. 'What you say is logical. Might I ask why you are sparing us?'

'I am not here to see the men of Pinrae slaughter one another. I am here to destroy the Witch Queen. Do not misjudge my mercy. If we meet again on the field of battle, I will crush you and any who stand in my path.'

269

The man bowed stiffly. 'My name is Agarin Pinder, and if I am ordered to stand in your path I will do so.'

'I would expect no less from a man of duty. Go now!'

Uther swung on his heel and returned to the plateau, calling Severinus to him. The young Roman followed him into the long building.

'Gods, I am hungry,' said Severinus, 'and what a wonderful feeling it is!' On the table was a flagon of wine and Uther poured two goblets, passing one to the Roman.

'We must leave the forest and march on Callia, a town nearby,' said Uther. 'There are insufficient supplies here to feed a legion.'

Severinus nodded. 'You chose not to fight. Why?'

'The Roman army was once the finest the world had seen. The discipline was second to none, and many a battle was turned on that. But your men were not ready, not after the creeping horror of the Void. They need time to feel the sunlight on their faces; then they will be truly Legio IX.'

'You are a careful commander, Prince Uther. I like that.'

'Speaking of care, I want you to take your men from the plateau and prepare your defensive enclosure below; there is a stream there. Do not allow your men to mix with the people of Pinrae. You have been part of their legends for hundreds of years and on certain nights they even watch you march. It is a trick of the Mist. But the important point is this: they believe

270

you are of Pinrae, and part of their history. As such we will gain support from the country. Let no one suspect you are from another world.'

'I understand. How is it that these people speak Latin?'

'They do not, but I'll explain that at another time. Send out a scouting troop to follow Goroien's soldiers from the forest. I will try to arrange some food for your men.' Severinus drew himself upright and saluted and Uther acknowledged the gesture with a smile.

As Severinus left the room, Korrin and Prasamaccus entered.

Korrin almost ran forward, his green eyes ablaze with excitement. 'You did it!' he shouted, his fist punching the air.

'It is pleasant to be back,' said Uther. 'Where is the man with the golden beard?'

'I do not know who you mean,' answered Korrin.

Uther waved his hand. 'It does not matter. Tomorrow we march on Callia and I want your best men, trusted men, to precede us. The Ghost Army of Pinrae is returning to free the land and the word must be spread. With luck, the town will open its gates without a battle.'

'I'll send Maggrig and Hogun. Gods, man, to think I almost killed you!'

Uther reached out and gripped Korrin's shoulder. 'It is good to see you smile. Now leave me with Prasamaccus.' The huntsman grinned, stepped back and bowed deeply.

'Are you still set on leaving Pinrae?'

'I am – but not until Goroien is finished.'

271

'Then that will suffice.'

After he had gone, Prasamaccus accepted a goblet of wine and leaned in close, studying Uther's face. 'You are tired, my prince. You should rest.'

'Look,' said Uther, lifting the sword. 'The blade of Cunobelin, the Sword of Power, and I do not know how it came to Laitha. Or why. I was trapped in the Void, Prasamaccus, and trying to find a way to tell almost five thousand men that I had raised their hopes for nothing. And just then, like a ghost, I saw Laitha raise a sword and cut the Mist as if it were the skin of a beast.'

Prasamaccus opened his mouth to phrase a question but stopped, his jaw hanging. Uther turned to follow the direction of his gaze. Sitting by a new fire was the golden-bearded man, holding tanned hands towards the blaze.

'Leave us,' Uther told the Brigante. Prasamaccus needed no second invitation and hobbled from the room as Uther approached the stranger.

'I owe you my life,' he said.

'You owe me nothing,' replied the man, smiling. 'It is pleasant to meet a young man who holds duty so dear. It is not a common trait.'

'Who are you?'

'I am the king lost to history, a prince of the past. My name is Pendarric.'

Uther pulled up a chair and sat beside the man. 'Why are you here?'

'We share a common enemy, Uther:

272

Goroien. But aiding you was merely a whim – at least, I think it was.'

'I do not understand you.'

'It is especially pleasant after so many centuries to find that I can still be surprised. Did Laitha tell you how she came by the sword?'

'She said she drew it through the air, and her hand was wet as if dipped in a river.'

'You are a bright man, Uther. Tell me where she found the sword.'

'How can I? I know of . . .' The prince stopped, his mouth suddenly dry. 'Hers was the hand in the lake the day my father died. And yet she was with me in the mountains. How is this possible?'

'A fine question, and one which I should like to answer. One day, if you are still alive when I reach a conclusion, I shall come to you. All I know for certain is that it was right that it should happen. What will you do now?'

'I shall try to bring her down.'

Pendarric nodded. 'You are much like your grandfather – the same earnestness, the same proud sense of honour. It is pleasing to me. I wish you well, Uther, now and in the future.'

'You are of the Feragh?'

'I am.'

'Can you tell me what is happening in my homeland?'

'Aquila is losing the war. He smashed one Brigante army at Virosidum, and Ambrosius has destroyed Cerdic. But the Saxon Hengist is moving north with seven thousand men, hoping to link with Eldared for a conclusive battle at Eboracum.'

'How soon will this happen?'

'It is not possible to say, Uther – any more than it is possible to predict your future. It may be that you will defeat Goroien and not be able to return home. It may be that you will return only to face defeat and death. I do not know. What I do know is that you are Rolynd and that counts for more than crowns.'

'Rolynd?'

'It is a state of being, a condition of harmony with the unknown universe. It is very rare – maybe only one man in ten thousand. In material terms it means you are lucky, but also that you earn your luck. Culain is Rolynd; he would be proud of you.'

'Culain is dead. The Soul Stealers killed him.'

'No, he is alive – but not for long. He also is riding to face Goroien – and there he will meet an enemy he cannot conquer. And now I must go.'

'Can you not stay and lead the war against the Witch Queen?'

Pendarric smiled. 'I could, Uther – but I am not Rolynd.'

He reached out as if to shake Uther by the hand, but instead dropped a Sipstrassi Stone into the Prince's palm.

'Use it wisely,' he said, and faded from sight.

15

Laitha found Uther sitting alone, lost in thought, staring into the flickering flames. She approached him silently and drew up a chair near him. 'Are you angry with me?' she asked, her voice soft and childlike. He shook his head, deciding it was better to lie than to face his pain. 'You have not spoken to me for days,' she whispered. 'Was it . . . was I . . . so disappointing?' He turned to her then and realised she did not know she had whispered Culain's name. He was filled with an urge to hurt her, to ram his bitterness home, but her eyes were innocent and he forced back his wrath.

'No,' he said, 'you did not disappoint me. I love you, Laitha. It is that simple.'

'And I love you,' she told him, the words tripping so easily from her tongue that his anger threatened to engulf him. She smiled and tilted her head, waiting for him to reach out and draw her to him. But he did not. He turned once more to the fire. A great sadness touched her then and she rose, hoping he would notice and bid her remain. He did not. She held back her tears until she was outside in the moonlight, then she ran to the edge of the stones and sat alone.

Inside the building Uther cursed softly. He had watched her leave, hoping this small punishment would hurt her, and found that it hurt him also. He had wanted to take her, to touch and stroke her skin; had needed to bury his head in her hair, allowing the perfume of her body to wash over him. And he had not told her that Culain was alive. Was that a punishment also – or a fear that she would turn from him? He wished he had never met her, for he sensed his heart would never be rid of her.

He stood and looked down at his ragged, torn clothing. Not much like a God, Uther – more like a penniless crofter. On impulse he took up the Stone and closed his eyes. Instantly he was clothed in the splendid armour of a First Legate, a red cloak draped over silver breastplate, a leather kilt decorated with silver strips, embossed silver greaves over soft leather riding-boots. The Stone still showed not a trace of black vein.

He moved out into the night and wandered down to the square ditch enclosure where the Legion had pitched their tents. The two legionary guards saluted him as he passed and he made his way towards the tent of Severinus Albinus. Everywhere huge fires were burning under the carcases of deer, elk and sheep, and songs were being sung around several of the blazes. Severinus rose and saluted as Uther entered his tent. The young Roman was a little unsteady on his feet and wine had stained the front of his toga. He grinned shamefacedly. 'I am sorry, Prince Uther. You find me not at my best.'

Uther shrugged. 'It must have been good to see the sunshine.'

'Good? I lost seventy men to the Void and many of them returned to stand outside the camp and call to their comrades. Only their faces were grey, their eyes red – it was worse than death. I will have nightmares about it for all my life. But now I am drunk, and it does not seem so terrible.'

'You have earned this night with your courage,' said Uther, 'but tomorrow the wax must stay firmly in place on the flagons. Tomorrow the war begins.'

'We shall be ready.'

Uther left the tent and returned to Erin, seeing Laitha sitting alone at the edge of the circle. He went to her, his anger gone.

'Do not sit here alone,' he said. 'Come join me.'

'Why are you treating me this way?'

He knelt beside her. 'You loved Culain. Let me ask you this: Had he taken you for his wife, would you have been happy?'

'Yes. Is that so terrible?'

'Not at all, lady. And if on your first night together he had whispered Goroien's name in your ear, would your happiness have continued?' She looked into his smoke-grey eyes – Culain's eyes – and saw the pain.

'Did I do that . . . to you?'

'You did.'

'I am so sorry.'

'As am I, Laitha.'

'Will you forgive me?'

'What is there to forgive? You did not lie. Do I forgive you for loving someone else? That is not a choice you made, it is merely a truth. There is no need for forgiveness. Can I forget it? I doubt it. Do I still want you, even though I know you will be thinking of another? Yes. And that shames me.'

'I would do anything,' she said, 'to take away the hurt.'

'You will become my wife?'

'Yes. Gladly.'

He took her hand. 'From this day forward we are joined and I will take no other wives.'

'From this day forward we are one,' she said.

'Come with me.' He led her to a small, still deserted hut behind the main building. Here he lifted his Stone and a bed appeared.

But the soaring passion of their first loving was not repeated, and both of them drifted to sleep nursing private sorrows.

*

The dragon circled Skitis Island twice before Culain directed it down to an outcrop of wooded hills some two miles from the black stone fortress Goroien had constructed. The edifice was huge, a great stone gateway below two towers, and a moat of fire – burning without smoke. Culain leapt from the dragon's back and spoke the words of power. The beast shrank back into the grey gelding it had been and Culain stripped the saddle from its back

278

and slapped its rump. The horse cantered away over the hillside.

The Mist Warrior took up his belongings and walked the half-mile to the deserted cabin he had seen from the air. Once inside he laid a fire, then stripped his clothing and stepped naked into the dawn light. Taking a deep breath, he began to run. Within a short time his breathing became ragged, his face crimson. He pushed on, feeling the acids building in his limbs, aware of the pounding in his chest. At last he turned for home, every step a burning torture. Back at the cabin he stretched his aching legs, pushing his fingers deep into the muscles of his calves, probing the knots and strains. He bathed in an icy stream and dressed once more. Beyond the cabin was a rocky section of open ground. Here he lifted two fist-sized stones and stood with his arms hanging loosely by his sides. Taking a deep breath he raised his arms and lowered them, repeating the movement again and again. Sweat streamed from his brow, stinging his eyes, but he worked on until he had raised each rock-laden arm forty times. As dusk painted the sky he set off for another run, shorter this time, loosening the muscles of his legs. Finally he slept on the floor before the fire.

He was up at dawn to repeat the torture of the previous day, driving himself even harder, ignoring pain and discomfort, holding the one vision that could overcome his agony.

Gilgamesh, The Lord of Battle . . .

The most deadly fighting man Culain had ever seen.

*

As Uther had hoped the town of Callia opened its gates without a battle, the people streaming out to strew flowers at the feet of the marching Legion. A young girl, no more than twelve, ran to Uther and placed a garland of flowers over his head.

Agarin Pinder and the army of Goroien had vanished like morning mist. The legion camped outside the town and wagons bearing supplies rolled out to them. Uther met the town leaders, who assured him of their support. He found it distasteful that they flung themselves full-length on the ground before him, but made no effort to stop them. By the following day six hundred erstwhile soldiers of the Witch Queen had come to him swearing loyalty. Korrin had urged him to slay them all, but Uther accepted their oaths and they rode with him as the Legion set off on the ten-day march to Perdita, the castle of iron.

Prasamaccus was sent with Korrin to scout ahead. Each evening they returned, but no sign of opposition forces was found until the sixth day.

Tired and dust-covered, Prasamaccus, gratefully accepted the goblet of watered wine and leaned back on the divan rubbing his aching left leg. Uther and Severinus sat silently, waiting for the Brigante to catch his breath.

'There are eight thousand footmen and two

thousand horse. They should be here late tomorrow morning.'

'How was their discipline?' asked Severinus.

'They march in good order, and they are well-armed.' Severinus looked to Uther.

'Do they have scouts out?' asked the prince.

'Yes. I saw two men camped in the hills to the west watching the camp.'

'Order the men to take up a defensive position on the highest hills,' Uther told Severinus. 'Throw up a rampart wall and set stakes.'

'But, Prince Uther . . .'

'Do it now, Severinus. It is almost dusk. I want the men working on the ramparts within the next hour.' The Roman's face darkened but he stood, saluted and hurried from the tent.

'The Romans do not like fighting from behind walls,' commented Prasamaccus.

'No more do I. I know you are tired, my friend, but locate the scouts and come to me when they have gone. Do not let them know you are there.'

For two hours the men of the Ninth Legion constructed a six-foot wall of turf around the crown of a rounded hill. They worked in silence under the watchful eye of Severinus Albinus. An hour after dusk, Prasamaccus returned to Uther's tent.

'They have gone,' he said.

Uther nodded. 'Fetch Severinus to me.'

Dawn found Agarin Pinder and his foot-soldiers twenty-two miles from the newly built fortress. He sent his mounted troops to engage the defenders and hold them in position until the infantry could follow. Then he allowed rations to be given to each man – a small loaf of black bread and a round of cheese. When they had broken their fast, they set off in columns of three on the long march to battle. He did not push them hard, for he wanted them fresh for the onslaught; nor did he allow the pace to slacken, for he knew that fighting men did not relish a long wait. It was a fine line, but Agarin Pinder was a careful man and a conscientious soldier. His troops were the best trained of the six nations and also the best fed and best-armed. The three, he knew, were inseparable.

At last he came in sight of the fortified hill. Already his mounted troops had circled the base, just out of arrow range. Agarin dismounted. It was nearing noon and he ordered tents to be set up and cooking fires lit. He broke the columns and rode forward with his aide to check the enemy fortifications. As the tents were unrolled and the soldiers milled about the new camp, the Ninth Legion marched in two phalanxes from the woods on either side. They marched without drums and halted, allowing their five hundred archers to send a deadly rain of shafts into the camp. Hearing the screams of the dying, Agarin swung his horse and watched in disbelief as his highly-trained troops milled in confusion. The Legion, in close formation, advanced into the centre of the camp, leaving two ranks of archers on the hills on either side.

Agarin cursed and hammered his heels into his horse's side, hoping to break through the red-cloaked enemy and rally his men. His horse reared and fell, an arrow in its throat. The general pitched over its neck, scrambled to his feet and drew his sword. Turning to his aide, he ordered the man from the saddle. As he was dismounting, two arrows appeared in his chest. The stallion reared as the dying man's weight fell to its back and galloped away. The thunder of hooves from behind caused Agarin to spin on his heel as Uther and twenty men in the armour of Pinrae rode from the trees. The prince dismounted, drawing a longsword.

'I told you once. Now you must learn,' said Uther. Agarin ran forward swinging his blade, but Uther blocked the blow, sending a vicious return cut through his enemy's throat. Agarin fell to his knees, his fingers seeking to stem the red rush of life-blood. He pitched to his face on the grass.

In the camp all was chaos, slaughter and panic. With no time to prepare, the men of Goroien's army either fought in small shield circles that were slowly and ruthlessly cut to pieces, or ran back towards the east in frantic attempts to regroup. Some two thousand men managed to break from the camp under the command of three senior officers. They ran the deadly gauntlet of shafts from the bowmen on the hillsides and tried to form a fighting square, but then four hundred cavalry thundered from the woods with lances levelled. The square broke as panic blossomed and the soldiers fled, pursued and slain by the lancers.

They received no help from their own cavalry who, seeing Agarin Pinder slain, rode south at speed. Within the hour the battle was over. Three thousand survivors threw away their weapons and pleaded for mercy.

The stench of death was everywhere, clinging and cloying, and Uther rode to the fortress hill where two hundred men of the Legion waited. They cheered as he rode in and he forced himself to acknowledge them with a smile. Korrin was ecstatic.

'What a day!' he said, as Uther slid from the saddle.

'Yes. Five thousand slain. What a day!'

'When will you kill the others?'

Uther blinked. 'What others?'

'Those who have surrendered,' said Korrin. 'They should all hang like the traitors they are.'

'They are not traitors, Korrin, they are soldiers – men like yourself. Strong men, courageous men. I'll have no part in slaughter.'

'They are the enemy! You cannot allow three thousand men – warriors – to go free. And we cannot feed and guard them.'

'You are a fool!' hissed Uther. 'If we kill them no one will ever surrender again. They will fight like trapped rats – and that will cost me men. When these survivors go back, they will carry the word of our victory. They will say – and rightly so – that we are superb fighting men. That will weaken the resolve of those still to come against us. We are not here, Korrin, to start a blood-bath, but to end the reign of the Witch Queen. And ask yourself this, my blood-hungry friend: when I leave this realm with my Legion, from where will you recruit your own army? It will be from among the very men you want me to slay. Now get away from me. I am tired of war and talk of war.'

Towards midnight, Severinus and two of his centurions entered Uther's tent. The prince looked up and rubbed his eyes. He had been asleep, Laitha beside him, and for the first time in weeks his dreams had been untroubled.

'Your orders have been obeyed, Prince Uther,' said Severinus, his face set, his eyes accusing.

'What orders?'

'The prisoners are dead. The last of them tried to break free and I lost ten men. But now it is done.'

'Done! Three thousand men!' Uther rose to his feet, his eyes gleaming and advanced on Severinus. 'You killed them?'

'The man Korrin came to me with orders from you. We were to take the prisoners away in groups of a hundred and kill them out of earshot of the others. You did not give this order?'

Uther swung to the centurions. 'Find Korrin and bring him here. *Now*!'

The two men backed away hurriedly. Uther pushed past Severinus into the night, sucking in great gasps of air. He felt he was suffocating. Laitha, dressed in a simple white tunic, came out and placed her hand on his arm. 'Korrin has suffered greatly,' she said. Uther shook her hand loose.

Minutes later the two centurions returned

with Korrin behind them, his arms pinned by two legionaries.

Uther moved back into the tent, returning with the sword of Cunobelin in his trembling hands.

'You wretch!' he told Korrin. 'You had to have your blood, did you not?'

'You were too tired to know what you were doing,' said Korrin. 'You didn't understand or you would have given the order yourself. Now release me. We have work to do – strategies to think of.'

'No, Korrin,' said Uther sadly. 'No more strategies for you. No more battles and no more murder. Today was the high point of your sad career. Today was the end. If you have a God, then make your prayer to him, for I am going to kill you.'

'Oh, no! Not before the Witch Queen is overthrown. Don't kill me, Uther. Let me see Astarte slain. It is my dream!'

'Your dreams are drowned in blood.'

'Uther, you cannot!' shouted Laitha.

The Sword of Cunobelin flashed up, entering Korrin's belly, sliding up under the rib-cage and cutting through his heart. The body slumped in the arms of the legionaries.

'Take this carrion and leave it for the crows,' said Uther.

*

Back inside the tent Uther slammed the bloody sword into the hard-packed earth, leaving it quivering in the entrance. Laitha was sitting on the bed, her knees drawn up to her chest.

Severinus followed the prince inside.

'I am sorry,' he said. 'I should have queried an order of such magnitude.'

Uther shook his head. 'Roman discipline, Severinus. First, obey. Gods, I am tired. You had better send some men to the other Pinrae leaders, Maggrig, Hogun, Ceorl. Get them here.'

'You think there will be trouble?'

'If there is, kill them all as they leave my tent.' The soldier saluted and left. Uther moved to the sword jutting in the entrance, the blood staining the earth. He made as if to draw it clear, then stopped and returned to the divan beside the bed. Within minutes the rebel leaders were assembled outside and Severinus led them in. Maggrig's eyes were cool and distant, his emotions masked. The others, as always, avoided Uther's eyes.

'Korrin Rogeur is dead,' said Uther. 'That is his blood.'

'Why?' asked Maggrig.

'He disobeyed me and murdered three thousand men.'

'Our enemies, Lord Berec.'

'Yes, our enemies. That is not the point at issue. I had other plans for them and Korrin knew that. His action was unforgivable. Now he has paid for it. You men have two choices. Either you serve me, or you leave. But if you serve me you obey me.'

'Will you replace the Witch Queen?' asked Maggrig softly.

'No. When she is overthrown I will leave

287

Pinrae and return to my world. The Ghost Army will leave with me.'

'And we are free to leave if we choose.'

'Yes,' lied Uther.

'May I speak with the others?'

Uther nodded and the men filed out. There was silence in the tent until their return. Maggrig, as always, was the spokesman.

'We will stay, Lord Berec, but Korrin's friends wish him to be buried as befits a war leader.'

'Let them do as they please,' said the prince. 'In a few days we will reach Perdita. Strip the dead of weapons and arm your own men.' He waved them away, aware that the sullen expressions were still evident.

'You have lost their love, I think,' said Severinus.

'I want only their obedience. What were our losses today?'

'Two hundred and forty-one dead, eighty-six seriously wounded and another hundred or so with light cuts. The surgeons are dealing with them.'

'Your men fought well today.'

Severinus accepted the compliment with a bow. 'They are mostly Saxon and, as you know, they are fine warriors. They take to discipline well – almost as well as true-born Romans. And if I may return the compliment, your strategy was exemplary. Eight thousand enemy casualties for the loss of so few of our own men.'

'It was not new,' said Uther. 'It was used by Pompey and by the divine Julius. Antony executed a similar move at Phillippi. Darius the Great was renowned for taking his Immortals on lightning marches, and Alexander conquered most of the world with the same strategy. The principle is a simple one: always act, never react.'

Severinus grinned. 'Do you always *react* so defensively to compliments, Prince Uther?'

'Yes,' he admitted sheepishly. 'It is a guard against arrogance.'

After Severinus had left, Uther saw that Laitha had still not moved. She sat, hugging her knees and staring into the embers of the brazier fire. He sat beside her, but she pulled away from him.

'Speak to me,' he whispered. 'What is wrong?'

She swung on him then, her hazel eyes fierce in the candle-light. 'I do not know you,' she said. 'You killed that man so coldly.'

He said nothing for a moment. 'You think I enjoyed it?'

'I do not know, Uther. Did you?'

He licked his lips, allowing the question to sink into his subconscious.

'Well?' she asked. He turned his face towards her.

'In that moment – yes, I did. All my anger was in that blow.'

'Oh, Uther, what are you becoming?'

'How can I answer you?'

'But this war was being fought for Korrin. Now who is it for?'

'It is for me,' he admitted. 'I want to go

home. I want to see Eboracum, and Camulodunum, and Durobrivae. I do not know what I am becoming. Maedhlyn used to say that a man is the sum total of all that happens to him. Some things strengthen, some things weaken. Korrin was like that. The death of his wife unhinged him and his heart was like a burning coal, desiring only vengeance. He once told me that if he won he would light fires under his enemies that would never go out. As for me, I am trying to be a man – a man like Aurelius, or Culain. I have no one to turn to, Laitha. No one to say, "You are wrong, Thuro. Try again." Killing Korrin may have been a mistake, but if I had done it earlier three thousand men would still be alive. And now – if we win – there will be no fires that never go out.'

'There was such gentleness in you when we were back in the Caledones,' she said, 'and you were a hunted prince, ill-suited to sword play. Now you are acting the general and committing murder.'

He shook his head. 'That is the sad part. I am not *acting* the general, I *am* the general. Sometimes I wish this was all a dream, and that I could wake in Camulodunum with my father still king. But he is dead and my land is being torn apart by wolves. For good or ill I am the man who can stop it. I understand strategy and I know men.'

'Culain would never have killed Korrin.'

'And such is the way of legends,' he mocked. 'No sooner the man dies than he becomes a wondrous figure. Culain was a warrior; that makes him a killer. Why do you think the Ninth Legion were in the Void? Culain sent them there. He told me about it back in the Caledones. It was a regret he carried, but he did it while fighting a war against the Romans four hundred years ago.'

'I do not believe you.'

'You are a foolish child,' he snapped, his patience gone.

'He was twice the man you are!'

Uther stood and took a deep breath. 'And you are a tenth of the woman you ought to be. Maybe that's why he rejected you.' She flew at him, her nails flashing towards his face, but he brushed aside her attack and hurled her face-down to the bed. Swiftly he straddled her back, pinning her. 'Now that is no way for a wife to behave.' She struggled for some minutes, then relaxed and he released her. She rolled to her back, her fist cracking against his chin, but he grabbed her arms and pinned her beneath him.

'I may not be right all the time,' he whispered, 'and I may have struck a bad bargain with you. But whatever I become I will always need you. And always love you.'

Outside, Prasamaccus heard the argument die away.

'I do not think they will want to see you now,' whispered a sentry.

'No,' agreed Prasamaccus, hobbling away into the darkness.

*

For two weeks Culain had toiled and struggled to regain lost strength and speed. He was now

291

fitter and faster than he had been for years . . .
and he knew it was not enough. Goroien had
been right. In accepting mortality, Culain had
lost the vital edge of youth. His doubts were
many as he sat on the hard-packed ground
before the cabin, watching the sun sink in fire.

Once, as Cunobelin the King, he had allowed
his body to grow old and grey, but it had been
a sham. Beneath the wrinkles his strength had
remained.

For two days now he had exercised not at all,
allowing his tired body to rest and replenish
lost energy. Tomorrow he would walk to the
Castle of Iron and seek a truth he felt he already
knew.

He was glad now that he had used up the
Stone in that wonderfully extravagant flight.
The temptation to use its power on himself
would today have proved irresistible. His
thoughts turned to Gilgamesh, seeing the warrior as he had first known him, strong and proud, leading a hopeless fight against an invincible
enemy. Goroien had taken pity on him, which
was unlike her, and helped him overthrow the
tyrant king. Gilgamesh knew glory then and the
adulation of a freed people. But it was not
enough; there was a hunger in the Lord of
Battle that no amount of victories could ease.
Culain had never understood the demon that
drove him. Three times Gilgamesh challenged
Culain, and three times the Mist Warrior had
refused to be drawn. Many in the Feragh had
wondered at Culain's reasons. Few had realised
the truth. Culain lach Feragh was afraid of the

292

strange, dark quality within Gilgamesh that made him unbeatable.

Then came the day when news of his death had reached Culain. His heart had soared, for deep inside he had begun to believe the Lord of Battle would one day kill him. He recalled the day well – the sun clear in a cloudless sky, distant cornfields glowing gold and the high white turrets of Babylon cloaked in dark shadows. Brigamartis had brought the news, her face flushed with excitement. She had never liked Gilgamesh. Before his arrival she had been considered one of the finest sword duellists in the Feragh, but he had defeated her with ease in the Shade Games.

'There was something wrong with his blood,' said Brigamartis gleefully. 'It would not accept Sipstrassi power. He aged wonderfully; in the last two years even Goroien would not visit him. He had begun to drool, you know, and he was half-blind.'

Culain had waited five years before crossing the Mist. Goroien was as beautiful as ever, and acted as if her affair with Gilgamesh had never taken place. His name did not cross her lips for another three centuries.

Now the Lord of Battle had returned and Culain lach Feragh would truly taste the terrors of mortality. It was galling to live so long, only to face such bitterness. Thuro and Laitha were trapped in a world he could not reach, victims of a goddess he could never kill and menaced by a warrior he could not conquer.

He lifted his lance and drew the hidden

sword. The edge was lethally sharp, the balance magnificent. He looked down at his reflection in the silver steel, gazing into his own eyes as if expecting to see answers there.

Had he ever truly known courage? How simple it had been for an immortal warrior to battle in the world of men. Almost all wounds could be healed, and he had on his side the knowledge and acquired skill of centuries. Even the great Achilles had been a child by comparison, the outcome of their duel never in doubt. Only his opponents had known courage. Culain smiled. His fear of Gilgamesh had made him run like a child in terror of the dark – and like all runners, he had hurtled headlong into greater fear. Had he killed Gilgamesh all those centuries ago Goroien would not now have taken into her body the dread disease that was killing her. From that he could reason that she might never have become the Witch Queen. So the terrors of this age came squarely to rest on Culain's shoulders.

He accepted the burden and sought the sanctuary of Eleari-mas, the Emptying. But his mind drifted into memory. He saw again the curiously beautiful end of the world. He was fifteen years old, standing in the courtyard of his father's house in Balacris. He saw the sun sink slowly into the west and then hurtle back into the sky. A great wind came up, and the palace of Pendarric began to glow. He heard someone scream and saw a woman pointing to the horizon. A colossal black wall was darkening the sky, growing ever larger. He had stared at it for some moments, thinking it a great storm. But soon the terror struck. It was a thundering thousand-foot wall of water, drowning the land. The golden glow from the palace spread over the city, reaching the outer sections just as the sea roared over them all. Culain had been rooted to the spot, desperate to draw the last second of life. As the sea struck him he screamed and fell, only to open his eyes and gaze at the sun in a blue sky. He stood, and found himself on a hillside with thousands of his fellow citizens. The horizon had altered; blue-tinged mountains and endless valleys stretched out before him.

It was the first day of the Feragh, the day Pendarric had rescued eight thousand men, women and children, turning Balacris into a giant gateway to another world. Atlantis was now gone, her glory soon to be forgotten.

Thus began the long immortal life of Culain lach Feragh, the Warrior of the Mist.

Unable to reach the heights of Eleari-mas, Culain opened his eyes and returned to the present. A thought struck him, easing the tension in his soul. Achilles and all the other mortals who died beneath Culain's blade must have felt as he did now. What hope was there for a mortal who stood against a god? Yet still they had taken swords in hand and opposed him, just as the mortal Culain would oppose the immortal, undead Gilgamesh. It was good that Culain's last earthly experience would be a new truth. At last he would know how they felt.

Later, as he sat in silent contemplation, Pendarric appeared, stepping into the cabin as if coming merely from another room.

Culain smiled and rose, and the two men gripped hands. A table appeared, then two divans, the table bearing flagons of wine and two crystal goblets.

'It is a fine night here,' said Pendarric. 'I have always loved the smell of lavender.'

Culain poured a goblet of wine and stretched himself on the divan. The king looked much as he always did, his golden beard freshly curled, his body powerful, his eyes ever watchful and masked against intrusion to his thoughts.

'Why did you come?'

Pendarric shrugged and filled his own goblet. 'I came to talk to an old friend on the night before he takes a long journey.'

Culain nodded. 'How is Thuro?'

'He is now Uther Pendragon and he leads an army. I thought you would like to know how he found it.'

Culain sat up. 'And?'

'He journeyed into the Void and brought back the Ninth Legion.'

'No?'

'And he has your sword, though I still do not know how.'

'Tell me . . . all of it.'

And Pendarric did so, until he reached the point of calling Laitha to the central altar. 'I still do not understand why I asked her to do it. It was like a voice in my mind. I was as surprised as she when she produced the sword – doubly so when the ramifications are considered. She reached back into the past, to a time and a place in which she already existed. As we both know, that is not possible. It is a wondrous riddle.'

'You should speak to Maedhlyn,' said Culain.

'I would, but I do not like the man. There is an emptiness in him; he does not know how to love. And I am not sure I want the riddle solved. One of the problems with being immortal is that there are few questions which escape answers over so many centuries. Let this be one of them.'

'Can Thuro . . . Uther . . . defeat Goroien?'

Pendarric shrugged. 'I cannot say. She has great power. But at this moment I am more concerned with Culain.' He stretched his hand over the table and opened his fingers. A golden Sipstrassi Stone tumbled to the wood.

'I cannot take it,' said Culain. 'But believe me, I want to.'

'Can you win without it?'

'Perhaps. I am not without skill.'

'I never liked Gilgamesh, and it seemed to me that his inability to accept Sipstrassi power was a judgement far above mine. But it has to be said that he was a towering warrior . . . truly Rolynd.'

'As am I.'

'As are you,' agreed Pendarric. 'But he, I think, has no soul. There is nothing of greatness in Gilgamesh – there never was. I think for him the world was grey. When Goroien brought him back she doomed herself, for the Bloodstone enhanced his disease, giving it the strength to infect her.'

'I still love her,' admitted Culain. 'I could not hurt her.'

'I know.' The king poured more wine, his eyes moving from Culain. 'There is something else – and I am not sure, even now, whether it will aid or condemn you.' Pendarric's voice trembled and Culain felt a strange tension seep into his body. The king licked his lips and sipped his wine. 'Goroien does not know that I am in possession of this . . . secret.' He lapsed into a silence Culain did not disturb. 'I am sorry, my friend,' said Pendarric. 'This is harder for me than I can say.'

'Then do not tell me,' said Culain. 'After tomorrow it will not matter.'

Pendarric shook his head. 'When I told you of Laitha and the sword, that was not all. Something . . . someone . . . bade me tell you the whole of the truth. So let it be done. You remember the days in Assyria when Goroien contracted a fever that brought her to the edge of madness?'

'Of course. She almost died.'

'She believed she hated you, and she left you.'

'Not for long!'

Pendarric smiled. 'No, a mere two decades. When she returned, was all as it should have been?'

'After a while. The disease took almost a century to leave her.'

'Did it ever truly leave? Did her ruthlessness

298

not grow? Was the gentleness in her soul not vanished for ever?'

'Yes, perhaps. What are you saying?'

Pendarric took a deep breath. 'When she left you she was pregnant..'

'I do not want to hear this!' screamed Culain, leaping to his feet. 'Leave me!'

'Gilgamesh is your son and her lover.'

All the strength and anger flowed from Culain's body and he staggered; at once Pendarric was beside him, helping him to the divan.

'Why? Why did she not tell me?'

'How can I answer that? Goroien is insane.'

'And Gilgamesh?'

'He knows – it is why he hates you, why he has always desired your death. Whatever madness infected Goroien was carried on into him. When he could not accept immortality, he blamed you.'

'Why did you tell me?'

'Had you accepted the Sipstrassi Stone, I would not have spoken.'

'You think this knowledge will make me stronger?'

'No,' admitted Pendarric, 'but it might help to explain why you were so loth to fight him.'

'I was afraid of him.'

'That too. But the call of blood was touching your subconscious. I have seen you both fight and I know that the Culain of old could defeat Gilgamesh. You were always the best; he knew that. It only added to his hatred.'

'How did you find out?'

'During the last years of his life, Goroien

would not see him. I went to him two days before he died. He was senile then, and calling for his mother. It is not a pleasant memory.'

'I could have raised him without hate.'

'I do not think so.'

'Leave me, Pendarric. I have much to consider. Tomorrow I must try to kill my son.'

16

The ten cohorts of Legio IX arrived at the plain before Perdita, the Castle of Iron, five days after the battle in which Agarin Pinder's army was crushed. Uther ordered a halt and the twenty wagons bearing supplies and equipment were drawn into a hastily dug defensive enclosure. The rebel army now numbered more than six thousand men and Maggrig had been placed in command of the Pinrae warriors.

With Prasamaccus, Maggrig and Severinus, Uther walked to the edge of the trees overlooking the fortress, a cold dread settling on him as he gazed on the black castle rearing from the mist-shrouded plain. It seemed to the prince to resemble a colossal demonic head, with a cavernous mouth of a gateway. No troops were assembled to defend it, and the plain sat silent and beckoning.

'When do we advance?' asked Maggrig.

'Why has no further attempt been made to stop us?' countered Uther.

'Why count the teeth of the gifted horse?' said Prasamaccus. Maggrig and Severinus nodded agreement.

'We are not engaging an enemy force,' said Uther. 'We are fighting a war against a Witch

Queen. No attempt has been made on my life; no other fighting force has been raised to oppose us. What does that suggest to you?'

'That she is beaten,' said Maggrig.

'No,' replied Uther. 'The opposite is the case. She used Agarin because his victory was the simple option, but she has other forces at her disposal.' He turned to Severinus. 'We have four hours before dusk. Leave a small force within the enclosure and march the Legion to where we stand.'

'And what of my men?' asked Maggrig.

'Wait for my order.'

'What do you plan?' asked Severinus.

Uther smiled. 'I plan to take the castle.'

*

On the high tower Goroien's eyes opened and she, too, smiled.

'Come to me, sweet boy,' she whispered. Beside her Gilgamesh stood, his dark armour gleaming in the sunlight.

'Well?' he asked.

'They are coming . . . as is Culain.'

'I would have liked the opportunity to kill the boy.'

'Be satisfied with the man.'

'Oh, I will be satisfied, mother.' Under the helm Gilgamesh grinned as he saw her shoulders stiffen and watched a crimson blush stain her porcelain features. She swung on him, forcing a smile.

'I wonder,' she said, her voice dripping venom, 'if it has occurred to you that after today you will have nothing to live for?'

302

'What do you mean?'

'All your life you have dreamed of killing Culain lach Feragh. What will you do tomorrow, Gilgamesh, my love? What will you do when there is no enemy to fight?'

'I will know peace,' he said simply. The answer shook her momentarily, for his voice had carried a note she had never heard from the Lord of Battle, a softness like the echoes of sorrow.

'You will never know peace,' she spat. 'You live for death!'

'Perhaps that is because I am dead,' he replied, the harsh edge returning.

'He is coming. You should prepare yourself.'

'Yes. I long to see his face and read his eyes in the moment I tell him who I am.'

'Why must you tell him?' she asked, suddenly fearful.

'What will it matter?' he responded. 'He will die anyway.' With that he turned and walked from the ramparts. Goroien watched him depart and felt again the curious arousal his movements inspired. So graceful, so strong – steel muscles beneath silk-soft skin. Once more she gazed at the line of trees in the distance, then she also returned to her rooms.

As she entered the inner sanctum, she stopped before a full-length mirror and closely examined her reflection. A hint of grey shone in the gold of her hair, and the finest of lines was visible beside her eyes. It was growing worse. She moved to the centre of the room, where a boulder-sized Bloodstone rested on a tree of gold. Around it were the dried-out husks of three pregnant women. Goroien touched the Stone, feeling its warmth spread into her. The corpses vanished and a shadow moved behind her.

'Come forth, Secargus!' she commanded and a hulking figure ambled into view. More than seven feet tall, he towered over the queen – his bestial face more wolf than man, his jaws slavering, his tongue lolling.

'Fetch five more.'

He reached out a taloned hand to touch her, his eyes pleading.

'Tonight,' she said. 'I will make you a man again, and you can share my bed. Would you like that?' The huge head nodded and a low growling moan escaped the twisted mouth. 'Now fetch five more.' He ambled away towards the dungeons where the women were kept and Goroien moved to the Stone; the black lines were thick in the red-gold. For some time she remained where she was, waiting for Secargus to bring the women to their timely deaths.

*

On the ramparts once more, Goroien waited patiently. The mist swirled on the plain, but her excitement grew as she waited for the inevitable moment of victory. With an hour to go before dusk, she saw the Legion march from the trees in battle order, ranks of five, spreading to form a long shield wall before their spearmen. On they came into the mist: five thousand men whose souls would feed her Bloodstone. Her hands were trembling as she watched them advance, their bronze shields gleaming like fire in the dying sunlight. She licked her lips and raised her arms, linking her mind with the dread Stone.

Suddenly the plain was engulfed in fire, white-hot and searing, the heat reaching even there on the battlements. Within the mist the soldiers burned, human torches that crumpled to the earth, their bodies blistering and burning like living candles. Black smoke obscured her vision and she returned to her rooms.

Culain would soon be arriving and she transformed her clothing into a tight-fitting tunic and leggings of forest green with a belt of spun gold. It had always been Culain's favourite.

Back at the edge of the woods, Uther collapsed. Prasamaccus and Severinus knelt beside him.

'It is exhaustion,' said Severinus. 'Fetch some wine!'

Maggrig stood close by, staring into the Mist where the vision of death had appeared. He was appalled, for he would willingly have led his own men across that plain and now would be lying scorched and dead on the blackened earth. Berec-Uther had halted the Legion within the woods, then knelt facing the plain.

Under the startled eyes of the rebel army Berec had lifted his hand, which glowed as if he held a ball of fire. Then a vision had appeared, of the Legion marching – a truly ghostly army. When the fire erupted and the heat washed over the watchers, Maggrig's stomach had heaved. The illusion had been so powerful he had almost smelt burning flesh.

Uther groaned. Severinus lifted him to a sitting position and held a goblet of wine to his lips. The prince drank deeply. Dark rings circled his eyes and his face was gaunt and grey.

'How did you know?' asked the Roman.

'I did not know. But she is too powerful not to have one more weapon.'

'This fell from your hand,' said Prasamaccus, offering Uther a black pebble with threads of gold. The prince took it.

'We will advance on the castle at midnight. Find me fifty men – the best swordsmen you have. The Legion will follow at dawn.'

'I will lead the raid,' said Severinus.

'No, it is my duty,' responded Uther.

'With respect, Prince Uther, that is folly.'

'I know, Severinus, but I have no choice. I alone have a source of magic to use against her. It is weak now, but it is all we have. We do not know what terrors wait inside the castle – Void warriors, Atrols, Werebeasts? I have the Sword of Cunobelin, and I have the Stone Pendarric gave me. I must lead.'

'Let me go with you,' pleaded the Roman.

'Now *that* would be folly, but I am grateful for the offer. If all goes well, the Legion will follow at dawn and I shall greet you in the gateway. If not . . .' His eyes locked to Severinus' gaze. 'Make your own strategy – and a home for yourselves in Pinrae.'

'I'll pick your men myself. They will not let you down.'

Uther called Laitha to him and the two of them wandered away from the gathered men to a sheltered hollow near a huge oak.

Swiftly he told her of the attack he would be leading – explaining, as he had with Severinus, the reasons for his actions.

'I will come with you,' she said.

'I do not want you in danger.'

'You seem to forget that I also was trained by Culain lach Feragh. I can handle a sword as well as any man here – probably better than most.'

'It would destroy me if you were slain.'

'Think back, Uther, to the day we met. Who was it that slew the first of the assassins? It was I. This is hard for me, for I accept that as your wife I must obey you. But please let me live as I have been taught.'

He took her hand and drew her to him. 'You are free, Laitha. I will never own you, nor treat you as a servant or slave. And I would be proud if you were to walk beside me through the gate.'

The tension eased from her. 'Now I can truly love you,' she said, 'for now I know that you are a man. Not Culain, not his shadow, but a man in your own right.'

He grinned boyishly. 'This morning I washed in a stream and, as I looked down, I saw this child's face staring up at me. I have not yet needed to shave. And I thought how amusing Maedhlyn would find all this – his weakly student leading an army. But I am doing the best that I can.'

'For myself,' she admitted, 'I saw a tree this

307

afternoon that seemed to grow into the clouds. I wanted to climb it and hide in the topmost branches. I used to pretend I had a castle in the clouds, where no one could find me. There is no shame in being young, Thuro.'

He chuckled. 'I thought I had put that name behind me, but I love to hear you say it. It reminds me of the Caledones when I did not know how to light a fire.'

Just short of midnight Severinus noisily approached the hollow, clearing his throat and treading on as many dry sticks as he could see. Uther came towards him, laughing, Laitha just behind.

'Is this Roman stealth I hear?' asked the prince.

'It is very dark,' answered the Roman with a grin.

'Are the men ready?'

The grin vanished. 'They are. I shall follow at dawn.'

Uther offered his hand, which Severinus took in the warrior's grip, wrist to wrist.

'I am your servant for life,' said the Roman.

'Be careful, Severinus, I shall hold you to that.'

'Make sure that you do.'

*

Culain lach Feragh stood before the gates of Perdita, the winds of Skitis Island shrieking over the rocks. He wore his black and silver winged helm and silver shoulder-guard, but no other armour protected him. His chest was

308

covered merely by a shirt of doeskin, and upon his feet were moccasins of soft leather.

The black gate opened and a tall warrior stepped into the sunshine, his face covered by a dark helm. Behind him came Goroien and Culain's heart soared, for she wore the outfit he had first seen on the day they met. Goroien climbed to a high rock as Gilgamesh advanced to stand before Culain.

'Greetings, Father,' said Gilgamesh. 'I trust you are well.' The voice was muffled by the helm, but Culain could hear the suppressed excitement.

'Do not call me Father, Gilgamesh. It offends me.'

'The truth is sometimes painful.' Now there was disappointment in the voice. 'How did you find out?'

'You told Pendarric, but probably you do not remember. I understand you were senile at the time.'

'Happily you will not suffer the same fate,' hissed Gilgamesh. 'Today you die.'

'All things die. Do you object to me saying farewell to your mother?'

'I do. My lover has nothing to say to you.'

Suddenly Culain chuckled. 'Poor fool,' he said. 'Sad, tormented Gilgamesh! I pity you, boy. Was there ever a day in your life when you were truly happy?'

'Yes – when I bedded your wife!'

'A joy shared by half the civilised world,' said Culain, smiling.

'And there is today,' said Gilgamesh, drawing two short swords. 'Today my happiness is complete.'

Culain removed the winged helm and placed it at the ground by his feet.

'I am sorry for you, boy. You could have been a force for good in the world, but luck never favoured you, did it? Born to a mad goddess and diseased from the moment you first sucked milk. What chance did you have? Come then, Gilgamesh. Enjoy your happiness.' The lance slid in two, revealing the slanted sword. Culain laid the haft next to the helm and drew a hunting-knife from his belt. 'Come, this is your moment!'

Gilgamesh advanced smoothly and then leapt forward, his sword hissing through the air. Culain blocked the blow, and a second, and a third. The two men circled.

'Remove your helm, boy. Let me see your face.'

Gilgamesh did not answer but attacked once more – his swords whirling in a glittering web, but always blocked by the blades of Culain. On the rocks above, Goroien watched it all in a semi-daze. It seemed to her as if she viewed two dancers moving with impossible grace to the discordant music of clashing steel. Gilgamesh as always was beautiful, almost catlike in his movements, while Culain reminded her of a flame leaping and twisting in a fire. Goroien's heart was beating faster now as she tried to read the contest. Culain was stronger and faster than he had been when the shade of Gilgamesh had defeated him. And yet he was failing.

Almost imperceptibly he was slowing. Gilgamesh, with the eye of the warrior born, saw the growing weakness in his opponent and launched a savage attack . . . but it was too early and Culain blocked the blows and spun on his heel, his sword snaking out in a murderous riposte. Gilgamesh hurled himself backwards as the silver blade scored across his stomach, opening the top layers of skin.

'Never be hasty, boy,' said Culain. 'The best are never reckless.' No blood seeped from the wound. Gilgamesh tore his helm from his head, his golden hair catching the last of the sunlight and Culain saw him with new eyes. How could he ever have missed the resemblance to the mother? The Mist Warrior was growing tired – but not as weary as his body appeared. He was grateful now to Pendarric, for had he not known the truth he would be dead by now. He could not have fought so well while struggling to come to terms with the awful knowledge.

'Are you beginning to know fear, little man?' he asked. Gilgamesh mouthed a curse and came forward.

'I could never fear you,' he hissed, his dead grey eyes conveying no emotion.

Swords clashed and Culain's hunting-knife barely blocked a disembowelling thrust which had been superbly disguised. He leapt back, aware more than ever that he had to maintain his strategy, for there was more to a battle than mere skill with a blade.

'A nice move, but you must learn to disguise

the thrust,' he said. 'Were you taught by a fishmonger?'

Gilgamesh screamed and attacked once more, his swords flashing with incredible speed. Culain blocked, twisted, moved – being forced back and back towards a jutting rock. He ducked under a whistling cut, hurled himself to the right, rolled on his shoulder and came back to his feet. A trickle of blood was running from a slashing cut in his side.

'That was better,' he said, 'but you were still open to a blow on the left.' It was a lie, but Culain said it with confidence.

'I never knew a man talk as much as you,' answered Gilgamesh. 'When you are dead, I'll rip the tongue from your head.'

'I should take the eyes,' advised Culain. 'Yours look as if the maggots still remain.'

'Damn you!' screamed Gilgamesh. His blades flashed for Culain's face and it was all the Mist Warrior could do to fend him off; there was no opportunity for a counter-strike. Three blows forced their way through his defences only partially blocked – the first slashing a wide cut to his chest, the second piercing his side and the third plunging into his shoulder. Once more he escaped by hurling himself sideways and rolling to his feet.

'Where are your taunts now, Father? I cannot hear you.'

Culain steadied himself, his grey eyes focused on the lifeless orbs of his opponent. He knew now with a terrible certainty that he could not defeat Gilgamesh and live. He backed away, half-stumbling. Gilgamesh raced forward but Culain suddenly dived to the ground in a tumbler's roll, rising into Gilgamesh's path. The Lord of Battle's sword plunged home in Culain's chest, cleaving through the lungs, but his own sword sliced up into the enemy's belly to cut through the heart. Gilgamesh groaned, his head sagging to Culain's shoulder.

'I beat you!' he whispered, 'as I always knew I could.'

Culain dragged himself clear of the body, which slumped face-first to the ground. He stumbled, his lungs filling with blood and choking him. He fell to his knees and stared down at the hilt of the sword jutting from his chest. Blood rose in his throat, spraying from his mouth.

On the rock above, Goroien screamed. She leapt to the ground and ran to Culain's side, grabbing the sword-hilt and tearing it from his chest. As he sank to the ground she pulled a small Sipstrassi Stone from her tunic pocket, but as she placed it over the wound she froze, staring at her hands. They were wrinkled and stained with brown liver spots.

Yet it was impossible, for five thousand men had died to feed her Bloodstone. In that moment she knew her only chance for life was in the small Sipstrassi fragment held over Culain. She stared down at his face.

He tried to shake his head, willing her to live, then lapsed into the sleep of death.

Her hand descended, the power flowing into Culain, stopping the wound, healing the lungs, driving on and on, pushing back his mortality. His hair darkened, the skin of his face tightening. At last the Stone was black.

Culain awoke to see a white-haired skeletal figure lying crumpled at his side. He screamed his anguish to the skies and tried to lift her, but a whisper stopped him. The rheumy eyes had opened. He crouched low over her and heard the last words of Goroien, the Goddess Astarte, the Goddess Athena, the Goddess Freya.

'Remember me.'

The last flickering ember of life departed, the bones crumbling to white dust that the wind picked up and scattered on the rocky ground.

*

Uther, Prasamaccus and Laitha walked in silence, the fifty swordsmen of the Legion moving in a line with shields raised on either side of them. The black castle grew ever more large and sinister. No lights shone in the narrow windows and the gateway was darker than the night.

Prasamaccus walked with an arrow notched. Laitha kept close to Uther. Behind them came Maggrig and six Pinrae warriors; his eyes remained locked to Uther's back, for every time he looked at the castle his limbs trembled and his heart hammered. But where Berec walked, so too would Maggrig, and when the Witch Queen was dead the godling would follow. For Maggrig knew that the prince would never relinquish his hold on the people, and he was not prepared to allow another Enchanter to torment the land.

With each step the attackers grew more tense, waiting for the fire to reach out and engulf them, as it had the phantom Legion which Uther had conjured. Slowly they neared the castle, and at last Uther stepped on to the bridge before the gate towers. He drew the Sword of Cunobelin, glanced up at the seemingly deserted ramparts and advanced.

At once a bestial figure ran from the darkness, a terrible howl ripping the silence. More than seven feet tall, the giant wolf-beast roared towards the prince and in its taloned hands was an upswept axe. An arrow sang from Prasamaccus' bow, taking the creature in the throat, but its advance continued. Uther ran forward, leaping nimbly to his left as the axe descended. The Sword of Cunobelin swept up, shearing through the huge arm at the shoulder; the creature screamed and the sword sliced down into its neck with all the power Uther could exert with his double-handed grip. Before the eyes of the attackers the giant body shrank and Maggrig pushed forward to stare at the dead but now human face. 'Secargus,' he said. 'I served with him ten years ago. Fine man.'

At that moment a sound drifted to the tense warriors and men looked at one another in surprise. A baby's cry floated on the wind, echoing in the gateway.

'Take twenty men,' Uther told a centurion named Degas. 'Find out where it is coming from. The rest of you split into groups of five and search the castle.'

'We will come with you, Lord Berec,' said Maggrig, his hand on his sword. He did not meet Uther's gaze, for he was afraid his intent would be read in his eyes. Uther merely nodded and moved through the gateway. Inside was a maze of tunnels and stairwells and Uther climbed ever higher. The corridors were lit by lanterns, faintly aromatic and glowing with a blood-red light. Strangely embroidered rugs covered the walls, showing scenes of hunts and battles. Everywhere statues of athletes could be seen in various poses – throwing javelins, running, lifting, wrestling. All were of the finest white marble.

Near the topmost floor they came to the apartments of Goroien, where a massive bed almost filled a small room which had been created of silvered mirrors. Uther gazed around at a score of reflections. The sheets were of silk, the bed of carved ivory inlaid with gold.

'She certainly likes to look at herself,' commented Laitha. Prasamaccus said nothing. He felt uncomfortable and it had little to do with fear of Goroien. All she could do was kill him. Something else was in the air, and he did not like the way Maggrig kept so close to Uther and the other men of Pinrae also gathered round the prince. The group moved through to the far room, where a five-foot tree of gold supported a rounded black boulder veined with threads of dull red gold.

'The source of her power,' said Uther.

'Can we use it?' asked Maggrig.

Without answering Uther strode to the tree and raised the Sword of Cunobelin high over his head. With one stroke he smashed the stone to shards. At once the room shimmered – the hangings, the carpets and the furniture all disappearing. The group stood now in a bare, cold room, lit only by the moonlight streaming in silver columns through the tall narrow windows.

'She is gone,' said Uther.

'Where?' demanded Maggrig.

'I do not know. But the Stone is now useless. Rejoice, man. You have won!'

'Not yet,' said Maggrig softly.

'A moment of your time,' said Prasamaccus as the wolf-like Maggrig drew his knife. The warrior turned slowly, to find himself facing a bent bow with the shaft aimed at his throat.

The other Pinrae men spread out, drawing their weapons. Laitha stepped forward to stand beside the stunned Uther.

'Did Korrin truly mean so much to you?' asked the Brigante.

'Korrin?' answered Maggrig with a sneer. 'No, he was a headstrong fool. But you think I am foolish also? This is not the end of the terror, only the beginning of fresh evils. Your magic and your spells!' he hissed. 'No good ever came of such power. But we'll not let you live to take her place.'

'I have no wish to take her place,' said Uther. 'Believe me, Maggrig, the Pinrae is yours. I have my own land.'

'I might have believed you, but you've lied

317

once. You told me we were free to serve you or leave, and yet the Legion archers were waiting in the shadows. We would all have been slain. No more lies, Berec. Die!'

As he spoke he hurled himself at Uther. The prince leapt back, his sword slashing up almost of its own volition. The blade took Maggrig in the side, cleaving up under his ribs and exiting in a bloody swathe. The other warriors charged and the first fell to Prasamaccus – an arrow through his temple – the second to Laitha.

'Halt!' bellowed Uther, his voice ringing with authority and the warriors froze. 'Maggrig was wrong! There is no betrayal! I speak not from fear, for I think you know we can slay you all. Now cease this madness.' For a moment he had them, but one man suddenly hurled a dagger and Uther swerved as the blade flashed by his ear. Laitha plunged her gladius into the chest of the nearest warrior and Prasamaccus shot yet another. The remaining pair rushed at Uther and he blocked one thrust, spinning on his heel to crash his elbow into the face of the second man. The Sword of Cunobelin cut through the man's neck, his head toppling to the floor. Laitha leapt forward, killing the last man with a dazzling riposte which ripped open his throat. In the silence that followed Uther backed away from the bodies, an awful sadness gripping him.

'I liked him,' he whispered, staring at the dead Maggrig. 'He was a good man. Why did he do it, Prasamaccus?'

The Brigante turned away with a shrug. Now was not the time to talk of the Circle of Life, and how a man's actions would always return to haunt him. Ever since, in his rage, Uther had killed Korrin, Prasamaccus had been waiting for the moment of Pinrae revenge. It was as inevitable as night following day.

'Why?' asked Uther again.

'This is a world of madness,' said Laitha. 'Put it from your mind.'

The trio left the room, slowly making their way to the courtyard. There Degas was waiting with more than forty pregnant women and one new mother. Some of the women were crying, but the tears were of relief. Two days ago there had been sixty women imprisoned in Perdita.

'This is a strange castle,' said Degas, a short powerfully-built soldier. 'There are three more gates, but they lead nowhere: just blackness beyond them and a deadly cold. And a little while ago all the lanterns vanished, and the statues. Everything! All that is left is the building itself, and cracks have already started appearing near the battlements.' As he spoke the gate tower creaked and shifted.

'Let us leave,' said Uther. 'Are all the men here?'

'All the Romans, yes, but what of your guards?'

'They will not be coming. Let's get the women out.' A wall lurched behind them, giant stones shifting and groaning as the legionaries helped the women to their feet and out through the yawning gateway. Once on the plain, Degas stopped to look back.

'Mother of Mitra!' he said 'Look!'

The great Castle of Iron was turning to dust, huge clouds billowing in the pre-dawn breeze. From the woods the men of the Ninth Legion swarmed down, their cheers ringing in the night. Uther was swept from his feet and carried shoulder-high back to the camp. As the dawn sun rose over the plain, the castle had completely disappeared. All that was left was a great circle of black stones.

Uther left Severinus and the others and walked to the entrance of the enclosure, looking out at the silent camp of the Pinrae men. On impulse he strode from the safety of the legion encampment and walked alone to where the Pinrae leaders sat. Their eyes were sullen as he approached, and several men reached for their weapons. They were seated in a circle with the warriors behind them, as if in an arena. Uther smiled grimly.

'Tomorrow,' he said, 'I leave the Pinrae. And there is no joy, now, in our victory. Several days ago I had to kill a man I had thought was my friend. Tonight I killed another whom I respected and hoped would lead you when I had gone.' His eyes swept the faces around him. 'I came here to aid you; I have no desire to rule you. My own land is far from here. Korrin Rogeur died because he could not control the hatred in his heart; Maggrig died because he could not believe there was none in mine. Tonight you must choose a new leader – a king if you will. As for me, I shall return here no more.'

Not a word was spoken, but their hands were

no longer on their sword-hilts. Uther looked at the men, recognising Baldric with whom he had travelled on the first quest of the Stone. In his eyes there was only a cold anger. Beside him sat Hogun, Ceorl and Rhiall. They made no move, but their hatred remained.

Uther wandered sadly back to the enclosure. Only a short time ago, as he had returned with Baldric, he had pictured their adulation. Now he felt he had learned a real lesson. During his short time in the Pinrae he had freed a people and risked his life, only to earn their undying enmity.

Here was a riddle for Maedhlyn to solve . . .

Prasamaccus met him at the entrance and the prince clapped him on the shoulder. 'Do you hate me also, my friend?'

'No. Neither do they. They fear you, Uther; they fear your power and your courage, but mostly they fear your anger.'

'I am not angry.'

'You were the night you killed Korrin. It was a bloody deed.'

'You think I was wrong?'

'He deserved to die, but you should have summoned the people of Pinrae to judge him. You killed him too coldly and had his body thrown in a field for the crows to peck at. Anger overruled your judgement. That's what Maggrig could not forgive.'

'But for you I would be dead now. I shall not forget it.'

Prasamaccus chuckled. 'You know what they say, Uther? That there are two absolutes with kings: the length of their anger and the short-ness of their gratitude. Do not burden me with either.'

'Not even with friendship?'

Prasamaccus placed his hand on Uther's shoulder. It was a touching gesture which Uther sensed, rightly, would never be repeated.

'I think, my lord, that kings never have friends – only followers and enemies. The secret is to know which are which.'

The Brigante hobbled away into the night, leaving Uther more alone than he had ever been.

17

At dawn Uther walked alone to the circle of black stones upon which Perdita had been constructed. The dawn shadows were shrinking now, and a cool wind blew over the plain. At the centre altar sat the man Pendarric, his large frame wrapped in a heavy purple cloak, sheepskin-lined.

'You did well, Uther. Better than you know.'

The prince sat beside him. 'The people of Pinrae cannot wait to see my back. And if they see it for too long, they'll plunge knives in it.'

'Such is the path of the king,' said Pendarric. 'And I *know*. You will find – if you live long enough – some splendid contradictions. A man can be a robber all his life, and yet do one good deed and be remembered in song with great affection. But a king? He can spend his life in good works, yet perpetrate one evil deed and be remembered as a tyrant.'

'I do not understand.'

'You will, Uther. The rogue is looked down upon, the king looked up to. That is why the rogue can always be forgiven. But the king is more than a man; he is a symbol. And symbols are not allowed human frailties.'

'Are you seeking to dissuade me?'

'No, to enlighten you. Do you wish to go home?'

'Yes.'

'Even if I tell you the odds proclaim you will die there within the hour?'

'What do you mean?'

'Eldared and the Saxons have linked forces. As we speak, fewer than six thousand of your troops are surrounded by almost twenty-five thousand of the enemy. Even with the Ninth Legion, your chances of victory are remote.'

'Can you get me to the battlefield?'

'I can. But think of this, Uther. Britain will be a Saxon land. They are many, but you are few. You cannot prevail for ever. If you stay in the Pinrae, you can build an empire.'

'Like Goroien? No, Pendarric. I promised the Ninth Legion I would take them home and I keep my promises where I can.'

'Very well. There is one other fact you should know. Goroien is dead; she died saving Culain. No, do not ask me why, but the Lance Lord is now restored to youth. One day he will return to your life. Be wary, Uther.'

'Culain would never harm me,' answered Uther, feeling a sudden premonitory chill as he pictured Laitha. His eyes met Pendarric's and he knew the king understood. 'What will be, will be,' said Uther.

*

Victorinus slashed his sword across the face of a blond-bearded warrior, who fell only to be trampled by the surging, screaming tide of men behind him. An axe crashed against Victorinus' shield, numbing his arm. His gladius ripped upwards to plunge deep into the man's side. A sword cannoned from the Roman's helm and down to slice into the leather breastplate. A spear took the attacker in the chest and two legionaries pushed forward to lock their shields before Victorinus. He leapt back, allowing them room. Sweat dripped from his brow, stinging his eyes. He glanced left and right, but the line held. On the hill to the right Aquila was surrounded, his seven cohorts forming a shield wall against the Brigantes. Victorinus and his six cohorts were similarly confronted by eight thousand Saxon warriors led by Horsa, son of the legendary Hengist.

This was the battle which the Romans had sought to avoid. Ambrosius had harried the Saxon army throughout their long march north, but had then been trapped at Lindum, his two legions smashed in four days of bloody fighting. With the three cohorts still left to him – one thousand, four hundred and forty men – Ambrosius had fled to Eboracum. Now Aquila had no choice but to risk the kingdom on one desperate battle. But he had left it too late.

Eldared and Cael had pushed the Brigante army of fifteen thousand men to the west of Eboracum, linking with Horsa at Lagentium.

Aquila had made one last attempt to split the enemy, attacking the Brigante and Saxon camps with two separate forces, but the plan had failed miserably. Horsa had hidden two thousand men in the high woodlands and these hammered into Aquila's rearguard. The

Romans had retreated in good order and linked forces on a range of hills a mile from the city; but now the Saxons had forced a wedge into the Roman line, which had buckled and regrouped as two fighting units. There was no hope of victory now and the six-thousand strong Romano-British army was being slowly cut to pieces by a force four times as powerful. Men fought merely to stay alive for a few more blessed hours, holding to impossible dreams of escape by night.

'Close up on the left!' yelled Victorinus, his voice straining to rise above the cacophonous clash of iron on bronze, as the Saxon axes and swords smashed at the shields and armour of the Roman soldiers.

The battle would have been over by now had it not been for the Roman gladius. The weapon was a short sword, eighteen inches from hilt to blade-tip; it had been designed for disciplined warfare, where men would be required to stand close together in a tight fighting unit. But the Saxon and the Brigante used swords up to three feet long and that meant they needed more space in which to swing the weapons. This caused problems for the attackers as they pressed against the shield wall, for the longswords became clumsy and unwieldy. Even so, sheer weight of numbers was forcing the wall to yield, inch by bloody inch.

Suddenly a section gave way and a dozen Saxon warriors, led by a tall man with a double-headed axe, raced into the centre. Victorinus dashed forward, knowing the rearguard would be following. He ducked under the swinging axe and buried his blade in the man's groin. A sword lanced for his face, his shield deflected it – and his attacker died with Gwalchmai's gladius in his heart.

The rearguard advanced in a half-circle, closing the gap and forcing the Saxons back into a tight mass where the longsword was useless. The legionaries pushed forward, their own blades plunging and cutting at the near helpless enemy. Within a few minutes the line was sealed once more and Gwalchmai, his rearguard reduced to forty men, rejoined Victorinus.

'It does not look good!' he said.

At the centre of the Roman square, the two hundred archers had long since exhausted their shafts and waited stoically with hands on the hilts of their hunting-knives. They had little armour and when the line broke they would be slaughtered like cattle. Some of them pushed close to the fighting line, dragging back the injured or dead and stripping them of armour and weapons.

Victorinus stared out over the sea of Saxon fighting men. Tall men they were, mostly blond or red-haired, and they fought with a savage ferocity he was forced to admire. Earlier in the battle some twenty Saxons had ripped their armour from their chests and attacked the line, fighting on with terrible wounds. These were the feared Bare-sarks, or naked warriors – called by the Britons, Berserkers. One man had fought on until he trod on his own entrails and slipped. Even then he had lashed out with his sword until he bled to death.

On the other hill Aquila calmly directed operations as if he was organising a triumphal march. He carried no sword and moved about behind the wall encouraging the men.

For two months now, Victorinus had experienced mixed feelings about the old patrician. He had been exasperated by his reluctance to take risks, but had always appreciated his courage and his caring for the welfare of the men under him. Under Aurelius he had been a careful and clever general, but without the charismatic monarch Aquila had been found wanting in the game of kings.

Three times the line buckled, and three times Gwalchmai led the rearguard into action to plug the gap. Victorinus gazed about him, sensing the day was almost done. The Saxons could sense it too; they fell back to regroup, then attacked with renewed frenzy. Victorinus wished the battle could fade away if only for a few seconds, so he could tell the men around him how proud he was to die alongside them. They were not truly Roman soldiers, merely auxiliaries hastily trained, but no Roman legionary could have bettered them on this day.

Suddenly thunder rolled across the sky, so loud that some of the Saxons screamed in terror, believing Donner the Storm God walked amongst them. Lightning speared up from a hill to the east and for a moment all fighting ceased. With the sun sinking behind him, Victorinus stared in disbelief as the sky over the distant eastern hill split apart like a great canvas to reveal a second sun blazing in the heavens. The field of battle was now lit like a scene from hell, double shadows and impossible brilliance blinding the warriors from both sides. Victorinus shielded his eyes and watched as a single figure appeared on the hill, holding aloft a great sword which shone like fire. Then warriors streamed out to stand alongside him, their shields ablaze.

And then the sky closed, the alien sun disappearing as if a curtain had been drawn across it. But the army remained. Victorinus blinked as he watched the new force close ranks with a precision that filled his heart with wonder. Only one army in the world could achieve such perfection . . .

The newcomers were Roman.

This thought had obviously struck the Saxon leader, who split his force in two, sending a screaming mass of warriors to engage the new enemy.

The shield wall opened and five hundred archers ran forward, the front line kneeling and the second rank standing. Volley after volley raked the Saxon line, which faltered half-way up the hill. A bugle sounded and the archers ran back behind the shield wall, which advanced slowly. The Saxons regrouped and charged. Ten-foot spears appeared between the shields. The first of the Saxon warriors tried to halt, but the mass behind pushed them on and the spears plunged home. From within the square the archers – with the angle of the hill to aid them – continued their murderous assault on the Saxon line and the Roman advance continued.

Back on the two hills, the Romano-British army fought with renewed vigour. No one knew, or cared, where this ally force had originated. All that mattered was that life and hope had been restored.

The Ninth Legion reached the bottom of the hill. The men left and right of the fighting square pulled back to create an arrow-shaped wedge at the centre which pushed on towards the Raven banner, where Horsa directed the Saxon force.

Inside the fighting wedge Uther longed to hurl himself forward, but good sense prevailed. As with the Saxons, the great Sword of Cunobelin would be useless at present. Yard by yard the Saxons fell back, unable to penetrate the wall of shields; they began to throw axes and knives over the wall. Severinus bellowed an order and the second rank of the square lifted their shields high, protecting the centre.

The early advance began to falter. Even with the addition of almost five thousand troops, the Britons were still outnumbered two to one.

On the western hill Aquila read the situation and signalled to Victorinus – raising his arm, bent at the elbow, and making a stabbing motion into the joint with his other hand. Victorinus tapped his breastplate, showing he understood; then he summoned Gwalchmai.

'We are going to attack,' he said and the Cantii grinned. This was the sort of madness

330

a Briton could appreciate. Outnumbered and trapped, yet holding the high ground, thcy would throw away their only advantage and hack and slash their way into the enemy ranks. He turned and ran back to the waiting archers.

'Arm yourselves!' he yelled. 'We march!'

The archers moved forward, stripping breast-plates from the dead, gathering swords and shields.

Gwalchmai ran along the line shouting instructions, then Victorinus pushed his way to the point at which the wedge would be formed. This was the moment of most extreme peril, for he would have to step in towards the enemy and the two men either side of him would turn their shields outwards to protect his flanks. If either failed, he would be isolated in the midst of the Saxons. A sword lunged for him but he turned it on his shield and disembowelled the warrior. Gwalchmai's hand descended on his shoulder. 'Ready!' yelled the Cantii.

'Now!' bellowed Victorinus, stepping forward and slashing open the throat of a Saxon warrior. The line yielded at the angles of the square. Victorinus, swinging his sword in a frenzy, forced his way deeper into the enemy line. The man to the left of him went down, an axe embedded in his neck. Gwalchmai hurdled the body and took the dead soldier's place. Slowly the wedge began to force its way downhill.

At the same time Aquila ordered his square to attack. The Brigantes fell back in dismay as the wedge clove the centre of their line.

In the midst of the battle, Uther watched the British cohorts struggling to join him. The battle ground was condensing towards Horsa's Raven banner and the Red Dragon of Eldared. Uther moved back alongside Severinus.

'Order your archers to drop their shafts around the Dragon standard. That is where Eldared and his sons will be standing.' Severinus nodded, and within moments a deadly hail of barbed arrows began to flash from the sky.

Eldared saw his closest carle fall beside him, along with a score of warriors. Others ran forward to raise their shields over the king.

The battle had now reached a point of exquisite balance when the three Roman forces, heavily outnumbered, were still closing slowly on the enemy banners. If they could be held, or pushed back, Eldared would have the day. If they could not, he would be dead. It was a time for courage of the highest order.

At the Saxon centre Horsa, a blond giant in a raven-wing helm, bearing a longsword and rounded shield, gathered his carles and launched his own attack on the new enemy.

But Eldared had no wish to die; in his mind there would always be another day. With Cael beside him he fled the field, the Brigantes streaming after him. Horsa looked at his fleeing allies and shook his head; he had never liked Eldared. He glanced at the sky.

'Brothers in arms, brothers in Valhalla,' he said to the man beside him.

'Let the swords drink one last time,' replied the man.

The Saxons charged, almost cleaving through the wedge, but fury and courage were no match for discipline. The Roman line swung out like the horns of a bull, encircling the surging Saxons. Victorinus and Aquila linked forces behind them and the battle became a massacre.

Uther could contain himself no longer. Pushing his way to the front line, he snatched up a gladius and a shield and stepped into the fray, cutting a path towards the giant Saxon leader. Horsa saw the fighting figure of the silver breastplate and black-plumed helm and grinned. He too pushed his way forward, shouldering aside his own warriors. Behind him came the banner-bearer and a score of carles. The men to the left and right of Uther fell. The prince stabbed an attacker with his gladius, which became embedded in the warrior's side. Dropping his shield, he drew the Sword of Cunobelin and began to cleave his way forward with slashing double-handed strokes, moving ever ahead of the square.

Horsa leapt to meet him and their swords clashed. All around them the battle continued, until at last only Horsa and Uther still fought. The Saxon army had been destroyed utterly. Several Romans moved in, ready to kill the giant war-leader, but Uther waved them back.

Horsa grinned again as he saw the massed Roman ranks about him. His banner-bearer was dead, but in death he had plunged the banner staff into the ground and the Black Raven still fluttered above him.

He stepped back, lowering his sword for a moment.

'By the Gods,' he said to Uther, 'you are an enemy worth having.'

'I make a better friend,' responded Uther.

'You are offering me life?'

'Yes.'

'I cannot accept. My friends are waiting for me in Valhalla.' Horsa lifted his sword in salute. 'Come,' he said, 'join me on the Swan's Path to glory. We will walk together into Odin's hall of heroes.' He leapt forward, his sword flashing in the dying light, but Uther blocked the blow, sending a reverse cut that half severed the giant's neck. Horsa fell, losing his grip on his sword. His hand scrabbled for it, his eyes desperate. Uther knew that many Saxons believed they could not enter Valhalla if they died without a sword in their hands. He dropped to his knees, pressing his own sword into the dying man's hand as Horsa's eyes closed for the last time.

The prince rose, retrieving the Sword of Cunobelin, and ordered Horsa's body to be draped in the Raven banner.

Lucius Aquila stepped forward, bowing low.

'Who are you, sir?' he asked.

The prince removed his helm. 'I am Uther Pendragon, High King of Britain.'

Epilogue

Uther returned in triumph to Camulodunum where he was crowned High King. The following spring he led the Ninth Legion into the Lands of the Wall, smashing the Brigante army in two battles at Vindolanda and Trimontium.

Eldared was captured and put to death, while Cael escaped by ship with two hundred retainers, sailing south to link with Hengist. Following news of the death of his son, Hengist had the Brigantes blood-eagled on the trees of Anderida, their ribs ripped open for the crows to devour.

Moret offered allegiance to Uther, who left him as the Brigante overlord.

Prasamaccus returned to the ruins of Calcaria and there found Helga, living once more with the servants of Victorinus. Their reunion was joyous. With the ten pounds of gold Uther had given him, Prasamaccus bought a large measure of land and set to breeding horses for the king's new *cohors equitana*.

Uther himself promoted Victorinus to head the Legions, barring the Ninth which the king kept for his own.

During the four bloody years which followed Uther harried the Saxons, Jutes and newly arrived Danes, building a reputation as a warrior king who would never know defeat. Laitha remained a proud yet dutiful wife, and rarely spoke of her days with Culain lach Feragh.

All that changed one summer's morning five years after the battle of Eboracum . . .

A lone rider came to the castle at Camulodunum. He was tall and dark-haired, with eyes the colour of storm-clouds. In his hands he carried a silver lance. He strode through the long hall, halting before the doors of oak and bronze.

A Thracian servant approached him. 'What is your business here?'

'I have come to see the king.'

'He is with his counsellors.'

'Go to him and tell him the Lance Lord is here. He will see me.'

Culain waited as the man timidly opened the door and slipped inside.

Uther and Laitha were sitting at an oval table around which also sat Victorinus, Gwalchmai, Severinus, Prasamaccus and Maedhlyn, the Lord Enchanter.

The servant bowed low. 'There is a man who wishes to see you, sire. He says his name is Lancelot.'